The Soft Room

Karen Heuler

Livingston Press
at
The University of West Alabama

Printed on acid-free paper.

Printed in the United States of America, Livingston, AL

Hardcover binding by: Heckman Bindery

Typesetting and page layout: Jessica Meigs & Gina Montarsi
Proofreading: Jessica Meigs, Christie Hise
Gina Montarsi, Becky Holland, Beaux Boudreaux,
Leah Schultz, Brandie Broadhead,
Audrey Hamilton

Cover concept & design: Heloisa Zero
Cover art: David Fratkin
Cover layout: Gina Montarsi

This is a work of fiction.
You know the rest: any resemblance
to persons living or dead is coincidental.

Livingston Press is part of The University of West Alabama,
and thereby has non-profit status.
Donations are tax-deductible:
brothers and sisters, we need 'em.
Printed and Bound by Publishers' Graphics, LLC

first edition
6 5 4 3 3 2

The Soft Room

"But it must be said from the outset that a disease is never a mere loss or excess—that there is always a reaction, on the part of the affected organism or individual, to restore, to replace, to compensate for and to preserve its identity, however strange the means may be . . ."
—Oliver Sacks
The Man Who Mistook His Wife for a Hat

Part One

Chapter 1

They were golden-haired, those twins. They were square-faced with thick eyebrows and strong chins. They had eyes of slate-blue, each with three golden flecks, and abnormally large, dilated pupils. Their mouths were generous and determined. Strong, vibrant girls, they grabbed immediately at anything in reach. Robust, lusty, big babies, their lungs like bellows, accordion-hearted, they expanded and contracted from joy to sorrow, trumpeting with outrage and gurgling with glee. And, no matter what the emotion, even with their crinkled eyelids half-shut on some large sensation, they checked each other to see if their responses agreed.

Abigail was the first-born, and she came into the world howling, no one had to smack her. Megan, however, yawned, gulped air, shook her fists and didn't cry, no matter how hard she was slapped. Enid, the new mother, strained to hear the second yell and had to be reassured that the child was silent but healthy. The nurse would say no more, exchanging a quick glance with the doctor. Time would tell if the infant was mute; perhaps the yawns were really inarticulate howls, the first of a series of pantomimes against the world.

By the time they all left the hospital—Abby in Enid's arms, Meg in Ralph's arms—both twins were equally noisy, faces turning pinched red and vocal chords working furiously when they were hungry or soiled or bored. Ralph held his child tentatively, afraid that the diapers and blankets wouldn't protect him from the warm, vibrant spill (for such small things, they had already managed to christen him— each one—and he had a new respect for small capacities).

Enid, still exhausted but feeling almost light enough to float now that the great weight had been lifted from her belly, crooned absently. She found herself humming whenever she had a baby in her arms, like a cat with a kitten. She felt accomplished, having two at once, saving herself an extra pregnancy and double bills. A shy, pleased, meditative smile crept around her lips; she had been *economical*. The future spread ahead of her—dressing the twins identically or not, being the only one to tell them apart, parading down the avenue with a double stroller. She would keep a record, a valuable record, perhaps, on the development of twins. She would join the Twin Society, she had looked it up when the doctor had detected the second heartbeat; she would find other magical mothers, bearers of twins, a new-found community. She had always wanted to join something.

Ralph followed his own thoughts. Enid hadn't noticed, yet, how kind he was about the fact that they were girls, not boys, and there was no way he could point out his own benevolence. Besides, he suspected that he might actually prefer girls. He imagined two radiant daughters, clinging to him prettily, adoring him, asking him endless questions and waiting breathlessly for his reply. In a few years, maybe, there would be a boy. With his own progenerative powers, probably two boys. For a few steps he walked as if his balls were huge enough to get in his way, two for the record books. But he corrected his step when it seemed to disturb the baby. It would be a while before they chattered and adored him, and for the moment it seemed best to let them sleep.

There were baskets in the back seat of the car for the babies, and Enid sat between them, smiling and glancing down left and right on the slow drive home. Ralph was talking about a station wagon—not immediately; he didn't think they would be driving around that much with babies in tow; they would be staying home with the sitter, he supposed, for years to come. But his voice had a satisfied, complaining quality to it as he listed the things they would have to get—in duplicate, too, just think of the expense—now that their family had increased so dramatically. He was harboring thoughts of a dog, already he was trying to imagine the situation where he would be obliged to acknowledge, "Children need a dog!" Would they have to get two? He liked dogs, he could handle two, complaining about the cost and having to walk them—or would they, by then, have moved into a house with a large yard? He thought, honestly, that they could soon afford one if he really worked harder at his job, truckled under a little bit more, studied the reports and things, threw out intelligent comments, worked a little later without being asked. It was all possible.

He pulled into the driveway of the house that would soon be too small for them and was certainly already too small for dogs. Luckily they had a four-door, so he could help Enid out, clutching one warm and already smelly daughter in the wicker basket he had thought was so clever of Enid to have gotten. Say what you would, Enid had style. He could imagine himself boasting, "We brought them home in baskets, they were on sale." He and Enid both liked that kind of thing, making the most of a situation, putting a little spin on the usual to make it original.

The girls' bedroom was ready. It was done in peach and green, very spring-like. Of course they had gotten the usual pastel clothes at the baby shower, but both Enid and Ralph agreed that they would dress their children in "real" colors—ochres and oranges, pine greens and gentian violets. Enid had hunted out bright colors and bold patterns in the fabric stores and had made simple dresses and shirts. These children would be distinctive even if their parents were not.

Enid kept the hospital bracelets on the twins until she could figure out a way to tell them apart. She crept in to look at them often while they slept, studying their features. As hard as she looked she saw nothing different. When their hair grew in, she figured she could make slight alterations in their haircut—cut Abby's hair shorter on the left, say—to mark them. But that would work only if they were together.

She found herself wondering if she could give one of them a small nick on the cheek—and flushed with shame. No doubt she would figure out a gentler way of identifying them.

Abby and Meg gained weight steadily. They were lifted and petted, fed and changed.

"Meg cries less than Abby," Enid said suddenly.

"Yeah?" Ralph asked. "I thought they both cried the same. Constantly."

"No," Enid said firmly. "Abby cries constantly. Meg cries in sympathy."

"It comes to the same thing."

Enid shrugged.

The children went to the pediatrician, Dr. Wolff, for their checkups and their shots. He was young and handsome and he had been recommended by Enid's friend Jill, who once rolled her eyes and claimed, "I'd *steal* a baby just to get in to see him."

Enid also fluttered when she took the children in. She dressed her best, no matter how distracted she felt, and she set her hair the night before. But she never permitted herself any fantasies. A mother of twins doesn't have time for daydreams.

"Ah, Mrs. Gallagher," he said, smiling and taking a child out of the stroller. "And which one is this?" He grabbed the nearest child.

"Abby."

"Sweet Abby," he crooned, weighing her, listening to her heart, letting her crawl across the table, observed clinically by his soft brown eyes, his wavy hair somewhat ruffled by the sticky hand of an earlier patient.

"Two more pounds, Mrs. Galloway. Healthy, healthy."

Enid blushed. Her hand fluttered lightly, at her throat. She puréed the baby food herself, scooping orange mush and green mush into her daughters' wandering mouths, hearing Dr. Wolff's voice praising her.

At nine months the girls were due for another inoculation. Enid pursed her lips, wondering what to wear. Her eyes were focused automatically on the twins, crawling on the floor. She could tell them apart fairly easily, now, by the differences in their scars and bruises. At seven months Meg had held on to the coffee table, stood up, and then fallen, splitting her chin open. It took three stitches and left a scar. She was an incredibly good child; she had let out one indignant howl and then crawled away, leaving a trail of blood. Dr. Wolff had been surprised at how docile she was—though he applied some kind of local anesthetic, the baby was still quieter than he expected her to be, and even tried to grab the thread. She was so unlike Abby, who screamed her lungs out at the least bump, who needed to be held and soothed and calmed and distracted. It was amazing how different their temperaments were. Enid was determined to be fair; still she was tempted to tell Abby, "Your sister would never cry about that!" as the child held up a hand pinched by a drawer and screwed her face into a prune.

And Abby was so difficult with needles. Enid automatically handed Meg to Dr. Wolff first. Meg would be good, staring and smiling or talking nonsense; but Abby would scream and howl and then Meg, her eyes narrowing in concern, would join in, looking around in distress for the source of the problem. Meg loved Dr. Wolff, Abby hated him.

Enid liked to believe she was a stoic herself; after all, she had gone through natural childbirth (and what is a pinched finger compared to *that*?). She hated to think that Abby would turn out to be a wimp, a hypochondriac. She saw herself the mother of Amazons.

Enid was running late for the appointment with Dr. Wolff. She was still dressing Abby when she heard a crash from the living room.

Meg sat on the floor looking worried. She had knocked over the

ironing board, and the apprehensive look on her face would degener-
ate into screams if Enid wasn't careful.

"You're such a good girl," Enid crooned. "See? The iron's all
right." She picked up the iron and grinned for Meg's benefit. The
child smiled tentatively.

"Good girl," Enid sighed, and put everything away, checking her
watch hurriedly and giving a final brush to her hair.

The two-seater stroller was already in the car, so she straddled a
twin on either hip (a very difficult way to walk), crawled into the
backseat with them, strapped them into their car seats, combing her
hair in the rear-view mirror, noting how ugly she looked when her
face was flushed, and drove off to Dr. Wolff, already ten minutes
behind.

She was feeling pressured and apologetic when she reached his
office. But the nurse smiled nicely and told her the doctor was running late anyway, and Enid noticed that Abby needed to be changed,
so she took her off to the changing room and by the time she got
back, Dr. Wolff was standing in the doorway, smiling and friendly.

Enid always made sure the twins looked their best on these visits. She had resolved the problem of whether to dress them the same
by putting them into identical outfits of different colors. Today Abby
wore a green corduroy smock with dark-blue shirt; Meg wore russet
and brown. Enid had observed proudly, while waiting with other
mothers at other times, how much her babies stood out among the
nursery colors of the wispy-haired toddlers around them, making
them pale by comparison. One or two mothers had asked about the
clothes, enviously. Enid searched the clothes out; she was on every
catalog list, even the most expensive. What she couldn't find she
made. But she was deliberately vague in her answers to the other
mothers. She wanted to keep the styles all to herself.

Dr. Wolff waited for Enid to pick a child.

"Meg?" He smiled as he got his twin.

"They're so different," Enid sighed. "If only Abby had her temperament." She shrugged. "But I'm afraid she's not quite—well, sturdy. She cries over every little thing."

"Abby's the normal one," Dr. Wolff assured her. "Babies cry. It's how they survive, after all. I've never had one like Meg before. I've even mentioned her to a few people. She's a real trooper." The baby reached out for his stethoscope, turning her hand over and opening it when she found it was out of reach.

He started to bring it towards her when he let it go and grabbed her hand. "What's this? When did this happen?" His shocked eyes looked up at Enid, who stepped forward quickly, bending her head.

"Why—her finger—" Enid began.

"Dislocated." Meg's little finger hooked out from her hand at a strange angle.

"I didn't see it," Enid said shrilly. "Why, she didn't even cry, how would I know? It must have been the iron, it must have just happened, it's why I was late and in such a rush. With two, it's so hard." She could hear the strident sound of her own voice and she was unable to stop it. "She knocked over the ironing board, and the iron fell. It must have hit her. I would have noticed if it had happened any other time, I take good care of them, I *notice* things."

"But it should hurt." Dr. Wolff frowned. Meg gurgled, amused by the attention. Dr. Wolff still held her hand gently, as if weighing it.

Enid was missing the point altogether. "I was rushed—I left the house less than an hour ago. And I had just washed and dressed her and left her on the floor while I did Abby. I washed her hands. Her hands were fine. So it had to be the iron. I heard the crash and went running." She took a breath. Dr. Wolff was moving Meg's finger. Just the sight of it made her cringe. "Stop that!" she said sharply, and Meg's eyes shifted to her mother's face. The smile left her mouth and she stared at Enid, waiting for the sound of her voice.

"I already set it," Dr. Wolff said, his voice low and surprised. "She didn't even notice. I wonder . . ." His voice trailed off and Enid decided that she didn't like this new sound, a hungry, scientific tone. The doctor's eyes rested brightly on Meg.

Meg looked at him once again and he smiled. "Pinch her, Mrs. Gallagher, while she's looking at me." He crooned it, not to arouse Meg's suspicions, and it shocked Enid as if it had been perverted.

"You're crazy," she breathed.

"Do something to hurt her while she's not looking."

"What *are* you?" Enid hissed. She thought she saw a hard, cold edge in the doctor's eyes—something utterly new and profoundly distasteful. Something alien and violent had taken him over, and she wondered how she could ever have liked or trusted him.

Suddenly he lifted his arm back and slapped Meg hard, then he immediately began laughing and talking nonsense to her. Enid let out a small, muffled cry and leapt for Meg, whose momentary surprise had shifted back into placid amusement as Dr. Wolff laughed.

"No!" Enid cried, grabbing the smock and T-shirt on the chair, lurching for the stroller with a red-faced and uncertain Abby in it. She whirled around and frantically began to push the T-shirt over Meg's head. She grabbed Meg's arm and then dropped it, remembering the finger, and then grabbed Meg's wrist and cupped her own hand over the child's hand, trying to dress her even though she was shaking badly.

"Mrs. Gallagher, stop," Dr. Wolff said. "They need their shots. And besides, we have to talk. Your daughter—I think your daughter has a very rare condition. I've never seen it, I've only read about it. Look," he said angrily as Enid continued to yank clothes on Meg, who was already beginning to whimper at the hostile treatment. Dr. Wolff reached for Meg's thigh and pinched as hard as he could, twisting the skin between his fingers as if he were killing something.

"Monster! Maniac!"

"She didn't even notice. She can't feel pain, Mrs. Galloway."

"She's crying! Don't you see she's crying?"

"That's because *you're* crying. Do you understand? She only cries sympathetically. Tests—we'll need tests—but I'm sure of it. You can see it too, can't you?" His face had taken on an almost be-atific expression, as if he could already see the important papers, the well-paid lectures suddenly coming his way. Enid saw only a child molester. His words hadn't hit her yet, she saw only those fingers of his, hitting Meg, pinching Meg, while he laughed and talked baby talk.

"I'm telling my husband," she cried. "I'm going to the police! I'll go to the TV stations if I have to! You're sick! God only knows what you're up to!" She managed to cram Meg into her half of the stroller and lurched to the door.

She met attentive faces in the waiting room, apprehensive moth-ers, whimpering children, and an indecisive nurse who stood just outside the door, wondering if she should go in.

"What he did is terrible," she said to the faces around her. "He's sick. He's perverted. Don't let him touch your children." The moth-ers stared at her silently. Some moved their children closer. One looked stonily away, her foot jiggling rhythmically. Enid left.

She was gulping for breath as she snapped the girls into their car seats, unlocked the trunk and put the stroller in, then turned the igni-tion with unsteady fingers that ground the gears. She realized, fi-nally, that she was shaking and crying, and so were the twins. She reached for the seat belt, snapping it locked, and took off surrounded by howls, almost blind with despair. If they all died now, it would be Dr. Wolff's fault.

She refused to hear what he'd said. She argued with him in her head all the way home. Meg wasn't sick, she was perfectly normal and healthy. She was a stoic; she just preferred not to make a fuss. That was unusual, of course, but not pathological. If anyone was pathological, it was Dr. Wolff, and the AMA would hear about it. Slapping, pinching, setting fingers without anesthesia! Was this good medicine? Shouldn't that finger be in a cast or sling or something? She would have to find a new pediatrician, someone older maybe, more traditional, easier to predict. She sobbed once; how everything was getting away from her!

She called Jill, who had recommended Dr. Wolff, but she wasn't home. She called her husband at work, but he was in a meeting. "I'll tell Mr. Gallagher you called, Mrs. Gallagher," the receptionist said, and Enid hung up. She wished the receptionist had said "Enid." She wished she had someone to talk to. She wasn't at all sure Ralph would call her. He claimed he didn't get all his messages, but Enid doubted that, it would be bad for business, very bad.

She examined Meg's hand carefully, but it looked fine. Maybe swollen, but the twins' fingers were pudgy anyway, it was hard to tell.

She put the twins down on the floor and sat down facing them.

She clapped her hands loud. Abby and Meg blinked at her.

"Good. You both heard that."

She lifted her hand up and waved at them. Both girls lifted hands and waved back.

"You can see."

She jumped up, ran to the kitchen, and came back again. She sat down, waited for their attention, and handed each of them a piece of chocolate. Meg was as happy as Abby.

"You can taste."

She waited until they were finished and then opened the container of spoiled milk she'd found. Each girl sniffed and moved away.

"You can smell."

She bit her lower lip and then jumped up again, this time disappearing for a longer period. By the time she got back they had crawled in opposite directions, and she had to shoo them back together again.

They looked at her with interest.

She held out a piece of sandpaper to Abby, who reached for it, stared with her mouth open briefly, and then dropped it. Then Enid offered a scrap of velvet, and Abby took it and held it, flapping it in the air.

Enid picked up the sandpaper and gave it to Meg, who had been watching all this carefully. Meg waved it in the air and then dropped it. She reached for the velvet in Abby's hands.

"It could just be the color," Enid said. The velvet was red; the sandpaper was brown.

She took the velvet and rubbed it across the twins' cheeks. They both smiled. She took the sandpaper and rubbed it gently against Meg's face, and the girl rested her cheek against it briefly, and then shook her head. Enid tried the same with Abby, who immediately took her head away.

"Not good enough," Enid sighed. Her head bent, she considered the possibilities. She could only prove Dr. Wolff wrong by using Dr. Wolff's methods. She began to sing "Patty Cake." Both twins began to gurgle along with her, and Enid carefully looked at Abby while her fingers inched over to Meg and pinched her hard, as hard as she possibly could, on the thigh. Meg smiled and continued her baby song. Then, her eyes on Meg, Enid's hand reached out and pinched Abby. Abby gulped, her eyes widened in betrayal, and her mouth let out a fierce, outraged howl.

Meg looked at her with concern. She stuck her thumb in her mouth, and turned her head to face Enid, who sat nodding to herself.

Meg held out a hand as if confused. It seemed an adult gesture. The finger she'd dislocated was swollen now, definitely twice its size. Enid thought she could see it throb. She nodded once more to herself, slowly, admitting how it all looked.

Abby howled, her stricken face even more astonished when Enid carefully picked up Meg as if she were delicate, and rocked her, like a sick child. "Shoo, shoo," she murmured, as if she thought it was the child in her arms wailing, and not the one on the floor. "Shoo, shoo."

Chapter 2

They moved into the house of their dreams when the twins were four. By then, of course, they knew that Meg could feel no pain, that she had an incredibly rare condition called analgia, and that the absence of pain meant that Meg could kill herself almost without knowing it. Both Ralph and Enid could spout a brief synopsis of the scanty knowledge on analgia without batting an eye, in a singsong voice, while they poured a drink or sliced an onion. They themselves never paid any individual attention to the words they spoke. Meg was frightening, a worry, a constant tight muscle in their stomachs, but they both found that if they described Meg rapidly, if they lifted glasses and allowed their eyes to wander while they reeled off the few precious facts known, then they could relax. It was all true, but if you said it often enough, it lost its power.

Ralph and Enid imposed rules on both the girls. They told Abby to be careful for her sister, because she wouldn't know when she'd hurt herself. They told Meg, over and over again, that she had to learn to watch her skin, that she had to tell someone if she started to bleed. They said it in definite, no-nonsense, matter-of-fact voices, as if they were saying, "You must come inside when it rains. Even if you don't think you'll get wet." The result was that Abby felt responsible for Meg, whom she understood couldn't figure out when she was hurt. Abby would often start to cry over some scrape or sprain and then look expectantly at Meg. If Meg had fallen, too, did she feel it? Was she hurt worse than Abby? Was Abby supposed *not* to cry but to run for her mother in case Meg was also hurt and couldn't tell? It got so that the two girls would gaze, frowning at each other after any tumble or accident, trying, as 4-year-olds, 5-year-olds, to figure out the damages done.

"You're crying," Meg said once, sadly, to her sister. "You must be hurt." Abby had tripped on the pavement.

"Hurry! Hurry!" Abby yelled, rolling over quickly. "Are you bleeding?"

Meg shook her head. "I didn't fall, so I'm all right. You fell all by yourself."

Abby drew in her breath and let it out again. She rubbed her shin, which had been scraped and was beginning to sting. In a minute it was stinging so badly that she began to cry.

"It doesn't look so bad," Meg said. She had the serious tone she always adopted whenever Abby cried. She'd been told about pain and hurting, and when it was explained to her, people were always solemn, also kind of annoyed.

"It *is* bad," Abby wailed, getting up and limping home. "What do *you* know anyway?"

"It's only a little skin," Meg said, shrugging.

This enraged Abby, whose wails reached a higher pitch as she headed for her own door. Enid opened it and rushed out, kneeling down on one knee in front of the girl and peering at her face. "Let me see," she said, and Abby pointed to her shin. Enid nodded and then looked around for Megan, who was standing nearby. "And you?" Enid asked, running over to her and kneeling down again, holding Meg out at arm's length. "Did you fall down too?"

"It's me, it's me, it's me," Abby screamed.

You just wouldn't believe the way she was yelling," Enid said with a twist to her lips. "For all the world like she'd been murdered."

Ralph shrugged his shoulders. "Same old story. I'm going to say you don't pay enough attention to Abby because of Megan, and then you get defensive."

"I don't get defensive. I just say you don't pay enough attention to either of them." She put her hands on her hips.

"Oh, yes," he sighed. "That's right. That's what you say."

"I worry about Megan *all* the time," Enid said. "She could kill herself when my head is turned and I wouldn't hear a peep."

"Not like Abby," Ralph agreed.

"Of course it's not Abby's fault," Enid continued. "But it's not my fault either."

"The doctors say it's the fault of a single chromosome." He unscrewed a light-bulb from a lamp he was working on. "Not yours or mine they say, but if you think about it—"

"They don't know," snapped Enid. "To them it's interesting."

"Sometimes I find it interesting too." Ralph unscrewed the socket.

Enid gripped her hands. "I know, I know, it's true, I do too." She sighed. "But never when she's around."

Ralph nodded. "It's much easier when she's not around."

"But you see what's happening," Enid insisted. "It's all coming out all wrong, somehow we're doing it all wrong. Abby is getting more and more demanding, we keep discussing it over and over again, and Meg—" she halted abruptly, swallowed and said, "I think I've seen Megan *sneer*."

Ralph calmly repaired the wires. "Can a six-year-old sneer?"

"This is a six-year-old who never said 'ouch.' From her point of view we're incredible sissies."

"I don't know what we can do about it, Enid. The doctors can't make her normal. All we can do is tell her, over and over again, that she *can* get hurt, that she has to be careful, that she can't just throw herself everywhere like she was made of rubber. We kept her in the yard for years—we moved out everything she could hurt herself on and she *still* broke her leg twice and dislocated her shoulder. Do you want to keep her locked up? Then you have to keep Abby locked up, too, because they can't be separated, Megan judges everything through Abby." He put the lamp down and folded his hands. "Besides, the truth is, she's fearless. She's absolutely fearless. She's reckless, too, I know, but it all comes together, it's all of a piece, and Enid, I love that fearlessness. I love to see it. When do we ever get the chance to see it? Anything as pure and simple and beautiful as that? Sometimes I look at her and think, My God, she's like another race, the way we were meant to be, there's almost no limit, she can do anything." He shook his head in admiration.

"She can die, too." Enid's voice had dropped.

"And I don't think it will bother her. It's the pain of dying that stops us more than anything—you know, 'What'll it feel like? How bad will it be? How long will it take?'—and none of that will matter to her, it can't possibly stop her. That's what I like, I guess, that we can't stop her, no one can. She's her own force, she's powerful."

"Oh yes," Enid sighed. "I know what you mean, it's like watching some wild animal, all instinct, no restraint. I know what you mean. But she's a child, after all, you can't forget she's a child. And she knows very little. We have to keep reminding her about death, it's not something she can understand. And there's Abby, too, she's very unhappy and I can't see how she'll ever grow out of it because she'll always suffer when Meg does not, and Meg will always get the attention; Abby will just be the normal one, just a side note, and she already knows it all too well."

"Handicapped by being normal," Ralph agreed.

"She watches us, she judges us. Is she getting enough? We ask her to watch out for her sister, to take care of her, when *she's* the one who feels pain."

"Contradictions," Ralph murmured, picking up the snout-nosed pliers. "They contradict themselves; they contradict each other. They look so normal. They smile so normal. You wouldn't know Meg's already bitten the tip of her tongue off—and it amused her when it happened."

"All that blood running out of her mouth."

"Sometimes I think she's a maniac."

"She's just different." Enid was defensive.

"Ma and Pa Kent, talking about Clark. 'Don't cheat, son, don't use your superpowers.' What do you think will happen to her?"

"She'll grow up. She'll learn her limits. Every child has to learn limits. Hers will be harder. How will she ever believe something is wrong because other people feel pain? She's like a god."

"After all," Ralph said dryly, "maybe we make too much of her. Maybe she'll grow older the way anyone else would, occasionally burning a finger off or losing toes to frostbite. We place too much importance on the physical; there's more to it than that. There must be." He looked tired and began to lay the pieces of the lamp out carefully, his interest gone. "I'll lock the door," he said, planning on leaving everything as it was.

"They'll get in; they always do. And if there's any way Meg can hurt herself, she will." Enid lifted a hand to pat him briefly on the shoulder. "She always does."

Ralph bowed his head, frowning thoughtfully. Then he began to put away the lamp and his tools in the locked overhead storage shelves. "Let's put them somewhere for a week and go away. Let's feel free."

She sighed. "We could never trust anyone enough. Too many instructions. And you know you made at least 20 phone calls to check on them the last time we went away."

"We always say 'them,' " he pointed out. "But it's 'her.' We always mean Meg when we talk about 'them.' "

"What can we do?" Enid asked. "I dread every phone call; I think it's some accident. I can't keep my eyes off her; I'm always checking to see how she walks, how she holds her hands, if she's too pale or too flushed." Her mouth twisted wryly. "I can't remember the last time I thought about you—or about me for that matter. It's like being ruled by a drug; it gets so exclusive."

"It's different with me," he admitted. "I'm jealous. I envy her. I want to be her. I want to be six and boundless and free of pain."

Enid looked at him and raised one eyebrow. Some other time she would have the energy to ask what pain he thought he had, what disorder so severe or yearning so hopeless that he would envy a child who couldn't notice when the tips of her fingers were charred or when her foot hung sideways. Why dream, she wondered, of numbness?

But Megan's world was far from numb or neutral. Pain had been explained to her many times over, and to her it was a fairy tale; she was a princess in a world with fragile glass people. She tried to be polite, but the warnings she always got seemed to apply to others. This pain they spoke about—and they always spoke about it—was like something in a ghost story: you couldn't see pain, but everyone lived in terror of it, having seen the demon, or been kissed by the demon, or swallowed by it whole. At odd moments, she wanted wistfully to be in pain, to be petted and soothed as her sister sometimes was, to be pale with a trembling lip. But it was fleeting; only a second later some slight movement on ground or sky would seize her, and she'd be off.

She and Abby were inseparable. If Megan had been born feeling pain, Abby might have been the dominant one, because she loved to be first, she always wanted to describe herself to other children in terms of action. Meg was the same way, but she won because nothing stopped her; she continued to run and shriek with a shoulder wrenched out of its socket, and Abby knew very well that she couldn't.

Enid had a notion that Abby was a crybaby, but it wasn't true. Enid would have learned a lot about Abby's pluckiness if she'd spent more time with children of pain. Abby knew she was at a disadvantage: she was as adventurous as Megan, but she felt every burn, scrape and broken bone; and when she was in the first flush of pain, outraged by it, then Enid automatically swept toward Megan, fear and concern bypassing Abby altogether. It was not a thing Abby could accept easily—how all eyes went past her to the smug, virtuously polite Megan, how pain never swelled Megan's lungs as much as outrage did, how she herself could never quite manage to articulate that it was unfair to compare her to Megan every time, that she was set up to fail, that it was, all the same, as important for her to be rated exceptional as it was for Megan, and she herself would have valued it more. But she was six years old; she only felt it all: injustice, pain, being second-rate, suffering when suffering was viewed as a character defect.

Neither Abby nor Megan was stupid, and they were twins, moreover, and knew each other's minds. Megan had a wild, silent cunning; she grinned, her eyes agleam, her arms flung wide, when she led the way in a new scheme. But she needed Abby, her other half, her contrast but still her confidant, and she knew enough to step back occasionally and let Abby lead, with her eyes flashing and her arms not perhaps so widespread, her elbows tucked in, a loud chortling sound issuing from her parted lips.

They were cautioned, constantly cautioned, and by and large they were well-behaved children. At least they never disgraced their parents in public: they could be counted on to keep their dresses clean for at least two hours, they would sit and stare with their mouths slightly open at visitors, they didn't pick their noses at dinner, and they always said please and thank you when it would be to their credit. Though Megan was regarded as odd or even suspect in the neighborhood, the twins were models for deportment up until they were around eight. The other children curled their lips when told to be more like Megan or more like Abby; there was something hypocritical about that command. But occasionally there would be a sudden, wild episode. A parent would stumble on the children at play, and afterwards there might be a question, "But don't you think those

Gallagher girls are a bit *rough?*" The question was eventually waved aside. The twins seemed so well-behaved.

The twins certainly demanded attention; once the other children accepted it, there was no problem. The only really dangerous times were when a new family with new children moved in, and the Gallagher children ran wild, intent on proving themselves: intimidating, challenging, conquering.

The Gallaghers lived on Hillside Court, the last street in a suburban development in eastern New Jersey. The road had petered out when the developer hit an escarpment of hard rock a few inches under the soil. Next to that, or technically below that, everything drained into a marshy, bushy area that drew birds for the birdwatchers (Enid was one) and furnished a great scouting area in high summer, where the neighborhood children crawled and hid and ambushed each other, eventually laying down in a sweaty sprawl of grass-stained elbows and scratched knees. Here the children were supreme, and here they played out all their struggles and developed, year by year, into the adults they were always destined to be.

There was a loose group of about nine children when the twins were eight years old; one girl was seven, one boy was their age, and the others were a year or two younger. The smallest were sometimes petted and sometimes roughly pushed aside, depending on the circumstances of their play. They were treated indifferently, except for David, four years old and the youngest of the group, who was very often dragged around by Meg or Abby—but Meg especially—only because he was too heavy to carry.

A typical summer's day consisted of the children loitering on the street near the twins' house. For some reason the children never burst into each others' homes; instead, they threw a ball against a fence or drew a stick against garbage cans, pretending to have landed accidentally and indifferently outside another child's house. This was almost certainly an outgrowth of Meg's attitude because in the heat of play she scorned any child who stopped for a scrape or a bump; she would force the others forward, pointedly ignoring a trembling lip (though she would glance at Abby first to see if she thought the injury significant). She kept a pace that demanded indifference to weakness; she never cried and she disapproved of crying when they were just children together; she created an almost stoical band, except for the fact that stoicism had no meaning for her. All this except for David; when David cried he was scooped and coddled. Of course there were days when David was simply too young; either Abby or Meg would say, "But David can't go with us," and the boy would be firmly turned round and pushed away in the other direction. He had learned to accept it (though he still cried sometimes), and his small reluctant footsteps headed dutifully home with only one or two backward glances.

As for the older children, they were merely fellow players and had no particular distinction for the twins. One of their favorite games was to divide the group in half—"you with me, you with her"— and start from opposite ends of the country, as it was called, in war parties. On some days they slunk low, trying to make no sounds; moving bushes were the only mark of their progress as they tried to capture an enemy. This was preferred in warm weather, when the bushes had leaves. On other days Meg would let out a whoop and the two groups of children would run all-out at each other, screaming and rolling their arms like helicopter blades. They ran full-tilt, slamming and falling down, then jumping up and slamming into someone else. Although Meg loved this game, it was played only in cool weather, when the bushes were bare and the children were padded, but even then someone generally ended up crying.

When there was fresh snow they all lay down on the top of the hill and began to roll. The one who reached the bottom first won. Once a striking dotted line of red was the only hint that Meg had bumped her nose while throwing herself down the hill.

Shrieks and shouts were the best indication to the houses along Hillside Court that everything was okay with the children. Ominous silence made everyone uneasy; it caused Enid to stop the wash, it made David's mother put her coffee cup down with a suddenly alert air, it made the man tinkering with his car lift his head from under the hood and wait for the howl of pain, the quick, low voices of urgency, the worried children appearing in clumps at the end of the street. It was better for all concerned when the children made the air shriek.

Of course there were quiet times when all was well, when the children got tired of the rocks and brambles of the hill and headed for the plush green, softly padded lawns and backyards, with faces flushed, hair tangled, shorts and shirts and socks at odd angles. They trudged back up the street, heading for shade and lemonade and one of the hunting games especially loved by Abby.

These consisted mostly of following a thing to its source. Abby would pick an object—a bug or a rock or a bush. If it was a bush the children had to find out how many there were in the area; someone had to dig one up and see its roots; its leaves, twigs and parts of its roots all had to be tasted by each of the children.

If it was a bug it had to be followed so they could find out where and how it lived. They had to try to find its food, and provide its food. Then they had to find other homes, based on this information; the child who found the most won.

Sammy, the oldest boy, had a book of insects. It had a hard, colorful cover and lots of illustrations—enough so that it was possible to find whatever bug Abby chose—but none of them could read very well, and the bug book was usually ignored until after they were finished, when Sammy would thumb through it, his index finger tracing the wings and abdomens of the beetles, his lips quietly trying to pronounce Latin names.

Sammy had respect for the signs of life around him, whether on the printed page or crawling on the ground; he was extremely interested in what a thing was. Abby wanted to find out what a thing did. Meg only looked at things for their use. She was cruel, she had no sentiments.

Meg's methods were direct. She would be sitting on the curb and an ant would pass—one of those big bulbous black ants. Without hesitation Meg's foot would stomp down on the ant—but not the whole ant. She always calculated her thrust so she squashed the back half of the bug. She leaned over, intently staring as the head and front legs of the ant thrashed violently. The other children stared at the ant—or spider, or caterpillar—when she started doing it, but it made them uneasy, and they looked away.

Abby didn't like it. The first few times she stared at her sister waiting for her to finish with it. After all, she knew very well herself that the bug would writhe and then die, every single time. She couldn't see the point of it. It just showed the difference between them. She couldn't see the fun of it, this nastiness.

She watched Megan watching the ant, and finally Abby slapped her. She lifted her hand with determination, and she hit hard enough to turn Meg's head.

Meg turned back to her. "What?" she said. Her eyebrows were raised. The other children watched closely.

"Don't do that. I don't like it."

Meg grinned slowly. "Don't like it? They don't feel anything."

Abby shook her head. "No," she said. "It feels something. Everything feels something. Except you."

The children waited quietly.

"So what?" Meg said.

"So don't do it."

"Or what?" Meg's upper lip was raised.

Abby stared at her with narrowed eyes. "We don't want someone who's mean," she said. "We don't like it. You'll have to play by yourself."

Meg shrugged. "I can play by myself."

"What can you play by yourself? Indians? War? Catch?"

Meg listened thoughtfully. "David will play with me," she whispered softly to the little boy. "Won't you, David?" He nodded.

"*I* won't," Sammy said abruptly. "I don't like it either."

"Smack her," Abby said flatly. Sammy looked at her and blinked. "Smack her and maybe she'll get the idea. It doesn't matter, it won't hurt her, but she'll know you mean it."

Meg laughed. "I don't care."

"She does care," Abby said. "Smack her." To demonstrate, Abby slapped her, hard. Meg's cheek turned red where Abby had hit her.

"She likes to hurt things," Abby said. "Smack her."

Sammy bit his lower lip, sighed, stepped forward, and slapped Meg.

"Too soft," Abby said. She turned to Mary and Carol, girls from down the street. "Now you do it." Mary smacked left-handed, so both Meg's cheeks were red. Then Carol hit her.

David was whimpering.

"Stop that or we'll have to hit you next," Abby said sternly.

"Now you did it," Sammy sighed. "He peed himself."

"He's too young to play with us," Mary said. "He's always doing that."

"Someone take him home," Abby ordered.

"I took him home the last time," Mary said.

"Really," Meg said. "Really it's your fault, Abby. You scared him again. You did the last time too."

Abby scowled. "Shut up. I'm mad at you. Shut up or we'll have to slap you again."

Meg's shoulders lifted and fell. "I don't know why you like it so much," she said coldly. "I don't see the point at all."

Abby slapped her again, hard.

Enid watched from the living room window, unwillingly. Slapping again, she thought, and she crossed her arms over her chest and hugged herself.

She tried not to interfere too much. She did sometimes and the children got sullen and she felt like a fool or a grotesque, vengeful mother.

Still, she didn't like this slapping business. Was it time to talk to them again? Would talking do any good?

She turned and walked back to the laundry room, where the washing machine jumped and thumped and kept a hectic pace. She was running Meg's clothes through twice, trying to get the bloodstains out.

It's better if I don't know, she thought with resignation. "Otherwise they're such well-adjusted children," she said out loud in that ironic tone she was taking more and more often with herself.

Chapter 3

"I don't want to dress like you today," Abby said.

"Why not?"

"I don't want to look like you today. I want to look like myself."

Meg frowned. She nibbled at a piece of loose skin on her finger. "We look the same."

"We don't have to. I want to wear my hair different, too, so people don't mix us up."

Meg sat on her own bed in their room. She stared soberly at Abby. "I was going to wear blue jeans and a sweater today."

"Go ahead. I'll wear something else." Abby started hunting through drawers.

"Unless you want to wear jeans and a sweater," Meg offered. "I can wear something else."

"I don't care what I wear as long as it's not the same as you."

Meg's voice was sullen. "Are you mad at me? I didn't do anything wrong."

"I didn't say it was wrong. I just don't want people mixing us up. They're always calling me 'Meg' at school. I'm not Meg. I'm Abby. I want something different, something my own. Like the way I look." She turned around to face her sister.

"So what? They call me Abby sometimes. I don't get crazy."

"You steal my friends," Abby said. "You pretend you're me and you tell them things."

Meg grinned. "So that's it. It was a joke. Besides, they're not really your friends if they can't tell us apart, are they? They don't know anything about us."

"I want my own friends," Abby said stubbornly. "I don't want them listening to you. I don't want you sneaking around being me. You're not me."

"You used to like doing that," Meg pointed out. "We did it in the third grade and you thought it was funny when we kept changing seats."

"That was a long time ago." Abby had put on black cotton pants and a T-shirt. She'd have to wear a jacket because it was a little chilly out. It would have been simpler to wear a sweater, but she wanted to mark her decision so that Meg would understand it completely.

Meg pulled on her jeans and sweater slowly. She sat down and began to tie her sneakers. "You're wearing sneakers too," she said.

"Sneakers are okay."

Meg nodded and Abby went downstairs. Now that she'd started defining herself, she wanted to go all the way.

She found Enid in the living room cleaning the blinds.

"I want to do something about my hair," Abby said quickly. "I want it so it'll be different from Meg's. I don't want to look like her. And I want my own clothes."

Enid put her rag down and turned her attention to Abby. "But you have your own clothes."

Abby shook her head. "We have the same clothes, just different colors. So we still look alike. I don't want to look like anyone else. I want to look just like me. And that means getting clothes Megan doesn't have. So they'll be my clothes and people will know it. And I want my own hair." She blinked earnestly at her mother.

Enid pushed her own hair back from her face. "How does Meg feel about this?"

Abby's lips tightened. "What does it matter?"

"Just asking," Enid said quickly. "Just wanted to know what was going on." She pursed her lips and cocked her head. "Do you know what you want to do with your hair?"

"I want it short, and parted on the side, and bangs," Abby said definitely.

Enid sighed. She'd always kept the girls' hair short when they were smaller, so Megan wouldn't catch her hair in something and pull half her scalp out. She'd only started letting their hair grow last year; it was only shoulder-length now. She had missed the chance to play with little girls' hair: braids and pony tails and barrettes. How sad. Well, there was no going back.

"You start looking through magazines," she smiled. "See if you can find what you mean and I'll cut your hair later."

"You're getting your hair cut?" Megan said as she came into the room. She had changed her clothes; now she was wearing the same slacks and T-shirt as Abby, only in a different color.

Abby flushed in anger. "My clothes," she said. "You're wearing my clothes."

"We'll get some new clothes next week," Enid jumped in soothingly. "We'll go shopping. That'll be fun." She smiled encouragingly.

"Why can't we go now?"

Enid sighed. "I'm sorry, Abby. I don't have any money right now. We'll have to wait till next week. In the meantime, let's see. Maybe I have a shirt or something you can wear. Come on." She led Abby to her bedroom. Megan followed noncommittally, as if she simply had nothing better to do.

Enid looked quickly through her closet. "Here's something, now. This sweater shrunk a little anyway, it's really too small for me. If we roll up the sleeves—there, that's better." She stood back and tilted her head. "A little waiflike. And here, we'll pull your hair back. A new look! What do you think?"

Abby looked in the mirror.

"It's too big. Everyone will know it's not yours," Meg said.

"It's okay," Abby said. "As long as you don't give one to Megan."

Meg shrugged. "I wouldn't want one. Who wants to look silly? I'm going out now." She turned to go.

"I'm going too," Abby said and followed her.

It was a beautiful fall day, sunny and clear. The sky looked bigger than normal, perhaps because so many of the leaves were down and the trees were bare.

"What do you want to do?" Abby asked.

"I'm going to the country." Megan's hands were in her pockets. She skipped along ahead of Abby, whistling occasionally with self-conscious nonchalance. Abby became more and more convinced that Meg had something in her pockets; moreover, she was sure Meg had something specific in mind, and the walk to the hill was no spur-of-the-moment decision. She forgot her fury as she tried to figure out her sister's plans.

"Are we meeting anyone?"

Meg pursed her lips. "I suppose if they're there we'll meet them," she said in an indifferent, grown-up voice.

Abby sucked on her lower lip. She thought, from the air Meg was adopting, that the other children *would* be waiting; that Meg had made plans without her, was maybe even excluding her. She saw Megan skipping ahead of her, without her, not missing her or thinking of her, and it filled her with hatred and longing. Her sister, her twin! Going on without her! She wanted to smack Megan again, grab her shoulder and whirl her around as she so often did, Megan's eyes calm and superior as she looked straight into Abby's eyes, not flinching as Abby hit as hard as possible. But this time she wanted to see tears slide from Megan's eyes, her lips crushed together, her nose running. Her sister, her twin! Ignoring her!

Abby considered these gloomy thoughts as she followed Megan down the street, up the slight rise with its low trees and bulldozed rocks, to the swamp.

"C'mon," Meg said happily.

There were no other children there. Abby knew she would have to wait a while to be absolutely sure, but it looked like Megan hadn't planned anything. It was just the two of them. She wondered what Megan had in her pockets; now that Megan's hands were waving in the air as she jumped over the rocks it was easy to see the outlines of some lumpy things in her pockets.

"What're you doing?" Abby asked, as if bored.

"I dunno," Meg said, equally bored. "Just walking."

"Me too," Abby agreed. "Just walking."

Meg leaned over and bent back a twig, snapping it off and then breaking it in half and in half again, into smaller and smaller pieces. She peeled the bark off the last piece she had and then bit into the woody stem with her sharp neat teeth (she'd managed to break or mangle every part of her body except her teeth). Abby heard her suck noisily at the sap and then spit it out in a vigorous, theatrical, lip-smacking flourish. Abby pretended not to hear it, as hard as she could.

"Look," Megan said casually, "a squirrel."

"Where? I don't see it." Abby's head snapped to where Meg was looking.

"It's gone. Poor squirrels." She walked ahead for a few feet. "They've got to find enough food for the whole winter, you know." She twisted one leg in back of the other.

"I know." Abby was alert. Putting one foot behind the other like that always meant Meg had a plan.

"So I got them some food," Meg said with a sunny smile. "Nuts. In my pockets." She stuck her hands in and jiggled them.

"I knew you had something in your pockets."

"I bet."

"I could *see* there was something."

"Maybe." She shrugged. "Anyway, I brought them food. For the poor little creatures. For the long hard winter." She put a saintly expression on her face, relaxing all her muscles except for the sweet, small smile on her lips.

She scrambled through the bushes down the hill, leading Abby over to the far edge of the lot where a few dozen oak and pine trees marked the edge of the development.

She squatted down and cleared an area in front of some bushes, brushing away rocks, leaves, twigs, and pulling out as much as she could of the sparse grass that grew there. Abby helped her. When had Meg gotten nuts, she wondered. Had she found some at home? Bought them? When? The day before they had walked to and from school together. Oh, no, wait; on the way home Abby had been talking to her friend Terry; it was Terry who told her that Meg had impersonated her during recess, and gotten the quarter that Terry owed Abby. Maybe Meg had slipped away at some point, getting a package of peanuts for that quarter.

Megan was humming to herself as, on her knees, she brought out the contents of her pockets and laid them in a pile on the ground.

Acorns. Fuzzy-balls from some of the trees. And yes, a few peanuts in their shells. Not a mix from a store; things Megan had collected, then.

"Are you sure squirrels eat these?" Abby asked doubtfully, picking up one of the fuzzy-balls. She turned it around between her fingers. There was a bruise on one side. She put it down and picked up a peanut.

"Squirrels eat all kinds of nuts. Nuts are fruits from trees. We had it in class," Meg said in her bossy voice.

"I know. I was in class too." Abby saw a spot on the peanut, too. And it looked like it had a hole in it. She squinted hard.

"Put it down," Meg said quickly, grabbing the peanut and placing it in the middle of the pile. "Maybe they don't eat it if it smells like people." She smiled innocently at Abby.

Abby sat back on her heels. She tried to look at the nuts without seeming to. She could see a bruise or a smudge on some of them; she imagined she saw a puncture wound in the middle of each dark spot.

Megan surveyed the pile with satisfaction. "Do you think they'll eat it?" she asked, grinning at Abby.

Abby nodded. "What now?"

Meg shrugged. "We'll come back tomorrow. We'll see if the squirrels took anything. Let's go." She stood up and brushed herself off. Abby did the same.

Megan hummed again on the way home, as if she'd done a good deed. Abby thought about the spots on the nuts. Had Megan put something in the nuts? She trudged silently behind her twin, thinking about the way Megan stomped on ants, the way she pulled the dogs' ears or pinched their necks. Was it possible to put something through those holes into the nuts so the squirrels would get sick or die? Would Megan do something like that, without being around to watch it? Or was she planning on coming back when no one was looking, squatting behind a bush and waiting to see what would happen with bright, staring eyes?

Abby considered it all slowly. She quickly dismissed any thoughts that the holes were either accidents or coincidence. Megan had put them there, no doubt of it.

Abby inched her hands into her pockets searching for change. She found a quarter and two dimes. "I'm going to the store," she said casually. "Maybe look at hair styles in the magazines." She jingled her money gently.

Meg stopped walking and turned to Abby with her face completely blank and still. "Do you want me to come along?"

"You'll be bored," Abby said indifferently.

Meg nodded.

Abby turned the corner to go to the store, walking as naturally as she could. She wasn't sure if Meg believed the magazine story. She had never lied to her sister and wasn't sure it could be done. Her neck prickled and she whipped around once or twice to see if she were being followed, but she wasn't.

She walked all the way to the store and looked at magazines just in case Meg was following her. Then she took the long way home, finally cutting through a vacant lot to get to the spot where Meg's nuts were heaped for the squirrels.

She squatted down, frowning seriously. She picked up each acorn and nut and found, as she expected, a hole in the middle of a damp area. Sniffing it told her nothing. She touched the tip of her tongue to one tentatively but she wasn't sure how far it would be safe to go. Maybe it was poison.

She thought it would be best to take the nuts away. She cracked a few and left the shells there in order to fool Meg, and she put the meats in her pocket, bound for the garbage can. The last acorn, however, somehow looked so nice among the peanut shells, and perhaps Meg wouldn't be convinced if everything were too neatly gone.

And she was also, suddenly, interested in what would happen if she left that last acorn there.

Enid watched the girls come and go by looking through windows as she cleaned, one room after the other. Front room, off they went. Kitchen, they passed across the yard, probably to meet one of the boys. Laundry room, passed back again, probably hungry, instinctively getting closer to food.

She could watch them forever. She wished she had been a twin, so close, inseparable, able to see herself all the time and yet be herself. She wished she were as young, and peremptory, and self-important.

Enid's hair was turning gray and it wasn't flattering. She had a stab in her side that had never been there before. She felt old and slow and she wasn't far past thirty. She felt her lips pursing; she could cry from the loss of it all.

Her favorite game when she felt this way was to imagine herself opening the door to a whole new world. Sometimes it opened into sunshine and a crowd of eager faces craving to see her; sometimes it held moonlight and a young man with burning eyes. She was becoming dreamier and dreamier, and sometimes she even felt guilty about how pleasant her thoughts could be, and how they carried her through one tedious task after another. She had only to imagine her hand turning a doorknob and a whole fantasy would spring from her forehead. She was as reliant on that as a drug, even when that stab of pain in her side hit her and she froze, holding her breath. The pain disappeared and her imaginary hand lifted to an imaginary door and she opened it to the roar of waves and the keening song of a gull.

Enid was so attuned to Meg-who-feels-no-pain and Abby-who-does that she overlooked herself. She was too busy, too enthralled with the fears of any parent for a child and the special fears of a parent with a special child. When she and Ralph sat down to formal discussions of bills and expected expenses, it all revolved around the children and what they needed. It was easy to forget herself.

Although, to be honest, it was just that she could more easily envision the children's lives than she could her own. She saw herself running off with them across the yard, down the street to the country, rolling down the hill, shrieking and self-absorbed. If she had had a choice she would be nine forever.

She realized that she was slipping away from reality, losing touch. When she jerked herself back, fiercely concentrating, she told herself she was ill, that it was a trick of her mind to escape the creeping pain, or possibly some sense of failure in life. Where would I have failed, she wondered, brows curled, as she raked the yard. She hit a root and immediately imagined it the corner of an old trunk, filled not with money but with rare, long-lost seeds for fruits and flowers, lost treasures that would make her fortune and tweak her interest with their startling, unfolding leaves.

Of course that was another fantasy and she caught it even as it happened, smiling ruefully and tolerantly. The root turned out to be a root after all, and that didn't mean that her life was limited or plain.

She had never stopped hoping, however, for neighbors stopping over for coffee, calling her over a fence. It was what she saw on TV, the shows like *Leave it to Beaver* or *I Love Lucy*, where neighbors were friends.

If the neighbors weren't all that warm, it was probably because Meg was such a rough girl that the other parents were suspicious of her, disapproving, even. And no wonder, with the kinds of stories their children brought home. Meg and the hatpin, testing how the children would react to pain (and of course one of the children had ended up with an infected arm). It made you wonder about children— not why Megan would do it, but why the other children let her.

She wondered if the children used Meg as an explanation for every cut or bruise they got. A ready excuse, Megan, no explanation needed. Did they hate the girl? If they weren't careful they would eventually be forbidden even to see her. She was already the neighborhood delinquent, and not yet ten years old.

So it must make the other mothers uncomfortable. Hard to be a chum with someone whose child is victimizing your own. Enid found it awkward, too; sometimes she believed Meg was capable of practically anything. She defied understanding sometimes, she seemed to lack an element, empathy perhaps.

Meg continued to be a celebrity in the medical community, however. She had been referred from one doctor to the next, and she almost always had a specialist who saw her on a regular basis, in addition to the pediatrician. It was the specialist who routinely stuck her with pins, testing her reactions, and giving rise, Enid was sure, to the hatpin incident. Meg wasn't really gratuitously cruel, or even all that imaginative, she thought; she merely had a certain obsessive interest in the difference between other children and herself. She didn't have to test Abby because Abby's most interesting reactions were emotional and psychological.

As, probably, were Enid's own. As far as she knew, no one in her circle had ever approached a psychiatrist, no matter what the magazines said. Sleeping pills and tranquilizers—well, yes, it wouldn't surprise her a bit, she'd gotten pills, too, easily enough. But there was a rash of articles about imaginary symptoms and psychosomatic illnesses; and she decided that her own pain, which took over a leg, then an arm, then her head or her side, never settling down to a consistent spot—well, this moving pain probably had something to do with Meg, it was almost as if she were making up for Meg's deficit, feeling it *for* her. This was a theory she arrived at after having spent two straight days toying with the idea that everything she felt was imaginary, that she'd been born like Meg, unable to feel pain, but had been brainwashed, somehow, into believing she did.

So she grew easily confused as her pains and her fantasies took over, uncertain when one began and the other ended, catching herself sometimes with a silly fond grin on her face staring into a corner of space as the washer turned or the water ran or the mail dropped through a slot in the door.

Ralph merely thought her calmer than most women, less demanding. She has adapted better than I have, he thought, watching her slow cheerful movements. He thought of himself as worried and anxious, no match for the alert unsympathetic eyes of his daughters; fretful because the bills kept such an even pace with his salary and there seemed no way out. He was constantly waiting for another recital of Meg's problems—which bone she'd broken without noticing, how much it would cost. Enid seemed proud that the doctors were interested in Meg, but it never mattered to Ralph until the day Enid mentioned that there was a medical college interested in keeping a close watch on Meg, that they would pay all medical costs. It would mean a move, if it came to that, and Ralph was surprised to find how little he cared for the house and the area. He felt peripheral; any move could only be beneficial. But Enid was hesitant and it was true, the offer smacked of labs and cruel experiments, he couldn't be sure, could he, what kinds of things they might do to a child who couldn't feel pain, what it might interest them to do in pursuit of a lazy theory; he distrusted their closed doors and their conveniently washable surfaces.

"Oh, Ralph, look at the girls," Enid said one day, leading him to the sofa so he could watch in comfort.

Abby and Meg kept blank faces. The girls stood in the center of the room. Their eyes looked into some far distance. When they first started playing the game, they had paid too much attention to each other, it had ruined things. They were naturally in tune; they had simply to let go of their own thoughts in order to fall into each other's thoughts. Meg yanked once on Abby's hand, and Abby yanked back.

They faced each other; the one hand they held was raised and spread open until they stood fingertip to fingertip. They made no mistakes as they went through a perfect pantomime of a girl fixing herself in the mirror. What was marvelous, as they cocked their heads in the same direction, raised an eyebrow, brushed back hair, was how perfectly they did it, so naturally. It all seemed unrehearsed, and it was impossible to tell which one was supposed to be the girl and which one the mirror. Enid watched them in delight, thinking how clever they were, how special. Ralph tried to figure out the trick of it; he thought someone had shown them, or maybe it just wasn't as difficult as it looked. He tried to remember if he'd seen anything like it, anything as good.

The girls continued. They brushed their hair, cleaned their teeth. And then it looked like they were cleaning a speck from the mirror, one hand circling vigorously.

They were fingertip to fingertip again, and they stopped.

"Oh, Ralph," Enid cooed, "aren't they wonderful?"

"I've never seen anything like it," he admitted. "Nothing at all. How do you do it?"

Abby shrugged. "It's easy."

"I caught them at it once," Enid said, boasting. "They said they do it sometimes when they're bored, just for fun. They do it 'until they stop.' That's what Meg said.—Children." She grinned. "And they say it's always different. Sometimes it's a regular mirror and sometimes it's a funhouse mirror. They won't show me that."

"It's a lot of pounding and making faces," Abby said. "We like it because we get to make fun of each other and point fingers."

"Think of that," Enid said, beaming.

They had been playing variations of this game since they were very small, but it had always been private. It had started when they noticed they yawned or scratched or stretched in unison. They finished the accidental movement off in another movement, never speaking. If one girl held her fingers tight together, as if she were picking up a cloth, it was the signal to face each other through the mirror. They were at their best around ten or eleven, they almost fell into a trance then, with their eyes half closed and their mouths half open. They spun around, exactly reflecting each other, and even with their backs to each other they went through the same steps, they danced, they swirled, in perfect synchronicity, done so naturally that they never understood why so much fuss was made. They just naturally behaved that way, it required no tricks or signals, it just happened, and adult praise was suspect.

"But how do you *do* it?" Enid used to insist.

Their eyes flickered once, back and forth, and then again to Enid.

"We start dreaming of something to do," Abby said slowly, "and we dream the same thing."

"*Do* you dream the same dreams?" Enid asked eagerly, her head jutting forward in excitement.

The twins stared back uneasily. "We don't dream at all," Meg said finally. "I meant, we *think* of the same thing to do."

"That's okay," Enid said quickly, sensing that she'd overstepped some private boundary. "You don't have to dream, not now. Most people forget their dreams, anyway. Although I like dreams," she said, smiling in encouragement. "Oh! and I like the way they seem to mean something!"

The twins looked at her politely. When she looked at their identical, smiling, formal faces, Enid felt despair.

Chapter 4

One day Enid went to the hospital and she stayed there for over a week. Ralph told the twins that she needed an operation to find out what was wrong. In the meantime, he took off from work for a few days, which he mostly spent at the hospital. David's mother, Mrs. Nunez, brought over a casserole one night and the twins set the table while Mrs. Nunez and Ralph talked in low voices in the kitchen. They seemed to be discussing whether it was too early or too late, their voices dipped up and dipped down. Mrs. Nunez kept referring to cousins, aunts, friends of friends—"and they said they'd never seen anything so bad!" she'd whispered, and Abby or Meg paused by the silverware drawer straining to make sense of it all.

"What do you think it is?" Meg asked.

Abby shrugged her shoulders.

They went to school, of course, and that was exactly the same, without any whispers or ominous absences. It seemed unlikely that anything would really change, although they made their own sand-wiches and took them for lunch, and their father either gave them too much milk money or none at all. But the teachers were the same, and the girls pushed against the same other children and were pushed back in turn.

And then, suddenly, their mother was coming home again. Any thoughts that life would go back on track, back to normal, were quickly dispelled by Ralph's distracted, nervous eyes. He looked uneasy, uncomfortable, as if he had to take on a role he wasn't sure of.

Ralph told them, "Your mother isn't feeling well. So try to be good." He trailed away, then lurched back. "Help out more. See if there's anything she wants." He looked at them in a sad, astonished way that made the girls uneasy.

"What's wrong with her?" Meg asked in her polite voice. All illnesses were a formality to her.

Ralph's face seemed to ripple, then regain control. "They're doing tests to find out the name. Right now, though, she has to take pills and they make her very tired. So you'll think of things to help, won't you?"

"Is she dying?" Abby asked in a soft voice.

Ralph rushed to answer quickly, his eyes slanted off to the right. "Everyone has to die sometime. But not now. Mommy won't die for a long, long time."

The girls stared at him.

"Will she make us dinner?"

Ralph shook his head. "Not now, anyway. Later, when she's better. You can help with dinner?" he asked encouragingly.

"Will she wash our clothes?"

"I think we can take care of that."

"Will she iron?"

Ralph shook his head.

"Who'll wake us up in the morning?"

"I will."

The twins glanced at each other. "And where will Mommy be?" Abby asked.

"She'll be here," Ralph said wearily. "If she's feeling better she'll be, oh I don't know, maybe in the living room, sitting, you know. Or lying in bed. You can talk to her. She'll still be your mother."

The twins looked pale and grim. They watched Ralph's face hypnotically.

"She'll be here when we come home from school?" Abby persisted.

"Yes."

"Will she eat dinner with us?"

"If she wants to."

"Will she go to the store?"

"No. No, I don't think so. Listen, we'll have to see, okay? It's going to take a long time before everything gets back to normal, but it will. You'll see, we'll forget all this in a while, we'll be surprised that it ever happened, that Mommy could ever be sick. You'll see," he said with fierce fervor. "You'll see."

What they saw was a drastically different Enid, her face pale and contorted with a grim cheeriness. She looked newly vulnerable to the girls, as if she were one of the "special" children at school who sat in wheelchairs and breathed raspily through cage-like chests. There was a greediness that hadn't been there before, you could almost see her watching everyone else's share. Of course they didn't know why or understand this. Enid walked through the house stiffly and carefully, she was often sick and the girls could hear her cataclysmic retchings through the thick old pine door, the monotonous sound of flushing, and the pungent acid reek of bile.

At first they had hovered anxiously in the hallway, waiting for their father to open the bathroom door and help Enid back into bed, with a washcloth to wipe her face. He always went back into the bathroom and they could hear water running in the sink, the sound of paper being ripped from a roll, the definitive sounds of cleaning up. They would not use the bathroom until Ralph had cleaned it up, and he changed subtly from this task, becoming less distant, more motherlike and human, from the accumulation of these details.

Then, later, as Enid's illness became a routine, they would steal out of the house when they heard her first miserable groan, gliding down the street until they were definitely out of earshot. "It's not respectful," Ralph told them sternly. "She knows you run out of the house whenever you hear her."

"Just when she's sick," Abby said defensively. "We don't want to hear that."

"She can't help it. And you're hurting her. You're avoiding her."

"When will she be all right again?" Meg demanded.

"Soon."

The twins glared at him.

"I mean it. It's the medicine that's making her sick. That will stop in a while. In the meantime," Ralph sighed, "remember she loves you and wants to see you. Imagine what it's like to be so sick and have people avoid you. Just imagine it."

Ralph had lost weight and, under the strain of keeping the household running, was developing new habits. He paid for a housekeeper to come in twice a week to clean and cook casseroles and stews and dishes that could be frozen or served cold to last the week. The housekeeper came while the girls were at school, and when the girls came home they would first go to the refrigerator to consider the new dishes and covered bowls, then to their closets to see what clothes were freshly ironed. They never discussed it and could never have explained it, but they went from room to room just looking at the subtle or obvious marks of the mysterious housekeeper. (There had been two temporary housekeepers before this one, but they pretended it was all the same woman, one who changed her form from week to week.) They were hoping, in fact, for clues, for evidence of a secret language or a whole other world of unknown rituals and intoned deeds. Something was happening around them; something that was never said in words. They looked for clues in odd places, and always away from Enid.

"Look," Meg said one day in a hushed whisper as they retraced the housekeeper's path, "all our dresses face one way except for this one." They regarded it seriously. "What do you think it means?"

"I think something different will happen to the one who wears that dress."

Meg nodded. "Good or bad?"

"Bad," Abby said solemnly. "Very bad."

Meg wanted to wear it because she couldn't be hurt anyway, and Abby swore to watch her every move. Meg wore it the next day; she walked carefully with her head held rigidly, checking the outside corners of her vision, her adrenaline fixed high.

They had a surprise test in geography. They got a homework assignment to outline an essay in English; they had lima beans for lunch.

"You know," Abby said thoughtfully on the way home, "I think maybe I turned that dress around. A couple of days ago, when I was looking for that pink blouse."

Meg nodded. "The dress is a dud."

"There's still home," Abby said hopefully. "Maybe there's something there." She bit her lip and cast a furtive side glance at her sister. Meg pursed her lips and crossed her eyes, which was the twins' hex sign against an accidental remark, but she didn't say anything, and Abby pursed her own lips automatically.

"Go see your mother for a change," Ralph said when they got home. At one time the twins had been the first to get home, but now they dawdled and he rushed, and when they finally got home it was usually time for dinner and after that homework and maybe TV. They were very careful about time now; with luck they could avoid the sounds of their mother's sickness for days on end.

They crept upstairs, pushing each other forward.

Enid must have had a good day. Her wispy hair was smoothed flat and she sat straight up in a clean bed. But the girls automatically started breathing through their mouths.

"Don't stand there," Enid said in a cheery voice, "I won't bite you. I'm safe. Give me a kiss." She held her arms out and the twins moved forward dutifully.

"What have you been up to?" Enid continued. Her voice was too loud, her shoulders moved when she spoke.

"School," Abby said.

"Of course school. Learn anything interesting?"

They shook their heads.

"What? Nothing at all? Nothing you didn't know when you got up this morning? Are you *sure* you went to school?"

"Predicate nominative after a copulative verb," Meg said.

"Adverbs modify verbs; adjectives modify nouns," Abby added.

"And prepositions?" Enid demanded, her voice getting louder with each word. "Do you know how to handle a preposition?"

"We had prepositions last month. We learned them all. We diagram sentences now."

"Diagrams? I don't think we ever had diagrams." Her voice was too loud, her face was getting pink from the effort, but Enid didn't seem to notice. "How interesting. Really this is interesting. What are the diagrams for?" When she smiled the skin stretched tight over her skull, as if it were being pulled.

"I don't know what they're for," Abby whispered. "We just have to do them."

"No matter. It doesn't matter at all," Enid called out hastily. "That's what school is for, isn't it? Spend half your life doing things that don't really make sense and then poof, they catch you on totally different things, you fail tests they never told you about at all, and who can remember what the point of a cosecant is?" Her voice sounded cheery but it worried the girls. She looked at them brightly, her face flushed. "We never have a chance to chat. So what do you think of this, huh? Life is different, isn't it?" She lowered her voice suddenly down to normal and said, "Please get me some water, would you? I'm dying of thirst." There was a pitcher and a glass on the nightstand. Abby was closest so she stepped forward and poured it for her mother, being careful not to spill anything on the collection of tissues, napkins and magazines overflowing on the nightstand.

Her mother gulped noisily, almost aggressively. She handed the glass back to Abby slowly, reluctantly, as if she already regretted something.

"You two are happy?" she asked, squinting at them.

"Yes, Mom, we're happy," Meg answered quickly. "We miss you, though. Dad keeps saying you'll get better soon." She offered this cautiously. Abby nodded in agreement.

"Actually, this is the cure," Enid said. "Getting so sick just for a cure. It confuses the hell out of me." She frowned. "I guess it's all right to say 'hell' in front of you. Your friends probably say 'hell,' don't they?"

"Yes, Mom, some of them do."

"Well, you save it for later. It has more impact if you don't use it all the time. Come back soon," she added, suddenly formal and anxious. "But go now. I'm not feeling well. Tell your father."

Abby turned and left, but Meg moved slowly, watching her mother swing her legs out of bed, clutching onto the table to steady herself as she stood up. She wore a knee-length gown, and her legs looked scrawny. Her face was contorted, her mouth shut hard in concentration as she swallowed over and over again. She was unaware of being watched, and Meg left before Enid had steadied herself enough to turn. She rushed down the hall to join her sister, trying hard to ignore the small grunts her mother made as she moved toward the bathroom. She passed Ralph on his way to Enid. He had the face of someone who was trying hard not to think about what he was doing.

Not knowing what else to do, she joined Abby at the table. They stared down at their plates with stony faces, listening, despite themselves, for their mother's groans.

One morning Abby woke up with a peculiar feeling in her gut. She had never felt anything like it before, and she twisted around, trying to find a more comfortable position. It was half an hour before

Ralph would come to wake them.

It was just starting to turn light, and because she couldn't go back to sleep and still couldn't find relief from the odd feeling, she went to the bathroom.

She froze in horror when she saw the blood on her pajamas. Her heart went dizzy and she blinked her eyes, looking around to see something wet and red she might have rubbed against. For a bewildering moment she thought it must be her mother's blood and she couldn't imagine how it had gotten *there*. Out of alarm she stuck her hand between her legs and saw in terror that it came back wet and sticky.

She was afraid she was going to be sick. She even moaned, and noticed it; it sounded like her mother's sounds. She must be dying. And it was all the more horrible because she was bleeding from a shameful place.

She thought maybe it would stop eventually, like a bloody nose always does. She took her pajamas off and began to run water in the sink, watching it turn rose pink as she stuck the pants in. As she stood there a small drop of blood began to run down the inside of her thigh. *I am dying*, she thought.

She cringed at the tap on the door.

"Abby?' Meg whispered. "Abby, open up."

Abby turned the lock and Meg crept in, closing the door behind her. She leaned against it slightly, looking at Abby's nakedness.

Finally she said, "I'm bleeding. You too?"

Abby nodded her head wildly. She was relieved of her loneliness. She didn't regret that this meant that Meg, too, was dying; just having Meg in the same predicament made her feel better. Dying together would be more comforting than dying alone.

"Does it hurt?" Meg asked.

"It feels awful," Abby confessed. "Like nothing else. Like something's eating me inside, scratching."

"I thought it might be more like a nosebleed," Meg said. "You said those don't hurt."

"They don't hurt. They just feel like something's running and when you hold your head back it gets stuffy."

"Not like a scraped knee?"

"A scraped knee burns in a lot of little places all at once and then it feels, too, like the whole thing's stretching tight, too tight, so the tightness hurts too, and it feels wet a little and you can notice a breeze, just a little."

"Is that what this is like?"

Abby concentrated, and then nodded. "Close. Like a scrape and like a bellyache when you don't get sick, just feel like you might."

"What did we eat yesterday?" Meg asked, suddenly bright. "Maybe that housekeeper gave us bad food?"

"Then Daddy would be sick too," Abby whispered. "Bleeding." She bit her lip. "But where would he bleed from?"

"What are we going to do?" Meg asked glumly. "I'm supposed to tell someone when I bleed."

"We can't tell Mom; we're not supposed to bother her."

"This is bad, I guess?"

Abby's lip trembled. "It's bad."

"Maybe we should tell Dad?"

"Tell him we're bleeding *where*?" Abby yelped. Meg nodded.

Quietly, they washed out their clothes. They rolled up toilet paper to stick in clean underwear, and then decided to take the oldest towel they could find and tear it in strips. They rinsed out their pajamas and tidied up the bathroom in silent communion. They hung their clothes in the back of the closet to dry and crept back into bed as usual and waited for their father to wake them.

They were quiet for breakfast, quiet getting their books and lunch together, feeling their blood seeping away, unable to say a word. They had decided that the best thing to do was to see the school nurse, since they would have to tell *someone*. They only hoped they could make it to school; they didn't know how long it would take to bleed to death.

They squirmed through the early morning; the nurse wasn't due until 10 a.m. When they sat before her finally, hand in hand and voices barely above a whisper, the nurse clucked and said, "What? No one told you about your monthlies?" and the girls eyed her warily.

They sat there silent, humiliated, and outraged as the nurse explained to them why they weren't dying. They felt tricked. It was some outrageous lie or bizarre betrayal. How come they'd never heard of it before?

"Most girls tell each other," the nurse said professionally. "Of course, you two, you're young. But you're not the first in your group. You've never heard of cramps, eh? You use it mostly as an excuse to get out of gym." She paused for a moment and looked at them gently. "Your mother's alive, isn't she?"

"She's sick most of the time now," Abby said.

"That's why, then." The nurse disappeared for a moment. When she came back she had booklets and boxes. "Here, we'll go through it all. Some schools tell their girls about this ahead of time. I hope someday they all will. It's nothing to worry about. You're not the first, you're not the last." And she showed them the diagrams and the belts and pads.

"A bit of a surprise," she ended cheerily. "But you'll get used to it. Everyone does." She sighed. "Believe it or not, you'll be sorry when it ends."

Abby and Meg left her office stiffly, and Meg stopped just before the door. "Is there anything else?" Meg demanded. "Anything else someone forgot to tell us?"

"You've probably heard about death," the nurse joked. She noted their stony faces and said seriously, "No. Nothing you have to worry about now."

The two girls held each other's hands as they slowly walked down the hall. They were furious; they believed that all the other girls knew about this business, that they had withheld the information. The other girls were necessarily guiltier than any adult because they were all children together and obviously at the mercy of adults. They were in school, after all, to be given information by adults, fed facts on schedule, like hamsters being given pellets in a cage.

And their friends knew facts as startling and personal as these, and had withheld them. Abby and Meg dismissed their classmates' possible embarrassment as inconsequential. They had been terrified, left out, and finally humiliated by that nurse, all because of something everyone else knew.

It was one of those times when the girls were conscious of thinking the same thought. There was an almost palpable echo in their heads. At times like this, Abby imagined she heard Meg's heartbeat, that they were synchronized from birth; she had already noticed they breathed in and out at the same time.

They walked down the hall together, hand in hand, thinking together how the world could withhold and the world could lie. They leaned closer together, sipping at the air, listening for heartbeats, their steps matching, their lips set, their eyes blinking like mirrors.

Chapter 5

It was just as if a very small but powerful key had been turned; you could almost see which bodies the key had touched. In the schoolyard the boys stood, runty, self-conscious, embarrassed yet pleased with themselves. They nudged each other with elbows as if outside it all, but they were perfectly aware that the girls were over there, giggling. The boys were conscious of the girls' eyes on them, and the way they walked reflected the knowledge that they were valuable to girls even before their voices broke. They developed a slow, loping gait, their chins held just a little bit high (not too much), their eyes bright, their mouths touched by that know-it-all smile, the one that said, "They love it, they're eating it up."

They had to know something was up the way girls clumped together, their eyes hungry and miserable, eaten alive by one crush after another. How many eyes were staring at this boy? How many girls held hands and whispered, tears streaming, over that one? It was an entirely sickening thing to see, how completely sensible girls were laid waste by this sudden plague, bled dry by their hormones.

Abby and Meg watched with hostile eyes; they had never forgiven anyone for their menstrual cycle. All the other girls had it too, as far as they could tell, certainly there were references to "the Curse" and "cramps" and anxious taps on one's forearm with a quick wiggle to denote the back of the skirt and "Tell me, do I show?" Meg always said "yes," and stopped getting asked.

The other girls clustered and sighed and groaned about it; they were drawn together. But the twins refused to give in; they might listen stony-faced to some comments, but they never offered any, like strict anthropologists taking it in.

Abby told one girl once that, because they were twins, she and Meg alternated their periods and that it was scientifically possible for them each to give birth to one of a set of twins in the next generation. Although—she said seriously—she was hoping to convince Meg to have all the children—hers and Meg's—because Meg wouldn't feel pain giving birth.

"They believed it all," Abby said, smirking as she repeated the story to Meg on their way home from school

"They'll get even when they find out." Meg stopped beneath the largest tree in the backyard and looked up. "We climbed to that branch last year, I think." She pointed half-way up the tree.

"We can go farther this year."

"If we want," Meg agreed.

"Or we can go inside. I'm getting hungry."

"No." Meg was firm. "He's not home yet."

Abby frowned at the tree. "She was okay yesterday," she said neutrally.

"I can't stand those noises." Meg, too, considered the tree. She squinted into the upper branches.

"She moans."

"I can't think of anything else when I hear it. I wait for more."

"Dad says she doesn't even know she's doing it."

"Then someone should tell her she is, so she can stop."

Abby's eyes followed Meg's up the tree and out along the branches. She pictured the branches bending under her weight—or actually under Meg's weight, since if she could picture someone looking like herself, it must be Meg.

"She's groaning because she's uncomfortable."

"Uncomfortable? Not in pain?"

Abby thought for a moment. "Not pain, I don't think. She's unhappy."

"Unhappy," Meg repeated. "That branch there, what do you think?"

"It's a skinny-looking branch," Abby said with interest. "I think it will break." She looked at Meg expectantly. "It will definitely break."

"Then you go," Meg joked.

"I'll get half-way out and freeze."

"Then I'll go," Meg said, and jumped up with energy.

"I'll be the crowd," Abby agreed. She watched approvingly as Meg took off her shoes and sweater. It was the way she preferred to climb, too, with her feet wrapped around the trunk like hands, her pleated skirt swinging in and out with each lunge up the tree as she grunted like a lumberjack. She got up to the branch and twisted round to look at Abby. "Okay so far?" she asked.

"You look awfully high," Abby said cheerfully.

"You look a mile away."

"If you fall, I think you'll live," Abby yelled.

"I think I'll live no matter what," Meg yelled back. She clung horizontally along her branch, inching forward like a caterpillar. It began to bend.

"You've gained weight."

"Ha! Not me!" she cried and the branch waved gently down, its farthest leaves touching those of the branch two feet below it.

"There's a wind." Abby laughed at the moving branches.

"*I'm* the wind!"

"Hot air! Hot air!" Abby squealed.

Meg crossed her eyes and stuck out her tongue. "You're always so jealous."

"I am *not*," Abby flushed.

"But you're not up here," Meg wheedled. "Look—I did it! I made sure it's safe. Now you don't have to worry." She had a nasty, pointed grin.

"I don't need you to tell me what I can do. I don't want to, that's all."

"But you love to climb trees. You just hate to fall."

"No one wants to fall."

"It's kind of fun," Meg snickered.

Abby shrugged her shoulders. "It doesn't count, you know, if you don't feel it."

"I do feel it," Meg whistled. "It feels good."

"Landing, then, I mean, hitting the ground."

Meg rocked on her branch, forcing it to sway even lower. "If you worry about how you land, you'll never have a bee-yoo-ti-full fall." She sang it out, dipping up and down in rhythm.

"You'll break that branch."

"So what? There are other branches."

"You don't care about anything," Abby said in a high tone. "You're destructive. Deliberately destructive." She said this with a certain amount of satisfaction. She had heard her father say it once; it had stuck in her mind.

"I don't have to care," Meg sang. "I'm a hero!" And with the last word she gave a dramatic bounce on her branch, meaning to make it bend so low that Abby would have to shut up from being so wrong. She believed that branch would bend as low as she wanted it to, that she *knew* its properties.

Instead, it snapped with startling suddenness and Meg was flung down—not heroically but in a tumbling, flipping way, her arms flung out to try to balance herself. She landed surprisingly digni-fied, however, almost cross-legged, leaning on one elbow. She took stock of herself quickly and rested lazily back against the tree, as if it had all been for show and very cleverly done. It happened so quickly that Abby had barely finished yelling "Watch out!" when it was already over. She stood over Meg, who blinked as if just waking up from a nap.

"Are you all right?"

"I'm always all right. I'm a hero," Meg said lazily. She stood up and started to brush herself off when her right leg gave way under her and she sat down again with a puzzled look on her face.

"You've done it now," Abby warned.

"Shut up. Give me a hand." She reached out and Abby hauled her up. Meg took a determined step forward and it happened all over again, just as if her leg were made of ribbon.

"Dad'll be mad," Abby said smugly.

"Maybe we can fix it before he finds out." Meg rolled down her sock and lifted her skirt. "If it's broken I can snap it back." She chewed her lip. "I don't see anything."

"That's why we have pain," Abby said with a superior air. "To find out where it hurts."

But they couldn't find out where, and it alarmed them both. After all, a broken bone was by now commonplace. Someone snapped it back in and Meg guarded it as carefully as she could to keep it from breaking again. That fit reasonably into the world of cause and effect.

Ralph studied the leg wordlessly as well. He couldn't find anything, and he foolishly asked once, "How about here? Does this hurt?"

His face got dark when both girls laughed, and his jaw set into a sharp, hard line. He stood up from leaning over Meg's leg, and Abby suddenly noticed that he wasn't as tall as he used to be.

He's really a small man, she thought sadly.

But almost as if he'd read her thoughts he glared at her and she became a child again, wary of a parent. "I suppose you're to blame as well."

"Not me. I was on the ground. I told her she'd fall."

"That's right, she did," Meg said smoothly.

"Stop it," Ralph sighed. "When you agree like that I know you've already decided who's going to take the blame. That's it. This costs money, that's the point. This always costs money, and there isn't much of that around. Your mother's sick—and there isn't much money left."

The girls listened politely. His eyes traveled unhappily from one to the other. "You see," he said softly, "when you don't have enough money you can lose things." He held his head lowered for a second and then looked at Meg's clear, appraising eyes. He smiled wanly. "I guess we go to the hospital. I can't tell what you've done, and I don't know if it can wait. So we're off." He held out a hand and hoisted Meg up, pulling one of her arms around his neck. Abby followed them. "Oh no," he said firmly. "You stay here, in case your mother needs you."

Abby looked worried. "Needs me for what?"

"Anything, anything. A glass of water. Hope. Just anything at all."

"She better sleep," Abby said meanly to herself. It was an odd thing; when Meg complained about Enid's sickness or noise, Abby said reassuring, adult things. She even *felt* them. At such times Meg seemed whiny and selfish. But when Abby was left alone—especially without her father around—then she felt resentful and put-upon. She was afraid she might be expected to do something distasteful, disgusting even, something unknown and problematic. *After all*, she thought defensively, *what do I know, what can I do?*

She stood outside the doorway to her mother's bedroom. She stood on tiptoe, holding her breath and leaning against the wall, listening. She couldn't even see in, she stood to one side of the doorway; if she couldn't see her mother, then her mother couldn't see her either. She heard the quick intake-outtake of her mother's breathing—self-pitying, Abby thought cruelly, even in sleep. It seemed to

Abby sometimes that her mother forced them all to be constantly aware of her illness, that the moans, the sounds of sickness, even the yellow color of her skin, were all demonstrations of a demanding nature. There wasn't an inch of the house that stood safe from Enid's overblown despair. The enforced quiet, the antiseptic smells, the jars and bottles on window sills and bathroom shelves, it was as if her mother's scrawny fingers (scrawny out of selfishness!) had patrolled and marked every surface everywhere.

She leaned back against the wall, sliding down to the floor, her arms hugging her knees. She wondered about what was happening with Meg. Her thoughts drifted back. She could remember her mother. She could almost remember her well.

Meg came back with her right leg in a walking cast from her foot to her hip. Abby noticed how companionable the two seemed, Meg and their father.

"Something broken?" she asked.

"Ripped," Meg said proudly. "Ripped every muscle and tendon. Set a record."

"She's proud of it," Ralph said. There was grudging admiration. "They say she missed one in the general area of her knee, but it wasn't an important one."

"I offered to try for it."

"I held her back."

Abby forced herself to grin. The two had a rhythm going, very much like the twins' own rhythm.

"And so?" she asked patiently.

"Ah yes," Ralph sighed. "Consequences. Facing facts. If she could be strapped in place for a month, that's what they'd order. Absolutely immobile. But they've got a record on her, they know her, they consult with each other and say things like, 'You know she won't, she never does,' and so they came up with this cast—much bigger and heavier than necessary, designed to slow her down. They say she might heal, if God has nothing else to do."

"I'll limp," Meg said with relish, "or my leg will shrink and my toes fall off."

"Not Olympic material, at any rate."

"I may need a wooden cart so I can push myself along."

"As long as you have fun," Ralph said, his mouth twisted. Abby could detect the small but dependable gleam in his eye.

"*And* I'll miss school for a week."

Abby looked shocked. "They insisted," Ralph said apologetically. "I told them she'd only last for a day; there's no chance she'll be still any longer. But they seem to think it's serious. They said she *might* be lame."

"Twisted with pain," Meg chortled, "howling and hunched."

"It's not pain they mean," Ralph said patiently. "I told you, they're talking about structural damage. That means that once you destroy a part of your body you can't use it again. Whether you feel it or not. You've got to learn," he said seriously, "that you've got to respect things even when they don't mean very much, personally. I mean even when you don't understand what it's all about. You're young, you heal fast. You won't be young forever. Even when things don't hurt you, you can feel the consequences."

"Yes, Daddy," she said prettily, turning her face up to him. She folded her hands together in her lap, her white leg stretched out in front of her.

He looked at her thoughtfully for a moment, nodded, and said "Yes." He turned to Abby. "How's your mother been?"

"Asleep the whole time."

"You didn't get her anything to eat?" he asked, surprised.

"You didn't say to wake her," Abby said defensively. "I didn't eat, either. I was waiting for you."

Meg smiled and her father looked uncomfortable. "We stopped

off," Meg said. "Pizza."

Abby's lower lip jutted slightly forward.

"Sorry," Ralph said in a low tone. "Sorry."

While Meg settled in for the night, demanding books, papers and pens close by, and extra pillows, fortifying herself for her week-long stay, Ralph sat on the edge of the bed and shook Enid awake.

"I have to talk to you," he said, and she blinked twice, three times, and then stared at him with narcotic, thoughtful eyes.

"Insurance only covers so much. So there's all the bills beyond it. And there's no one, really, to look after the girls. And, I don't know, it doesn't seem right, somehow, how removed you are." He sat back in the shadows, his chin on his chest. Enid continued to look at him steadily.

"Do you understand?"

"Yes," she whispered. "I keep on drifting. It's so hard. To pay attention."

He drew in his breath. "You said there was a place that wanted to observe Megan."

"Oh yes. They liked her. They liked the thought of her."

"Enid, we're losing everything. I can't think straight for the money. I worry. I don't know what life is without worry anymore." He took another long pause. "I barely made the payments this month. They were late. Next month they'll be later, it will be hard to know which month they'll be for." He laughed shortly. "I can wait until we lose everything or I can make a move now."

"Now," Enid whispered calmly. Her eyelids were already beginning to close.

"It will mean changing everything," he said.

"Then there's nothing to lose," she whispered back faintly, and fell asleep.

Chapter 6

Life changed rapidly and immediately. Before Meg's cast had come off, the house was sold, the family had moved into the city, and all medical expenses were taken care of by the Towers Research Institute. This included Enid's treatment. The grim uneasiness Ralph may have felt at being taken over (as he saw it) by Towers, was soon dispelled by Enid's recovery. They evaluated her condition, took her off all drugs for two weeks, ran tests, and insisted on a less overwhelming treatment. She was alert now, her head craned eagerly when there was any movement. She was out of bed most of the day, often sitting expectantly on the sofa. Towers supplied a visiting nurse and a wheelchair. The doctors who saw Enid and spoke to Ralph always had upbeat lifts to their voices; they used phrases like "quality of life" and spoke casually of Enid's recovery. The day nurse, too, had the same friendly, cajoling attitude, insisting that Enid do more each day and—just as important—enjoy more each day.

Certainly their lives had changed, and little by little Ralph relaxed into it. All the people around him bloomed: his wife smiled again, the girls laughed and stayed home. He looked at them all at dinner and thought, *Thank God. I've done the right thing.*

With the house sold there was now even a small but secure savings account. They had an apartment in a good neighborhood—not the best part of the city, but safe and relatively quiet. His family was whole again. The Institute wanted to see Meg twice a week, once with her sister in what was described as a talk session. Ralph supposed it was psychology, and he thought it was a good thing for a girl so different from normal; two girls, really, because Abby spent every minute tied to and compared with Meg. Saturday mornings Ralph left Meg at Towers for three hours. Meg said she mainly walked and talked. Sometimes they blindfolded her and asked her what she felt. They checked her reflexes constantly. Sometimes she couldn't understand in the least what they were doing, though the air of excitement made her watch carefully. They did x-rays and made her describe every injury she'd ever had as best she could. They took blood samples, skin samples, hair and nail samples. They gave her exercises in coordination, in various kinds of sense memories, in imaging. She was constantly describing sensations and making guesses at what pain was like.

When Ralph asked her—with an obvious air of restraint—if it was possible that they were actually *hurting* her without her being aware of it, she snapped, "I can *feel* it when they do things. I can't feel pain but I can feel, you know." Ralph nodded, but he kept his worried air.

"Besides," Meg said, "they talk about it all the time. 'How can they hurt me if I can't feel hurt?' It's their favorite question. 'Is there pain if there's no one around to feel it?' That's what they say."

"You *are* there," Ralph objected strongly.

"It's a joke. I understand the joke."

Ralph frowned. Meg was developing an attitude, a superior, select attitude. She was becoming a specialist in herself and he had no idea how to stop her. He continued to worry, and one day he took the opportunity to talk to a young doctor while he was waiting for Meg to come out. The doctor seemed happy to talk; he was going over Meg's folder, and he allowed Ralph to interrupt him.

"We do various tests, that's all. Oh, any kind of test. There's no set scheme for her." He grinned. "We try anything. Even sensory deprivation. It's a new thing. It doesn't make her meditative," the doctor said. "It brings on a kind of frenzy. Very interesting."

"But what does it mean?" Ralph asked anxiously.

"There's been a lot of debate. But frankly . . . well, I don't think it *means* anything at all." The doctor looked slightly pleased with himself, perhaps even magnanimous. Ralph blinked at him steadily.

"It's just the way she is," the doctor said genially. "Science has come a long way. Some things just are, you know. They exist. They don't ask to be interpreted."

"And Meg?"

"Meg's a challenge," he said enthusiastically. "She demands explanation. Trouble is, she's so rare it's hard to tell what's Meg and what's her condition, if you see what I mean."

"I see," Ralph said, trying as hard as he could. "And then what comes next?"

"Why, we keep on testing! I expect a breakthrough eventually. We're all fascinated with her. She's got such an easygoing personality."

Ralph raised his eyebrows. "Easygoing? I've never seen that."

"Well, maybe from your point of view you don't see that. But from ours, you know, she's very good. She never complains unless she's bored. That's wonderful."

"And what would she complain about?" Ralph asked sharply. "What do you do to her that others would complain about?"

"Relax," the doctor said, suddenly snapping back into his professional, removed role. "I mean some of the others are paranoid and scream, or they repeat themselves with memory losses and bore us with the same complaints. Or their brain deficits keep them responding in the same way to the same situations. We've read all the books. It's very disappointing to us when there are no surprises. Your daughter is news, undiscovered territory; we're all secretly writing articles on her. We see her and think of grants and awards. She's our pot of gold. We love her disease and it doesn't bother her. It's not messy, you see, she's perfectly normal except for this one odd thing, and it's theoretical, almost, we all just try to map it out. We couldn't hurt her if we wanted to." He grinned quickly. "And absolutely no one would want to."

Meg's specialness had, for the most part and except for Abby, kept her apart from others. She was rough because she was different and her personality was such that she turned difference into defiance.

The move was disorienting, but the Institute adored her. They did not worry over her, they did not guard her, they liked her differences, her challenge. At first she became severely conceited, but that passed; she was a freak in an institute of freaks and she was intelligent enough to see it. It happened each time she sat in a waiting room with an assortment of other "cases"—and she quickly caught on to the references. There was the Frontal Lobe, the Fleeting Feeling, the Long-Term Memory, the Coma Lady. Some of them grinned in ecstasy, some winced prematurely. Very quickly, Meg learned her place, and if she was proud that she could stand gracefully in a room of the spastic and wheelchair-bound, she still knew that the contrast was superficial. In some strange, neural area, they were all firmly bound together, charted, and identified.

So much so that Meg sometimes felt pulled in two directions on the days when Abby was with her. Abby gained entry into this new world with its strange catalogs only through Meg, so she was a guest and an outsider. But Abby had the same mix of pity and annoyance whenever the Man Who Forgets came up to them and repeated, the same way every time, "Where am I? Someone tell me. Am I in prison? What is this place?" The inflections were always the same. The panic was always the same. Abby and Meg both passed quickly from pity to mockery.

When Abby was with her, Meg felt more of an us-against-them solidarity. She divided the other guests into "mental cases" and "not."

And sometimes, of course, Meg couldn't be certain if it was mental; Abby, too, got confused about the *order* of events, typified by her distress when she met The Hand, who came up to her with his elbows out, crying, "Listen. Explain this to me. Do you see this hand? It's not my hand. Dear God, they put someone else's hand on me! I can't get over it! It's so ugly. It's not mine, you see, it's obvious, don't you see how different it looks, grotesque, beyond belief. They won't admit it, they'd all lose their jobs, they want to convince me it's mine." His face stretched even wider into shock. "Do they think I wouldn't know my own hand? I've seen it every day of my life. This one's cold and lifeless and it looks like sticks, just sticks covered with pink plastic. I swear I'll chop it off some day just to get rid of it."

"No, of course there's been no accident," their counselor assured them. Dr. Waltz was a small woman with curled brown hair turning to gray. She was only slightly taller than the twins, who at 13 were just above average height for their age. Dr. Waltz wore glasses on a gold chain, although she never took the glasses off her nose. She spoke slowly and thoughtfully, with very little emotion in her voice. "He's had a stroke. There's a part of the brain that operates by recognizing all the parts of the body. That's where he had a stroke, and the particular cells that are capable of understanding that the hand is his—those cells are dead. It's very confusing for him and it makes him unhappy. Because that part of his brain is dead, he can't accept an explanation, no matter how many times we offer one. We've tried a variety of different directions, but as yet we haven't found a working cure. But that is his hand."

"It's all he ever talks about," Abby whispered.

"That's how important every part of the self is. We're always trying to make ourselves 'whole.' When we can't, we get stuck. Haven't you ever noticed that? When you think you've failed at something, for instance, don't you find it almost impossible to *stop* thinking about that? Or, on another topic, don't you sometimes want to melt in, to be unconscious of your uniqueness—to not be a twin, for instance?"

Abby and Meg cast troubled glances at each other. "But we *are* twins," Abby said, frowning. "That's what we *are*."

"And is it always good to be a twin?" Dr. Waltz asked smoothly.

"It's always a good thing," Abby said firmly, staring at Meg with wide-open eyes.

"It's a wonderful thing," Meg agreed, trying to open her eyes even wider.

Dr. Waltz's neutrality remained unspoiled and she made just the slightest mark with her pencil on the notepad in front of her.

The twins' passive dislike for Dr. Waltz was confirmed one day. They were early, and Dr. Waltz was running late, and they decided to sit on the wooden bench in the corridor rather than in the stuffy little waiting room.

There was another girl there, perhaps the most beautiful girl they'd seen. She had straight, shiny hair in a variety of blond shades, ranging from the darkest to the palest, that hung exactly to her shoulders, and when she moved her head the shades parted and fell forward or back against other shades. Her eyes were hazel with extremely dark, long lashes, and she had very fair, smooth skin. She smiled at them as they came towards the bench and patted it for them to sit with her.

"Oh good!" she said happily. "I was getting so bored. And you were going to see the Waltzer? That's what I call her, you know, I had to see her too for a while until I said I wouldn't do it, she put me to sleep, and what was the point of her analyzing my snores? I don't really snore," she said, behind her palm, "it was just a point I was making. So now I'm seeing Dr. Rippard, a man even if he is very old, and I'm having much more fun. He likes to hear dreams and I make them as dirty as I possibly can because he likes that and he says it's perfectly natural and healthy, even though it takes a lot of my time. I have to go to the library, you know, to get enough material for these dreams, because I'm still too young to get into some of the really *good* movies." She sighed. "That would make it easier, but I like to read, anyhow, and it *does* make him so happy."

"So you can change doctors?" Abby asked with interest. "I didn't know that."

"Well, you have to find the right way of doing it. I don't think they'll believe it if the two of you start sleeping during your session, you know. And you can't say you don't like her or you think she doesn't do anything because they'll just say it's resistance or something and part of the cure. Of course, too, maybe they'd only do it for me because I'm so sad. They feel sorry for me."

"What for?" Meg asked. She was fascinated by the girl, who was so beautiful and so friendly.

The girl blinked her eyes and then sighed once with her head slightly tilted to the side. "I'll go completely insane when I'm a grownup. It's hereditary, it happens in my family. Only with the women, though; the men are unimportant. But it happens all the time, they've been trying to trace every part of the family for their research. In the meantime, my mother's getting strange and they're telling me I shouldn't marry. Just have lovers and things." She looked proud of herself. "And you?" she asked politely.

"They told you to have lovers?" Abby asked in astonishment.

"Oh not exactly. They can't tell you things like that exactly. Not when you're fourteen. I think you have to be sixteen for *that*. But I tell my mother what they say, and she tells me what they mean."

"But doesn't it make you feel weird? Knowing you'll go insane?"

"After all," the girl said smiling, "it won't happen till I'm my mom's age, and by then, you know, I don't think there's much fun anyway. My mom is smart, but she never has fun. Maybe it's better to go crazy." She whispered the last sentence, her hand laid on her throat, her eyebrows raised to the ceiling.

"I think it would scare me," Abby said firmly.

"Really?" she asked, interested. "I guess I'm just used to it. My name's Greif, by the way, short for DeGreif Dundee, all family names. I know it sounds strange, but I'm the last one on either side they think, and I'm supposed to carry the name."

"I've never heard of that," Meg said.

"Oh yeah, and I'm supposed to make sure the names get passed on and don't die and isn't *that* a joke? I mean, being told not to have children and all." She smiled happily. "I guess you two aren't going crazy?" She had a suddenly wistful quality in her voice.

They shook their heads.

"You're twins, aren't you?" Greif asked simply. "You *look* like twins but you can never be sure here."

"I'm Meg. This is Abby. Abby can feel pain. I don't."

"Oh, *you're* the one," Greif said brightly. "I've heard of you. But that must be like being crazy, you know, cause not related to effect, as Grippard says, that's the definition of insanity, or at least inappropriateness. But I bet *we* all seem insane to you—I mean, you must think, 'What's the fuss? What's the noise? If it's broken, fix it.' How wonderful. No pain. But do you think it's had a *psychological* difference?" She furrowed her brow. "How silly. Of course it has. *Everything* makes a psychological difference."

"You're very smart," Abby said, impressed by the volume of Greif's words.

She blinked happily. "That's why I think I'll go *very* crazy."

The door opened and the nurse beckoned to Greif. "Come early next week and I will too," Greif said in a loud whisper. "There's so much to talk about." She rolled her eyes up, promising infinite revelations, and the twins felt their hearts quicken gladly. They were mildly surprised to see that Greif was several inches shorter than they were; indeed, her head was barely higher than theirs as she stood and they sat. She was so beautiful that they had thought she must be tall.

The twins stared at Waltzer during the session, thinking how they could get rid of her, maybe even share Grippard with Greif. They liked the idea of researching odd sexual practices, or even normal ones; maybe Greif could bring them up to date on what she'd already said.

Waltzer kept her hands on her desk, her eyes traveling from one twin to the other. The twins gazed solemnly back, turning various plans over in their minds. "You girls are quiet today," Waltzer said in her monotonous voice, and she got no reply.

"I'm so glad you're better," Ralph said. "God, I got so lonely."

"You don't mind losing the house?" Enid asked. They were peeling potatoes in the kitchen, peeling the skins away slowly with sharp knives on to newspaper. Enid's fingers were still bony and white, but the skin around the bones in her face had loosened. She looked young and thin, not dying.

Ralph shook his head, gripping the edge of the table, the knife in his right hand pointed upward. "I dreaded walking into it. I dreaded every window, every doorway. Every inch of it seemed unmanageable. You weren't there any more, and no part of it worked the right way."

"The girls didn't even want to come near me. I knew it. I felt it. I don't suppose I can blame them."

"It was very hard for them to understand. And I suppose I didn't help. I didn't know what to tell them."

"What did you tell them?"

"I said that you were sick and that the pills would make you better, eventually. But then I stopped believing that." He looked ashamed of himself and horrified at the same time. He laid down the knife and reached over to Enid's wrist.

She went on slowly peeling. "At first I just told myself to get through it," she said, "just get sick and get it over. But it went on too long, so I started looking for the sickness before it even came—you know, as if I were listening for footsteps. I recognized it sooner and sooner, I think, I sort of crawled inside so there was never any real relief, just trying to figure out what part of the wave I was in. I felt like I was in a wave, pushed, floating, sucked under, tossed, rolled, and every pocket of air would be temporary, ripped from me. Just being so constantly sick. I forgot about every one but me and I got so terribly lonely." She cut the potato into pieces, dropping the pieces into the pot of cold water.

"It's over now."

"Thank God for that," she said fiercely.

"We're back together and you're getting better. It's more than enough. The girls are getting along. I think I made the right move. You feel good, don't you?"

"I feel like health."

"And that doctor seems good."

"Good? Maybe he's God. He brought me back to life." She smiled to herself. "He must be God," she said softly.

The day after they met her, Greif shouted down to the twins from a second-floor window at school.

"Hey! Hey! Hey!" she yelled. "Abby! Meg! Look at me!"

The twins waved back wildly. It was the first friendly gesture from anyone at school. They had gotten used to the other girls standing together in twos and threes, their heads dipped together, their eyes switching from one girl to the next. Intent on ending their isolation, Meg and Abby studied the way everyone dressed, and they started wearing knee socks with stripes just as everyone else discarded stripes and went with solid. Their efforts to figure out the dress code kept them in a perpetual frenzy; they went through their clothes every night, trying to find items that matched what the popular girls wore that day.

It was easy to tell who the popular girls were. They never stood alone, trying to look busy. They always *were* busy, their heads locked in perpetual discussions. Every so often, conscious of her importance, one girl would slowly and casually step away from her friends and, as if walking on sand, go over to the most popular boy on his side of the hall for a brief, smiling word.

Try as they would, the twins always seemed to dress wrong. The popular girls smiled at them and dipped their heads together, the boys jostled and joked with each other and hunched away.

"That's so silly," Greif said the next week. "There isn't any dress code. They won't talk to you because you belong to the Institute." The twins looked alert.

"Of course," Greif said breezily. "You're new, you don't know yet. They think we're contagious or something. You see, a lot of us from the Institute go to that school. The ones who can blend, you know, the ones who can take tests."

"How many?" Meg asked.

"It varies," Greif said casually. "Let's see, in my year there's the spitter and the curser. Now *he's* funny. He says fuck! bitch! prick! all the time, but his answers are always right, he's the best student in his class. And—let me tell you—you know, no one else curses. Afraid of the association, I guess. The school never complains about us. There's some sort of financial business between the school and the Institute, but I think the regular students don't like it. They stick together. They don't talk to you much. Every once in a while someone smiles and then you realize the smile is some sort of disease, it's someone else from the Institute. Like a secret sign. If they smile at you, you're one of them."

"Who else?" Abby asked. "Who else is here?"

"There's Topsy. I think. I'm not sure. She's not my year. She's got a tumor that destroyed the bottom of things. She's officially learning -disabled. She can read, but slowly, because she can only see the top of letters, and she says so many of them look alike—l's and d's and b's are the same on the top half, she says, unless they're capital letters. She's very fond of f's because they're always distinct. but she can't do math because she can't see the bottom half of fractions and things. She might have moved out because of that. Plus she sometimes forgot to wear half her clothes."

"Joke?" Meg asked.

"Serious. It wasn't just that she couldn't *see* the bottom, the concept was gone. She'd only drink half a soda, button the top buttons. I'm not sure she's ever seen her own feet; if she has, it would only be the top of them."

The twins glanced at each other. "We're not like that," Abby said hastily. "In fact there's nothing strange about me at all."

Meg glared at her, curling one side of her lip.

"It doesn't matter," Greif said. "They know you, they've labeled you. People will smile at you, once in a while, but they'll be our people."

"Dribbling," Abby said disdainfully.

"Spitting," Greif corrected. "It's a hostility thing. Crossed circuits. Just a gesture."

"I'm not like that," Meg said softly. "My brain is perfect."

"Perfect?"

"Normal. And without the error of pain."

Greif grinned. "I like arrogance."

Abby frowned at her sister. "You have a defect in your brain cells. You could die without even noticing it. That's 'without the error' you're talking about."

Meg shrugged. "You learn. You watch for signs."

"It'll work as long as your mind stays clear," Greif said. She had a self-conscious look.

"Why wouldn't it stay clear?" Meg's lip got belligerent.

"Things happen. That's all. You could get a bump on the head—one you wouldn't even notice, I suppose—and then you'd be strange. Strange to yourself."

"Never."

Greif smiled contentedly. "I never did find any point in worrying."

Meg smiled back.

Chapter 7

They were all sitting down to breakfast one Sunday morning the following winter.

Meg saw the exact moment when her mother froze.

Enid was just staring through the doorway, as if she'd suddenly remembered something odd. She began to blink rapidly. Her lips were parted; her right hand still gripped her fork, her head was slightly cocked, as if listening.

Ralph and Abby were passing salt and pepper, and clicking their forks faintly against their plates.

"Mom?" Meg asked.

Enid raised her left hand and spread the fingers out. She held them up and touched the air in front of her tentatively. It was a slow, cautious movement.

Ralph and Abby saw it too. Their eyes were on her.

"Enid?" Ralph asked softly.

Enid stretched her lips wide, so wide that there was something bizarre in her appearance. Her hand kept shifting back and forth as if gently rubbing a face in front of her own face.

"I can't see," Enid said without any surprise or alarm. "I'm blind." She kept that stark, alarming grin.

Ralph settled his fork on the table. The twins put their hands on their laps as if they were at school. No one answered her.

"Did you hear me?" she hissed. "Did you say anything?" Her face had changed during their silence: alarm, even terror had taken over. Her eyebrows were stretched up, her bottom lip had stretched down, revealing her gums; her eyes were open so wide that the whites could be seen above and below her iris.

Ralph was quick to grab her hand, which was still rubbing some unknown form in the air. "We're here," he said quickly. "We're all here. You can't see anything?" His voice was harsh and yet, somehow, professional, as if he were prepared to be responsible no matter what.

"No shapes," Enid whispered. "Not even any light. Nothing. Like my head's in a cave. I thought—I thought for a moment I couldn't hear either. You were so silent. Don't ever do that again." She gripped Ralph's hand so hard he winced.

The twins were crying. "Does it hurt?" Meg whispered.

"It doesn't hurt," Enid whimpered. "I wish it hurt. I wish it felt *wrong*. Oh God," she said in a hopeless way.

"Get your mother's coat," Ralph said firmly. His face was suddenly lined. "You girls stay here. I mean it; don't go out. I'm taking your mother in." The way he said that phrase, "taking your mother in," seemed suitably defeated to them all. She had been out, released, for half a year, but it had been a false freedom.

From that day on, time had a run-together aspect. There were no moments when Enid was out of their thoughts. They woke, conscious of her absence; they went to the hospital after school.

The entrance to the hospital was a different doorway from the doorway they ordinarily used on their visits to the Institute; the corridors were painted green to elbow height, and white above that, shiny oil paints that had already become dull in places.

Enid was in a room with a woman who never woke, and from whom a network of varicolored tubes came and went. At first they whispered so as not to disturb her, but after a few days they forgot her altogether. She never had visitors.

Enid was propped up in bed. Since her sudden blindness she always faced forward, and cocked her head slightly in the direction of the talker, like a priest at confessional. Her facial muscles were starting to slacken, as if she no longer had any need for expression.

The twins could not adjust to her blindness. They moved themselves where her eyes would be looking if she could see; they even began to make exaggerated gestures while they spoke to her, as if encouraging her to trade in blindness for deafness.

The nurses and attendants came regularly, armed with generic kindness that was curiously close to indifference. They took blood, inserted tubes, rolled patients over with quick hands and neutral faces, saying, "Over in a minute!" or "That doesn't hurt!" when a sick body cried out or raised an arm in its own defense.

If a nurse came to Enid while they were visiting, they would all step back with respect, giving her room to work. They watched uneasily, poised to scoot out of the room at the slightest indication that anything intimate was about to happen. They were becoming hypersensitive to smells, embarrassed easily, groaning spiritually as Enid was moved farther and farther away from them, not only by blindness, but because she was now so obviously a body to be handled.

Her blindness was permanent and in fact Ralph thought he could detect a white cloud beginning to spread in one eye and it was this cloud he checked every time he saw her, bending down to kiss her cheek.

As the muscles in her face grew slacker and the cloud Ralph believed he saw spread (he was ashamed to ask about it), Enid insisted that anyone who visited must talk to her nonstop. She felt no obligation to respond or even pay attention; she wanted to be sure she could still hear, and they all began to chatter senselessly as soon as they heard her cry, "Who is it? Who is it? Speak to me! Tell me!"

The twins happened to hear her talking to herself one day. They had stopped in the corridor at the sound of her voice. "Oh my God, what is this? What's going on? I'm dying, I'm dying," and the twins were stunned with horror. No one had said that word in front of them;

when they sat down to dinner with their father, or stood silently together in the hallway while nurses closed the door between them and their mother, they had never said the word, and it was easier to believe that the word didn't apply.

"Oh God," their mother moaned. "Oh God." And the twins stood in the hallway, trembling and clutching each other until their father came.

"Oh Daddy," they cried to Ralph like very small children. "She said she's dying."

He patted their shoulders absently, his eyes staring through the doorway. "It's all right," he whispered. "Let me talk to her."

The door closed again.

"Do you think," Meg asked stonily, "that she could die?"

"Why? Why would she die?" Abby asked desperately.

They shuddered and waited.

"Who is it?" Enid rasped as Ralph closed the door.

"It's me," he said, and he kissed her. The cloud in her left eye had spread to her right. He sat down next to her sadly, holding her wandering hand (which automatically rubbed an invisible face in front of her own face) in his own hand. "Do you want to come home?" he asked gently.

"Home," she repeated avidly, blinking her clouded eyes. "Oh Ralph—can I go home?" There was a touch of her voice from her younger days—Ralph heard it and shuddered. A 20-year-old girl seemed to be begging him for hope. His eyes traveled around the room, barely registering white tiles, white nylon curtains on white metal tracks, the faint odor of disinfectant seeping over everything. In the corner of the room near the window the comatose woman snored.

"They want to do more tests, of course," he said, patting her hand. "But let me talk to them. I miss you. We all miss you. We want you to come home." And he spoke to her soothingly, until even her slack face softened into a smile and her clouded eyes glittered. "I want to go home," she quavered, and she was no longer 20 years old but 35, and dying.

Still, everyone avoided the word. He spoke to doctors and technicians, who used words like "invasive" and "recurrent" and "extensive." They hesitated and recommended more tests. They paused in their headlong flight down the corridor to blink at him and hem and urge patience. Ralph could see their desperate effort to recall who he was, and then the snap and pullback when they did, the consciousness and reluctance flooding forth together; the embarrassment.

By then, of course, Ralph had noticed the difference in the nurses' tones as they spoke to patients. They lingered over those who would recover, stopping to chat, to exchange life. But the losing patients, the ones who would never be cheerful again, were washed and powdered in a haze of speed, handled without being looked in the eye, heartened with childish, automatic words, their first names used only as a command.

Such as "Enid! Enid! Twist over there, to your left, there's a dear, this won't take long, hold onto the railing! Now that was easy, wasn't it? All done, I'll tuck you in. Want anything? Have to go now!" And a brisk, cheerful exit, even as Enid called, "Where are you? Have you gone? Are you here? Answer me!"

But it was Ralph who heard her call and answered, casting his eyes over the whiteness of the room, the clean white tiles, looking for traces of blood.

"**Oh?**" Greif said later with interest. "Your mother's here?"

"In the hospital," Abby said. "She's lost her sight."

"Blind?" Greif said. "They don't keep you in the hospital because you're blind. There must be more."

"Well, yes," Abby said reluctantly. "She's been sick for years." She and Meg got smooth looks in their faces, which Greif noticed and respected. "I see," she said.

"They're doing tests," Meg said with authority.

Greif bit her lip and didn't answer, looking away.

"To see what's wrong," Abby continued.

"Have you seen her?"

"Every day," Meg said. "We see her every day."

"Oh," Greif said, relieved. "That's okay then."

After a pause Meg asked, "What did you think?"

"I know where they do the tests," Greif said, shifting her eyes back and forth along the corridor.

"I do too," Meg said with surprise.

"Not *our* tests. Other tests."

The twins looked at her solemnly.

"Want to see?" Greif whispered again in too loud a tone to be a real whisper. They nodded.

"After you see Waltzer, then. Meet me here."

Dr. Waltz, who knew about Enid's condition, looked neutrally at the twins. They expected, and got, the usual questions from her:

"And how is your mother?"

"The same as last time."

"And how do you feel about that?"

"Why, good. Yes, good. It's better than her getting worse, isn't it?"

"But if she does get worse?"

"Why should she get worse?"

"But if she does?"

"Why are you saying that? The doctors don't say that!"

Caught by a potential breach of ethics, Dr. Waltz considered her words. "You must remember that anything can happen. We could all die tomorrow."

"Oh well," Meg grinned, "as long as we *all* die tomorrow, then there's no problem, right?"

Abby nodded in support.

Dr. Waltz blinked and made another check mark on her yellow pad.

"This way." Greif motioned them through a doorway at the very end of a series of turns along the corridor past the doctors' doors. They went down enough flights of stairs to realize that they were now below street level. The walls and ceilings were dull green.

The stairwell doors all had a rectangle of glass, and Greif stood on tiptoe at one of these. She ducked her head up and then down a number of times and then, after putting a finger warningly to her mouth, opened it slowly and motioned them to follow. She led them a few yards down and then opened another door and they all went inside.

They were in a utility room. There were boxes and bottles ranged on shelves, with larger boxes stacked on the floor.

"We have to wait a few minutes," she whispered, almost in pantomime.

The twins were excited, and a little bit afraid, but the fear itself was pleasurable. At this moment they admired Greif enormously. The Institute was so powerful, so large, and after six months they still felt ignorant of the Institute's system. They expected this; they were, after all, still in school so they understood rules. But the Institute, more than anything else, symbolized the adult world, full of strange solemn forms and superior manipulations.

Yet Greif could get around them all. She had sounded so clever and self-sufficient about besting Waltzer, but the twins had to take that on faith, and they were at the age when faith was waning. Prowling through the body of the Institute, the way the Institute prowled secretly through them, was thrilling. They felt almost as clever as their jolly, empty-mouthed doctors. Their arms had goose bumps. Whatever it was that Greif wanted to show them, they were ready.

"Now," Greif said, checking her watch, and she opened the door. Whether it was necessary or not, the precautions against exposure added to the thrill. They crept out into the hall, heading past a series of doors whose top halves were glass.

Inside each door they could see a long Formica counter with deep sinks running along one side of the room. Two rows of cages lined the opposite wall.

Greif did not comment when they stopped at one door and looked through it.

The cages they could see most clearly had a single cat in each. The cats lay down or sat quietly, barely moving. Some of them had parts of their scalps rolled back (like a lawn had been scuffed, Meg thought), with wires and colored pins running into their skulls. They had square index cards taped to the fronts with words and crudely drawn zigzags, and a date in red.

Some of them were bandaged and one of them, they could see, was opening and closing its mouth silently in a quiet howl. It was the only movement they saw.

They turned to Greif anxiously.

"There's something I want you to see," Greif said, and they moved on.

She took them to another door, and after looking through the window quickly, she opened it and went inside. Their hearts were beating now, they expected an alarm or an angry voice, but there was nothing.

This one had monkeys, and some of them were violently active, slamming themselves against the bars and walls and baring their teeth in an aggressive chatter. They walked past these carefully until Greif reached one monkey in particular.

"This," Greif breathed exultantly. "This one is mine."

They looked at her curiously and then turned their eyes back to the cage.

It was a small monkey with beautiful hands. It groomed itself mechanically, picking through its fur while watching them intently. At first it backed away from them, turning slightly to look over its shoulder from the corner of the cage. The card on the front had a long number and then columns of dates in different colors. There was an envelope taped to it.

"That's my number," Greif breathed. "You have numbers too. I know mine. When they take samples from me they come down and do something to the monkey. I've kept track." She pointed. "See? That's yesterday's date. They took my blood yesterday and they gave part of it to the monkey."

The monkey crept closer, still keeping its eyes on them.

"My blood," Greif said. "My monkey." She stared at it hypnotically. Its brown eyes watched Greif intently and then it raised one hand and stretched it forward, hooking it around a bar and pulling itself back in an impatient leer. There was a small shaved area on the back of its neck and a fresh scab. It settled down and stuck one hand out, palm upward.

Abby went closer and reached out to stroke its fingers.

"Don't!" Greif cried. "It could be crazy, you know. I never touch it. I just come down to see if it's alive." Abby took her hand back.

"Let's go," Greif said abruptly and turned on her heel. "They found me once and I had to cry and pretend I was lost. I'm small, you know. I can look very young." She checked her watch. "We have to go. We have to go now."

They retraced their steps back to the stairway. When the door closed behind them, Meg turned to her. "Is there one for me? With my number?"

"I suppose so. At least they'll try. But I don't know if they've got an animal without pain." Her voice lowered harshly. "I've heard them scream, you know. Whatever they do in there, I don't know what it is. When they have a red date on their cards, they disappear.

I think they kill them."

"No," Abby protested.

"My mother said it's for our good."

They didn't answer.

"My mother's mad," Greif said bitterly.

The next time Meg's doctor took blood from her she asked, "Do you like cats?"

"Oh, yes," Dr. Smallwood said airily. "I have a cat. Persian. Leaves hair all over the place but what a face! You won't feel a thing," he joked as he stuck the needle in.

"Have you ever seen a monkey?" she asked.

"Of course," he said, drawing back the plunger.

"I saw my first the other day."

"Cute, huh?" he said absently.

"They have hands just like us."

"Pretty close," he admitted. "Does that bother you?"

"It doesn't bother me. Do their hands feel cold or hot?"

He looked at her, somewhat surprised. "I've never noticed."

"Your hands are cold," she said.

He pressed his fingertips quickly against his cheeks. "So they are," he laughed. "I'll have to keep them in my pockets."

"Your doctor is Smarts!" Greif said in awe.

"No, Smallwood, Dr. Smallwood," Meg said.

"We call him Smarts," Greif crooned. "I've read his name in the paper. He was once on TV. I heard one of the nurses say he was a genius. Oh, you're so lucky! He's so cute! So adorable!"

"He's all right," Meg said.

"I've never seen him," Abby said with interest. "Is he really so cute?"

"He's cute," Meg admitted. "I just never think of him that way.

He's not our age. He's much older."

"Oh, pooh," Greif said, belittling. "He's got delicious buns. Round, you know, a nice slope out from his waist. Not flabby; not like most men. Like fruit; you want to weigh them in your palm and—umm—squeeze."

Meg and Abby both gaped at her.

"I've never paid attention," Abby said.

Greif glowed with satisfaction. "I look at men. It's something to do. But you have to stay with it. Perseverance. There aren't so many nice ones around."

"There aren't?" Abby asked, her mouth drooping open.

"Not with buns. Trust me."

This was a revelation to Abby, who had never heard that a man's body could be attractive. She thought "good looks" meant the right height and a great face. But now she found herself looking at men, staring at their buns, wondering what Greif would say. Meg caught her doing it and pinched her every time.

Chapter 8

Meg could not bear to look at her mother walking slowly, one arm stretched out in front of her, down the hall. Enid was seized by restlessness now that she was home; she stalked each room, she felt every object in it, over and over, sometimes moving papers and trinkets from one pile to the other, her lips moving. She was memorizing and categorizing everything all at once.

"I hate it," Meg confessed.

"I think it makes her feel safer," Abby said. "I've been trying to think why she does it. She can't see but she wants to know what's around her. We're always looking around, to make sure nothing's changed. We can see if something's changed; she can't."

"You're *explaining* it," Meg protested. "I'm telling you how I *feel*."

"I hate it too," Abby sighed.

Enid was gaunt again, and her endless, restless movements seemed to work away what little flesh there was on her bones, but even so things weren't so bad until the day Enid started screaming.

Ralph and Abby had gone to the supermarket; it was Meg's turn to stay home. Enid had been calmer that morning and they were all relieved when she announced she was going to lie down again. She was bones, a walking cadaver. She drank milk when she took her various pills; other than that she was too restless to concentrate on eating. Sometimes they followed her around with sandwiches, cookies, fruit, imploring her to take a bite.

Meg was reading a magazine when the first scream rang out. It caught her off guard, it was loud and gruesome and frightened. It hit her so loud that she flung herself onto the floor and shivered in terror.

She wanted to wait there until her father got back; she wanted no part of it. She covered her ears with her hands; she took pillows from the sofa and pressed them over her head, she groaned and tried to listen only to her own groans. But the piercing wail continued, it rose up and then broke off; it began again with a sob, a dismal, desolate cry, and then it rose in fury and despair, gaining an awful power until Meg felt that she must, absolutely must, lift up her voice and scream with it, crying against death.

There was a pounding on the door. "What is it? What is it?" Meg recognized Mrs. Pearl's voice, the landlady, and she flung herself at the door, not even realizing that she was sobbing too.

Mrs. Pearl grabbed her, thinking there was something wrong, but Enid's shrieks continued, and still holding Meg, she dragged them both into Enid's room, whispering, "Dear God! Dear God!"

Enid was lying flat on the bed, her fists beating against her forehead. Her eyes were wide open and tearless. Other than those merciless hands, her face and her body were rigid.

"Mrs. Gallagher! Mrs. Gallagher!" the landlady cried. Meg threw herself into the corner of the room and huddled there, watching and crying.

Mrs. Pearl grabbed one of Enid's hands, then both of them, but the fists kept rising up and hitting the sides of her head. "Stop it!" Mrs. Pearl screamed. "You've got to stop it!" Uncertainly, unnerved by the screams, she stuck her own hand in and smacked Enid, thinking that it was some fit of hysteria, hoping to startle her, but the screams continued, and she immediately began again to try to grab one hand at least and stop it.

They heard footsteps running in the hall and then, miraculously, Ralph was there and he dropped his packages on the floor, spun around and then came back with a vial of pills and a glass of milk.

"Enid! Enid" he yelled. "Stop it! Take these! Take these! They'll help you, Enid!" And between him and Mrs. Pearl they were able to prop Enid up and get some of the pills down her outstretched throat, slopping milk and pills all over the bed until Enid's sobs took on a hiccupping, defeated quality and she began to quiet down.

They stood around her, panting, checking her with cautious eyes. When she got quiet, they left the room and closed the door, escorting Mrs. Pearl out in silence.

She turned to them before they left, saying, "God have mercy on you all," and at that the girls began to cry again, big beefsteak tears.

"We have to talk," Ralph said.

They sat around the kitchen table, so Ralph could see down the hallway in case Enid's door opened. He didn't realize this was impossible now.

Ralph sighed, clasping his hands. He looked up at his daughters, his eyes mixed with sympathy and resolution.

"Your mother is dying," he said quietly. "I think you should know. We had hope before, but I don't think there's any hope left. It's spreading through her brain now, destroying her. Not her mind. She can feel it happening to her, each snap, each loss. And she's in pain.

"We have two choices. We can send her back to the hospital. You've seen what that's like. There'll always be someone there to take care of her. They'll keep her quiet, maybe all the time. We won't know everything they do."

He stopped for a moment, looking at them. A picture of the cages in the basement flashed through the twins' minds. No one knew what was done there either.

"If we keep her here," Ralph continued, "we can get a nurse if we want, like the last time, but even then we'll always have to be here, and if she screams we'll hear her. We won't be able to walk away from her."

"What does she want?" Abby asked.

"She wants to stay here."

"And you?"

"Yes. I want her here."

"Not in the hospital," Meg said quietly.

"I agree," Abby said.

Ralph stared down at his hands. "Thank you."

"Dad?" Abby asked fearfully. "How long will it be? How bad?"

"I don't know. They tell you different things. We can give her pills for the pain. She'll sleep a lot. Like the last time." He looked at them seriously. "You're older now. You can help."

"I thought they were helping her," Abby said.

"So did I," he sighed. "Maybe we just didn't understand."

"Well, I don't understand," Meg said. "This is it? She'll scream like that, and we don't know how long—and then she'll die?"

"It's the best we can offer her," he said helplessly.

Meg felt a strange fascination making her do shameful things. Yes, she was horrified and repulsed; at times her mind absolutely refused to believe her mother would die. But sometimes, too, she began to speculate: maybe these people who felt pain were really just making it up? She would give her mother the wrong pill when it was her turn to give the medication. It seemed to her that her mother screamed without any predictable causes. Mrs. Pearl sometimes came up trembling, whispering, "Please! Please! I understand it all but you must do something about the screams." Eventually they got stronger pills, and Ralph learned to give injections.

Then Meg began to creep into her mother's room and stand in the corner, watching her. If Enid stirred and whispered fretfully, Meg held her breath and didn't answer. She studied her mother's open eyes. There was so much pressure inside her skull that her eyes bulged out. Enid could no longer close her eyes, and there was a wash and drops by her bed to keep her eyes wet. The headaches made her scream with pain, and the only relief was in the series of pills, all labeled by Ralph and kept out of Enid's reach. He had a pad by the bed, listing the pills and the times she was given them.

Meg watched the onset of one attack, standing silently in the corner as a ripple of consciousness fled across Enid's face. It was odd enough to watch her sleep with her eyes open; odder still to try to catch her waking up without the obvious signs. Her lips widened, grimacing over her teeth, so it seemed that they, too, protruded. Her hands clenched and unclenched, and she let out a low animal groan, deeply felt and harsh. Meg guessed that the groan meant Enid remembered she was dying.

She shot out her hand, scrambling for the eyewash on the table and putting drops in with an almost addictive desperation. Her hands seemed to be alert, even intelligent; they were always trying to do something. After using the eyewash they scrambled across the bed-clothes, hopelessly straightening things out. They probed her forehead, as if feeling for sore spots. Then they paused, fragilely, like butterflies, and Enid raised her chin slightly. Meg could tell that it was going to be one of those rare moments when her mother seemed alert, almost healthy.

"Someone's here," Enid said sharply. "Who is it?"

Meg hesitated.

"It's you, isn't it?" she rasped. "You're watching me again, aren't you? Like a little god with a fly. Like a boy with a fly." She huffed angrily. "It's you, isn't it? You want to see if I'm in pain when I'm alone, is that it? You think maybe it's all an act, just for you, right, when the lights are on, or maybe we've overlooked something you might just catch. Tell me who's there!"

"Yes, it's me," Meg said. She stepped over to Enid's side of the bed. "I wasn't sure you were awake. Do you want anything?"

"Liar," Enid said sadly. "You stand in that corner like a spider and watch me. I know you do."

"Are you in pain?" Meg asked gently.

"Am I in pain," Enid repeated bitterly, her hands flinging themselves back against the bedspread. They rose up and searched blindly for the drops, dripping the liquid into her eyes. "And I can't even blink! My God, they're torturing me!" She turned her head to the side, her mouth twisted. She had no tears or she would have cried; she went through the motions dry; a dry convulsing of the chest, furtive gasps, little choking sighs. But then she was still with a complete suddenness.

Meg understood. "It's starting again, isn't it?" she asked with that mixture of fascination and dread in her voice.

"No. Stop," Enid whispered, and then her hands raised themselves in protest around her head. "Oh God, it's coming now, it's coming like a knife, an ax splitting my head open, it's burning me. I can almost hear it hiss, it hurts so much. It will split my head open any minute, I'll die, I'll die." Her voice rose. "If I could pull it out, I'd pull it out!" She began to pound the heels of her hands against her head. "Oh God." She began to sob. "All this and I'm going to die, too!" She wailed. "Ralph! Ralph!"

"He's not here," Meg said.

"Oh, I can't stand it!" Enid cried. "I can't stand it!"

"This pill," Meg said nervously. "Take it."

"Pill? Is it time?"

"Dad gives it to you when you're like this."

"I'm always like this," Enid said, reaching out her hand. "There's nothing else. Oh give it to me! Now!" She leaned forward in the direction of Meg's voice, grabbing at her. Meg picked up the vial, tapped out a capsule, then gave it to Enid.

Her breathing eased almost immediately; Meg had noticed this before.

"What does it do?" Meg asked, watching as her mother grew calmer.

Her mother's chest heaved up and down, slower and slower. "It makes everything so easy. When I think, 'No more, not a minute more,' then I find another minute's gone and I drift away somewhere. It doesn't even have a look to it, a wonderful blank picture and soon I think, 'I can hang on longer, who knows what will happen, who knows?'"

"And pain?"

"That's what I think," she said drowsily. " 'And pain?' It gets . . . distant. I can think about it, it doesn't seem so bad. But I know it's there. If I look for it very hard I can find it again, but it's smaller, it's quiet." Her hands lay still, curled around her arms. "Like a piece of music. It drifts past you, you try to catch it. And while you try to catch it, you think of something else." Her voice got slower and slower and finally ground down to a whisper. "It's so peaceful. So sad." She sighed, moved slightly, and began to breathe softly.

Meg took a step back, frowning. She bit the edge of her finger, a favorite spot peeled raw. She wished Abby were around, but she had gone with Ralph to carry packages.

She watched her mother sleeping. Her cheekbones stuck through her skin, her nose was sharp and pointed. Her fingers—when they touched you—were twigs. You could feel the joints like knobs. And the way those eyes never closed, and the lips stretched back over her teeth. Meg sucked in her breath. She felt nervous about it, tentative, as if at any moment she might feel a tap on her shoulder and it could happen to her.

She tiptoed to the bureau, looking over the bottles. She picked up the painkillers, turning the plastic vial to left and right. She turned it over and spilled out two, rolling them across her palm. They looked simple. White, with a notch down the middle. She picked up her mother's glass. It was half-full.

She swallowed the pills.

She stood still, wondering if she would feel anything. The only pills she'd ever taken were for antibiotics.

Eventually, her arms and legs felt warm and loose. She smiled sleepily. She went over to her corner and sat down, leaning against the wall. She stopped worrying about Enid, and worrying about pain. She felt good being in the same room with her mother sleeping. She closed her eyes.

One day, more than a month later, Ralph woke up in the middle of the night, feeling cold. He got another blanket, he turned up the thermostat, and when he got back into bed, inching himself in so as not to disturb Enid, she was dead.

His hand stayed at her throat. He thought, *Five minutes ago she was alive*, and he was surprised because he felt nothing. *I had to turn up the heat*, he thought. *It was too cold.* And he remembered how he had almost turned to Enid because it was cold, and how in the old days he would have hugged her to him for warmth.

But of course I can't do that anymore, he thought, and he touched her again blindly, thinking, maybe her pulse was just slow.

He studied her chest and thought he saw a faint breath, but after a while he knew that was a mistake, too.

Until finally he admitted she was dead and he had no feeling to connect to the slow tears that rolled down one, two as he held her hand. He had been waiting for death and now it was here and he was surprised and not at all surprised at the same time. He couldn't get over, he told himself, how she had waited for him to leave the room before she died. If he'd only stayed another minute. If he'd only turned to her and held her. Gone five minutes at the most and every night he'd slipped in beside her, counting her breaths.

The girls cried, of course, with scared faces, crying together and holding each other as he wished right now he'd held Enid, some-how known enough to have held her. They slip away even when you're watching them, he thought, and the guilt was so hard he couldn't imagine releasing it.

But of course the girls came in, inching into the room together, and he began to smooth Enid's blankets and her hair and those eyes stared out even blinder than before, and it was almost as if every movement was a chain reaction, because he picked up the phone and made his calls.

They sat together in the living room with their mouths shut, like an awful visit they had to make, aware of time and death in the other room.

When the ambulance came Ralph showed them where she was, and they suggested that it might be good for the family to leave, so Ralph put a hand on the shoulder of each twin, and they went down-stairs to Mrs. Pearl.

They heard the thump on each step and they stood at the win-dow watching as the stretcher rolled out front. The sound of the thump and the sight of the stretcher drove them all mad, and they howled for Enid, with her teeth bared and her eyes open, for Enid who was dead.

Chapter 9

A kind of lassitude overcame Ralph after Enid's death. He kept everything in place—his job, his apartment, the Institute to take care of the girls—not because they were positive choices, but because they were already there. Anything else would have been too much effort, incongruous, suggestive of hope after death.

He smiled sadly at the girls sometimes. He spoke to them softly and occasionally looked at them intently, as if trying to focus.

The twins continued tightly bound to each other, covering uncertainty by stepping forward with the same foot, matching their movements, occasionally speaking simultaneously. They parted their hair on opposite sides, however, continuing the mirror game of their childhood. But it didn't make telling them apart any easier. Everyone knew they could be lying.

The older they got, however, the easier it actually was to tell them apart if you knew how to look. Meg had a slight limp from having ripped her tendons twice; she had an extensive burn scar on her right arm near the elbow. In general, she had more scars.

Greif, for instance, could tell them apart instantly, by a small scar above Abby's eyebrow. Greif never mentioned it; she knew instinctively that it would be a very easy—and interesting—thing for Meg to cut an exact scar above her own eyebrow. Greif merely saw it with her inquisitive eye, and kept it to herself.

After the funeral, Meg and Abby had gone to school expecting special treatment. They certainly felt special and cried when they couldn't explain why. They dressed in dark colors for a week because they needed to do something. Their world had become odd and fragmented. Mrs. Pearl clucked when she saw them. One of the doctors who had taken care of Enid while she was at the Institute came to the wake. He had frowned at the casket, and only the fact that he was known to be nice (one of the nicest) had kept them all from exploding when he'd said, finally, "What a shame. If she'd only lived longer maybe we could have saved her."

But as usual, the other students kept their distance at school, maybe even more. Everyone was self-conscious and loud, and their eyes went right past Meg and Abby. Greif started high school three blocks away, and she said she'd made sure not to mention the Institute. It was easier that way. Though sometimes, she admitted, she thought there might be a certain erotic appeal in announcing you were a freak. "I think I'll hold it in reserve," she said. "Maybe whip it out at the right moment." She fluttered her eyelids.

Meg hated it without Greif; she felt the hostility of all the other kids, even when Abby claimed it wasn't true, that no one ever noticed them any more. Meg couldn't understand it when Abby made her periodic attempts to talk to the other students. "They're ants," she said angrily. Abby shrugged and replied, "They're people. Like me." Meg glowered.

She even began to dress sloppily the more Abby primped. That stopped when she saw a boy stare at Abby, then walk over and talk to her. After that Meg spruced herself. She smiled at the boy and then looked away.

But she hated the school, she hated Abby's interest in it; she preferred the Institute, and Greif, and the shadowy corridors Greif showed her. She liked excluding Abby; she wanted Abby to feel left out. And there was a quality in Greif that pleased Meg: Greif really didn't think anything was odd. She seemed to know everything and judge nothing.

Greif took her to the cold room, with the vials and jars of body fluids. The bloods were kept in plastic bags. The other vials were too revolting to name, both Meg and Greif got dizzy with disgust and their faces contorted unconsciously, but they went there more than once. Occasionally they brought fake jars and labeled them with fake patient names and old dates. These jars would stay there for months and then—all of them together—disappear.

Greif said she was looking for the room with the used parts. She said that there had to be a room with tumors and bad hearts and a whole lot of tonsils and appendixes. "I mean, my God, they can't throw them out with the garbage, can they?" she breathed. Meg wondered if there was a sort of partial graveyard somewhere: "Here lies the kidney of John Smith, awaiting him."

They found where the clothes were washed, the great presses that ironed them, they found the morgue but it was empty. "Isn't that eerie?" Greif said. "Isn't that weird? Where did the bodies go? What are they doing with all those bodies?"

"Are there so many bodies?" Meg whispered.

"Half the people who come into a hospital never leave."

"Half?"

"At least."

They ended up walking the long underground tunnel between the hospital and the research building. There were metal containers and plastic garbage cans near each exit. A thought seemed to strike them both at once: were the missing bodies *there*? Liquids seeped from the containers, some of it dark. Was that blood and gore? Their steps picked up. Meg wished Abby were with them. Whenever Greif said the word "dead," Meg always thought of Enid and it confused her; she didn't know what to do with the thought and she would have liked seeing how Abby handled it.

They went down to the research rooms to look at Greif's monkey, going through the usual elaborate ritual of ducking and hiding. Meg was beginning to think it was all show; maybe everyone went home at five and Greif knew it.

"My Dundee," Greif crooned. "Do you think it looks crazier?"

"Definitely crazier," Meg agreed. The monkey plucked at its fur and bared its teeth. It hurled itself against the front of the cage.

"They go crazy, anyway, from confinement," Greif said, pursing her lips. "I looked it up. I don't know what they think they can prove. It's not a good test."

Meg walked down the rows of cages. "Where's my monkey? I know my number now, and I don't see it."

"Doesn't have to be a monkey," Greif said. "There are cats and dogs here, even mice. It could be any animal. Maybe even a fish. Hey, how about a lobster? They say lobsters don't feel any pain, that's why you can boil them alive or even just slice their stomachs open to stuff them and bake them alive. And you don't have to feel guilty. They say," she trailed off.

"Not a lobster. I'm sure it wouldn't be a lobster." Meg was offended.

Greif shrugged. "It's true, I've never seen one here."

"A lobster," Meg repeated in disgust. She was stiff with anger.

"I've been thinking," Meg said to Abby later. "Do you believe Greif? Do you really think she'll go crazy? Or do you think she's normal?"

"She doesn't seem crazy to me," Abby said judiciously. She was brushing her hair. "Silly sometimes."

"Likes attention."

Abby smiled. "If she's not going crazy, what's she doing at the Institute?"

"*I'm* not going crazy. Maybe there's something else wrong, only not as interesting. Maybe she's there because she *thinks* she'll go crazy, or because she *wants* to think it. It could be tricky."

"If she wanted to believe she was going crazy, that would be a form of craziness, too, wouldn't it?" Abby was interested.

"See what I mean? Tricky."

"It's the monkey thing, isn't it? You're jealous."

"How do I even know she's telling the truth? *She* says it's got her number, but maybe she just wants to believe it does."

"I really don't know; I don't see her as often as you do. You think about her too much. She's not the only person on earth."

"Who is? Besides, she's my friend."

"I'm not even sure you like her."

"I'm not sure either."

"You never ask me to come with you anymore. I'd like to see the monkeys, too."

"There wouldn't possibly be one for you, you know."

Abby sighed. "I just want to see them."

After a minute Meg said, "Sure."

Abby kept brushing her hair, frowning into the mirror. "You're doing it for that Jeff person," Meg said flatly.

"I'm doing it for me."

"You got nail polish. I saw it."

"It's to keep me from biting my nails."

"There's nothing wrong with biting your nails."

"No, nothing wrong. It's just not elegant."

"Don't talk to him, Abby. When he turns away from you, he laughs."

"He doesn't."

"Watch him the next time," Meg said sorrowfully. "Watch him like I do."

Abby put the brush down, looking at her sister in the mirror. Unconsciously, she tried to smooth out hair, then stopped. The messy hair was Meg's, not hers.

"You come here every week now?" Abby whispered as they all hid behind the stairway door.

"Almost," Meg said.

"I remember hiding here the last time. Do you hide every single time?"

"If they found out about us, they'd get careful. Then we couldn't check on the progress," Greif said.

"Progress?"

Greif nodded. "I have to know when the monkey goes insane. I have to see how it looks. Be careful!" she hissed, ducking against the wall.

They waited. "There's no one there," Meg said finally, and they crept out into the corridor.

"That sound," Abby said urgently as they passed one of the lab doors.

"It's a cat howling," Meg said.

"Why?"

"I don't know," Meg said. "It's uncomfortable? It's lonely?" She looked deliberately unconcerned.

"It's in pain," Abby said.

"Okay."

"Meg said you have a boyfriend," Greif announced suddenly.

Abby flushed. "I don't."

Greif nodded. "It's okay. I understand. Even at our age they're so unreliable. My mother says it just gets worse."

"How *is* your mother?"

Greif shrugged. "The same. Here it is." They slipped into the lab room, walking past the rows of rats to the monkey section. The Dundee bared its teeth and rushed at them.

"She's annoyed today," Greif said sadly. "I thought maybe our moods matched, but I feel happy as a clam today." She fingered the card on the cage and sighed. "The dates match, though. They took blood Monday. That's this." She pointed to the last date.

The monkey grasped the bars and flung itself at them, back and forth. They stared soberly.

"It'll get hurt," Abby said, worried.

"It never gets hurt, though," Greif said.

"Why should it get hurt?" Meg asked.

"Things get hurt." Abby stood carefully away from the cages, her eyes traveling around the lab.

Greif turned to her suddenly and smiled. "Do you think men matter?" she asked, and waited expectantly.

"Matter?" Abby repeated, surprised. "Of course they matter."

"I mean, are they important? Important as they say? Important to us?"

"How could they not be? Who else would we marry?"

"But necessary? Necessary, do you think? Do you think we can do without them, as easily as not?"

Abby blinked at her, perplexed. "Why?"

"I was just thinking," Greif said dreamily, her eyes shining. "If there were only two of you left on earth," she said, "who would you rather it be? Your best friend or a man?"

Meg laughed. "What about the propagation of the species?"

"Even then you might have only one child. Or all the same sex. That could happen."

"It's a silly question," Abby said suddenly. "As if you could choose who the other person would be."

Greif shrugged. "I like philosophy, that's all."

She returned to tapping the plate on her monkey's cage. Meg walked up and down the rows, checking the numbers and dates on the cards. One of them might be hers.

They could hear a dog howling through the walls.

"I don't like that," Abby said nervously. "Why is it howling like that?"

Meg was indifferent. "Lots of them do that. It stops."

"Maybe something's wrong." She hesitated. "I'm going to see."

Meg followed her casually. She didn't want to seem interested. Abby peered through the window in the door, then opened it carefully. Meg had been in this room once before, with Greif. Then it had been silent, almost drugged with silence. Today it mewed and whined and moaned. She heard Abby's quick intake of breath. Abby walked down the row on her tiptoes, her eyes pegged to the cages. The cries continued. Meg watched.

"Their legs are all broken," Abby said in a choked voice. "Their back legs. They can't even sit right."

"Leave them alone, Abby."

"We have to go now," Greif said urgently.

"Just leave them? Just like that?"

"Maybe they're trying to fix them. Maybe that's why they're like that."

Abby shook her head.

"We can't do anything about it," Greif said. "Not now, anyway. And if someone finds us, we won't be able to come back, ever. And then you'll never know."

Abby nodded reluctantly and followed them down the corridor. Greif chattered on endlessly once they'd made it to the relative safety of the stairway. "I think she looked good today, my Dundee-monkey, don't you? She's emotional, certainly, but they say emotions make life deeper. Or is it cheaper? I'm sure I heard it somewhere, one way or the other. So, what's your boyfriend look like? Is he tall? Is he handsome?"

"He's not my boyfriend." Abby's face was pink.

Greif paused, up ahead of them on the stairs. "You don't have to worry about *me*. I wouldn't tell anyone. Does he have a lot of hair?"

"What do you mean?"

"Oh, don't worry," she laughed, waving her hand and squinting her eyes. "I mean his head. My mother always said to pick bald men. She said they're so *grateful*."

The girls sucked their lips, trying hard to think what this gratitude might mean.

"Maybe he'll be bald when he's older," Greif said encouragingly. "You can't tell right away, but you *can* tell by the way he dances. My mother says that a man who dances well makes love well too."

"Did she?" Abby asked, with a flat, almost challenging accent.

"She said to pick out a man who can keep the beat," Greif drawled.

Abby's breath was coming in quick annoyed bursts, so she had to control her voice when she asked, "But, Greif, isn't your mother crazy?"

"Oh yes," the girl answered cheerfully, "crazy as they come. She always tells me she'd have to be crazy to be my mother."

"I don't know whether she's nuts or not," Abby said to Meg later that night. "But I don't think she's at all nice. Do you like the things she says?"

"She's funny," Meg said, smiling. "She doesn't care what she says."

"She doesn't care about much of anything." Abby's fingers were trembling as she picked through the combs and clips on her dresser. Meg watched her coolly, waiting to hear what had upset her.

"Like what?"

"Like those animals. What's going on there? What are they doing?"

"Medicine. Science."

"It looks horrible to me. If you could have seen those dogs—"

"I've seen them." She concentrated on catching every move Abby made. The little jerks, the frown, the too-bright eyes. Abby was picking combs up and putting them down again without paying attention to what she was doing.

"People like you—" she began angrily.

"Like me?" Meg said slowly.

Abby put one hand over the other to keep them quiet. "They have feelings, you know. Or maybe you *don't* know anymore. They can feel pain. They can feel lonely."

"And people like me can't?" Meg whispered.

"You can't feel pain."

"Pain is an electrical impulse passing along the nervous system to the brain. Like a lightbulb."

"More than that," Abby insisted.

"I don't think so," Meg said, bored with Abby's anger. "And science doesn't think so either."

"Science," Abby repeated miserably.

"Besides which, you're the only people like me," Meg said soothingly. "We're exactly the same except for this. We don't even have to talk. We think the same things."

Abby climbed into bed and shut out the light. "It used to be like that, when we were little. Now I don't think I know what you're like."

"Yes," Meg whispered soothingly. "I know what you mean. It's nice, isn't it?"

A month later Greif was stunned when she found her monkey was missing.

"Oh no!" she said, louder than she'd ever been in the lab. "She's gone! She got out! Oh what'll I do?"

Meg looked closely. She opened and closed the door. "The card's gone," she pointed out. "The cage is clean and it closes fine. I don't think the Dundee got out."

"I'm sorry," Abby said.

Greif looked stricken but unenlightened, so Meg plunged on. "We think she's dead, Greif."

Pathetically, Greif stepped backwards, flailing against a counter.

"Dead!" she said, as if the concept came as a horrible surprise.

"Maybe they even killed her," Abby said bitterly. "After all she was just a series of electrical impulses." She looked at Meg with a certain proud bitterness.

Meg nodded, acknowledging it. "I'm sure they killed her," she said pleasantly, "no matter what happened." In fact she was pleased to say the phrase, "I'm sure they killed her." In her mind she was coldly aware that she was mentioning death without meaning her mother, and that she was able to think of the word and the sentence with clinical compassion. Death was an event.

Greif sagged even more bonelessly against the counter. Abby stepped next to her, touching her arm. She was worried that Greif might, finally, choose this moment to go insane, that Greif had been right all along and her fate was irretrievably tied to the Dundee. The hand she placed on Greif's arm was there to restrain her, to keep her on the side of sanity, to prevent trouble.

"How will I know what's happening to me?" Greif quavered. Meg and Abby, unable to supply an answer, waited uncertainly. "How will I know when I've gone mad?" Greif whispered.

"We'll tell you," Meg said quickly, thinking how could she not know when she was changed.

"But what if you don't believe us?" Abby asked, worried.

"I'll believe you, I promise. I'll swear right now." She placed her hand on her heart. "But don't ever lie to me about it. I'll believe you, whenever you tell me."

"And then what?" Abby breathed.

Greif stared down at the ground. "I'll turn myself in or something." She bit her lip and frowned.

Greif seemed even more interesting than usual. They were all silent for a moment until Meg asked, "Do you think they just threw out the Dundee?"

Greif looked up, startled.

"I mean, they do research, don't they? Maybe they'd keep her. You know, dissect her."

"She'd be pickled," Greif exclaimed.

At the end of the counter, against the wall, stood a huge refrigerator. Without a word they all headed towards it. Meg and Abby stepped back politely, leaving it to Greif. She stretched her hand out, the fingers curled slightly like the Dundee's hand, and she gripped the handle on the door, pulling it open in a jerky motion that made the jars inside rattle. She opened the door wide and stared in. The lightbulb made her blink, and Meg and Abby stepped forward, blinking as well.

"That's a brain," Greif whispered, pointing to the contents of a white enamel pan covered in clear plastic.

Meg lifted it slowly and brought it to the counter. The three stood around it solemnly, their eyes examining every loop and curve.

"It has clips," Abby breathed. And indeed it had, small metal clips and tags with letters and numbers on them.

Meg's hand reached out, gently pressing against the plastic covering.

"Don't touch it!" Greif cried and her face turned as white as the enamel pan before she grabbed at the counter weakly and slumped to the floor.

The twins watched her, stunned, as she lay on the floor. "She always sounds so tough," Meg said in surprise. Her hand strayed back to the glistening mound on the counter. She pushed it with one finger. The tip of her tongue hung out the side of her mouth. She picked it up, out of the pan. It felt in her hands like an overripe fruit, so soft that it lost its shape. It needed its housing, its bony walls, to give it dignity.

"Oh, put it back," Abby said, exasperated. She hated the look on Meg's face. "We've got to get her up and out of here." She ran water in the sink and sprayed handfuls at Greif, who began to rally.

Meg put the tray away reluctantly, closing the refrigerator door as quietly as she could. She grabbed Greif under her arms and lifted her up. "Whatever you do, don't say the word 'brain' until we're out of here," Abby said in an undertone to Meg. And with Greif leaning heavily on them, they made their way out the door.

Chapter 10

Almost without warning the twins were in high school and Ralph found himself living with two young women instead of children. The girls had noticed, even before Enid died, that Ralph seemed to be shrinking; by junior year in high school they were taller than he was, and he felt it, too, confused by those startlingly adult eyes staring back patiently at him, just tall enough so that he had to tilt his head. It made him twist his mouth when he was alone after their noise had left with them; he was rueful and he felt silly and extraneous. He might have stood a chance with boys, he thought occasionally, but girls—well, you never knew what they were thinking, did you? And he continued to grow smaller, no doubt because he fit into his widowerhood so easily. Thoughts of seeking a new wife were thwarted by an immediate sense that there would be too much required of him. Even in his own mirror, away from his daughters' eyes, his hair was wispy, his shoulders bowed, and his eyes had a weak, moist look to them.

And dating—he tried it occasionally when a coworker or Mrs. Pearl introduced him to another stranded, middle-aged individual like himself—but it seemed ridiculous to him to begin dating just when his daughters were doing the same. The three of them ended up supremely uncomfortable together when it came time to go out. Freshly washed faces, clean clothes, brushed hair—none of them could figure out how to do it right.

Ralph asked Abby, or Abby asked Ralph: "Where are you going?" And the answer was always, "Out."

Then everyone froze, looking pained, and Ralph asked Abby, or Abby asked Ralph: "On a date?" And the answer was always a wrinkled, thoughtful frown and, "Sort of."

The thought had crossed Ralph's mind that dates were roads leading eventually to sex. The same thought had occurred to the twins about Ralph. Sex was on everyone's mind, though purely speculative for all of them and, for the twins, somewhat unsubstantiated. Too much of what they heard came from Greif, even though they now saw each other infrequently. Ever since the Dundee's death she had refused to go to the research labs, and for a while she had harbored a grudge against Meg for her callousness, but that had eventually worn off. She stayed in touch with the twins because they were her social link with the Institute. She told outsiders now that she was checked occasionally for a rare "nerve disease" because she had discovered after a surprisingly long time, that she never got a second date when she mentioned potential insanity. "Boys," she concluded bitterly, "were not at all the way they are in books." In addition to books, she quit reading *True Confessions* because of all the lies.

She announced, finally, "I have a boyfriend now. I stick my tongue practically down his throat. It's the most disgusting thing I've ever done." She grinned.

"Can't be that disgusting," Meg grumbled, "if you do it." She disliked the way Greif bragged about anything to do with sex.

"But aren't you curious about it? Don't you want to know what it's like?" Abby asked Meg later.

"Just watch. She'll tell you she heard explosions when it finally happens. She'll blink her eyes and tell you she knows what it means to be a woman, and she couldn't possibly describe it."

"But you know she's bound to have sex before we do," Abby protested.

"At least that's what she'll say."

Abby could see that Meg was resistant about sex or boyfriends or some aspect of the matter that she didn't understand. Meg had only cold, contemptuous things to say about boys, and about girls who giggled over boys; "moon-faced, pie-eyed ninnies," she muttered when she saw girls leaning together and whispering.

On the other hand, Abby had already gone through a dozen crushes and would doubtless go through more. Her heart slammed into her stomach at the sight of each of her secret lovers, one after the other. It was a fabulous, heart-rending cycle, it made life worthwhile, and she couldn't imagine why anyone would dismiss it. Here she differed from her sister, who seemed to be as immune to crushes as she was to pain. Abby didn't know what the connection was; it was entirely possible that there wasn't one. Maybe it was simply Meg's superior attitude and exacting standards that were to blame. Although she could see Meg's point. There were times when she, too, found all those whispers, shrieks, and wild surmises too much to bear, really beyond belief. But she fought the sneer as soon as she felt it coming on: Let Meg have her sharp tongue and her snooty ways; as for herself, she wanted to be as normal and as popular as she possibly could be, and she wanted a steady boyfriend as soon as possible, a place in the world and a place in the heart.

Alliances in the hallways shifted rapidly, and while everyone was morbidly sensitive about their popularity, occasionally a rogue would appear, someone who was proving a point by talking to a twin, tricky business when you considered that one of them was a medical freak. So she was eager when boys talked to her, open-eyed and grinning, happy to pretend a boy was clever even when he hemmed and stalled and stuttered.

Of course some of them disappeared just as quickly, escaping back to their own tittering group, snapping their heads down, scoring some obscure point. It hurt Abby to see a potential encounter turn into—what? A dare, a bet, a cheap challenge? And it angered Meg, who watched with a jealous, contemptuous eye. But then Abby quickly accepted it and went on. Her reward in the last year in high school was Danny. He was thin, quiet, tall; a pointy chin and high cheekbones gave him an almost elfin look, though elongated. He had a shock of dirty-blond hair that constantly fell to his eyes. He was the kind of student who generally knew the answers but never had enough confidence to raise his hand. He was gentle, and he wanted to judge things for himself. He was invited to parties because he was tall, but he was never in the first or even second rank of importance at school. He spent an entire school term considering the twins; in retrospect, Abby supposed he was weighing the merits of one against the other.

He went from saying hello to asking her opinion about the books they read, or the fairness of a math problem. He pointed out cars to her and asked which ones she liked. When he heard she no longer had a dog, he brought her as far as his own yard to meet his dog, Duke. And then he walked her home. He was silent and then explosively talkative. The silences allowed her to imagine almost anything.

At last he asked her out, and they had a polite first date. He kissed her awkwardly at her front step, and in the next movie they held hands formally, both conscious of perspiration, and pretending they didn't really notice it.

He lived in a different direction or they would have walked to and from school together. Instead, he waited for her at the main doors, always standing straight up and self-contained, like one of those birds that can stay immobile for long stretches of time.

"It's embarrassing to look at him," Meg muttered as she saw him once again in front of the school doors. "Like a dog waiting for a biscuit."

"We had to give our dogs away because of you," Abby pointed out. "You pinched them." Their arguments now contained references to unresolved issues, an oblique jockeying for position.

"I pinched them to keep them from begging," Meg answered.

"Really," Abby said, not even a question. Her eyes were steadily on Danny, and she wore a smile that Meg very much wanted to rip off her face. She felt continually betrayed; she was supposed to take second place to Danny. As if second place would do.

She heard how Abby spoke to Danny—quick to laugh, to flatter, to hesitate, to be flustered—and she hated it. Where had Abby's sturdiness gone? She blamed it all on Danny, on some sort of paralysis that sprang from him to Abby.

She couldn't do anything about it until the day she answered the phone and Danny thought she was Abby. Instead of denying it, Meg played along, bouncing her voice, making it lighter, the way Abby did.

"I'm going to be late meeting you tonight," he said.

"Oh no!" she wailed faintly.

"It's okay. I won't get to Dale's before seven, not six-thirty like I said. That's all. I have to watch my kid brother till my dad gets home."

"No problem," Meg said. "Dale's at seven, then." She hung up, smiling to herself. She didn't mean to go further with it, she would tell Abby that Danny would be late, and step out of it. She would be the only one to know she pretended to be Abby.

But then, even as she heard Abby's quick step on the stair— even as she saw Abby's face light up, expectant and proud, when she said, "Danny called. . ."—well, something changed inside. She said, "He can't make it. He has to watch his brother tonight."

"No," Abby said, disappointed.

"Sorry," Meg answered.

Abby hesitated as she passed the telephone, but she had never called Danny. Meg watched her and relaxed.

Abby flung herself on the bed and picked up a magazine. Meg took her sister's usual spot in front of the dresser, brushing her hair, trying out barrettes and clips. "Which is better?" she crooned to Abby, holding out a comb.

"Wear that one," Abby said. "I always liked that one on you."

"You mean on you. I never wear it." She smoothed her hair back and angled in the comb. "You're right. This does look good with our face." She pursed her lips and smiled and patted her hair, all in imitation of Abby.

"I didn't know you were going out."

"You don't know everything. I have a date. Anyway, it's almost a date. See, I can be popular too."

"Who is it, Meg?" Abby asked, with real curiosity. She forgot her own disappointment; she was relieved that Meg was meeting someone. With any luck that would divert Meg's attention from concentrating so exclusively on her.

Meg patted her hair. "It's that new boy. He was talking to me while you were on the lunch line. He said he'd be at Dale's. And he asked if I was going."

"Oh. Dale's," Abby sighed.

"So don't go there, okay?" Meg asked. "I'd feel self-conscious."

"Of course," Abby said. "You're on your own. You'll be great." She sighed again. "I'll think of you there and imagine it's me."

"You do that." Meg grinned wickedly.

Meg had a few misgivings, but went out with a purpose. She suspected Abby had a secret life: that she and Danny had pet jokes, private words for each other, maybe she'd even allowed him to kiss her or touch her. On the way to Dale's she began to smile the way Abby smiled; she tossed her head a few times for practice; she giggled with her hand over her mouth. It was fun; it was a game.

He was there already. She slid into the seat opposite him, lowering her head shyly and then looking up. He grinned, held out his hand and withdrew it. He was as awkward as ever. But his eyes were happy to look at her. At first she didn't notice it, but as she played

Abby, as she laughed and swooped and complimented him, his eyes kept bumping happily into hers and she found herself liking it. He wanted to join up with some friend who had a car, so they could go for a ride. His face got flushed, and Meg suspected there were strings to this ride, but the strings seemed pleasurable and desirable. He was a nice boy, after all, with a slow kind of humor and a genuine likeableness.

She didn't quite catch the names of Danny's friends in the front seat, a boy and a girl whose heads were so close and moved so mechanically together from side to side that they seemed on one stem.

Danny crowded in next to her in the back seat, lifted his arm and said, "Your spot. I kept it warm." She moved in against him, he lowered his arm around her and from then on—with the car moving or parked—they clung innocently to each other, murmuring short phrases, notations on their moods: "The moon." "Is your arm asleep?" "That cloud." "Ummm." "Here. Move here."

At first Meg pretended to like it, but without warning her liking became real. She wanted to whisper small things to him. She wanted to tell him she liked the wind in her hair, she liked the sun in her face, and she liked the grit of sand in her toes, all human things, she wanted to tell him she felt normal.

When he kissed her with small, quick rabbit kisses and his hand moved diligently to cover her small breast, she felt almost smug with normalcy.

How easy it is, she thought, and sighed, and he froze, his hand around her breast, not quite pressing on it, and he gasped, "It's okay?"

She could tell by the surprise in his voice that it wasn't, and she wriggled. "Oh, Danny," she said sadly, and he muttered, "Sorry."

It was so nice that only a phrase or a nudge was needed. All conversation took place in the early part of the date; after that life became a touch, a grunt. It was all so elemental, it seemed unlikely she would be found out.

She liked him more and more, his very human presence, his breath and his hesitant hand. His eyes, when they were open, were kind.

Abruptly, it seemed to her, the car drew up and stopped.

"Here you are," the voice up front said.

Meg struggled up from the seat of the car, blinking around her. "Home," she said with surprise.

"You're always surprised," he smiled.

She looked at him, suddenly cold. She had been feeling totally herself, and his comment made her realize that she had been indistinguishable from Abby. Irrationally, she was annoyed.

He slid out first and held the door open for her. She didn't want to leave, she wanted to remain inside, with him, where all things were predictable and pleasant. She wanted him to know who she was, and still like her. She hated the fact that Danny still didn't know who she was.

She got out, the door still open. She stepped back slightly, against the car.

He squeezed her shoulder. "Maybe next week?" he whispered.

The night was running out, this was her last chance. She put her hand against his shoulder. "I need to tell you something—something about me—"

"What's the holdup?" the front seat asked impatiently.

"Yeah, what is it?" the second head snapped.

"We'll talk tomorrow, Abby," Danny said hurriedly. "Gotta go."

"Oh, all *right*," Meg snapped. She could tell Danny wasn't going to listen to her. She slammed the car door shut even though Danny was still on the sidewalk. She was annoyed at all of it, at all of them.

She tugged at something caught in the car door, as Danny stared, his jaw dropping. "No, wait," he gasped.

"*You* wait," she said rudely, and tugged again, her mind blurred with disappointment. "Why didn't you notice?" she wanted to say.

"Can't you see I'm *me*, not her? Don't you know the difference?"

"Your thumb," he said weakly, and then he stumbled slightly backwards, caught himself, and threw up.

Meg turned slightly, into the surprised looks of the two heads up front, and saw something sticking out of the seam of the car door. She looked down at her hand; it was her thumb.

"Oh hell," she sighed, and she opened the door, holding her dangling thumb carefully with her right hand.

Danny held his arms out blindly and then crumbled to the ground.

Meg climbed into the back seat. "Emergency room," she said without urgency, her lower lip ragged with annoyance.

It didn't take long to figure out; Danny called Ralph to tell him about Abby; he got Abby. They went automatically to the Institute. Meg was already in surgery, sedated to keep her still and to reduce the trauma that her body still experienced whether she could feel it or not.

It wasn't until the next day that Abby got a chance to talk to her, and when she saw her sister's white face and lethargy, she thought it totally unfair. She was angry, and she had never seen Meg look so unwell.

"How do you feel?" she asked quickly.

"Just tired," Meg said. "I've never felt so tired." Her whole arm was wrapped up and immobilized.

"I think what you did was lousy," Abby blurted out. She glared at Meg.

Meg gave the equivalent of a shrug.

"I liked your Danny," she said slowly. "And I didn't even mean to." She looked steadily at her sister, who frowned and softened at "your Danny."

But she wasn't about to give up entirely. "You lied. You said you were me. We stopped doing that."

"Did we? I don't remember saying that."

"We didn't have to. It's okay with kids. It doesn't matter who a kid is—you know what I mean. But it matters now. I'm me. You're you. We're different. Don't lie about it. It makes me feel disgusting and slimy. I feel like you're my enemy. A liar! You can't be me!"

"Danny thought I was," Meg said weakly. Her eyes were barely open, but the dark edge of her pupils showed through the slits, following Abby's moves.

"What were you two *doing*?" Abby hissed.

"The usual, I guess." Meg sounded innocent. "What do you two usually do?"

"I hate you."

"Do you think he knew, or do you think it didn't matter?" Her voice was barely a whisper. "Maybe there are other girls, too, maybe he just likes everyone? He was so friendly. I liked that. I liked how friendly he was."

Abby glared. "I know why you did it, Meg. You did it to show me up. You did it to prove that you could be me if you really wanted to, that you're superior to me. You want to make sure I understand that it's not that you can't find a boyfriend; you just think it's too silly, it's beneath you. But you liked it, didn't you? Danny said he couldn't tell because you're always so cold to him but you were nice last night. You probably thought you'd make fun of him, that you'd do something to break us up without our ever really knowing why. But it wasn't the way you expected, was it?"

Meg patiently waited for her to finish. "I had a nice time. He's a very nice boy. Did he tell you he fainted like a Southern belle? Heaved his guts up and fell over in a heap. Delicate for a boy, isn't he?"

"He's not used to you. You liked him, didn't you?"

"Kisses like an angel. Soft little itty-bitty kisses."

"I bet you liked that, too, didn't you? That's why you're trying to make it sound silly."

Meg opened her eyes fully and considered Abby more carefully. "That was clever. Did someone tell you that?"

"I guessed."

Meg nodded, then sighed. "It was fun for a while, pretending to be normal. It's a very nice world you live in."

"Oh, don't be like that. It's your world too."

"Not me," she said evenly. "I can see what you like, and why you like it. And it's even fun for me, for a while." She moved restlessly, a slight, automatic adjustment. "But I can't imagine it lasting forever."

Abby sat on the edge of the bed. "Give it a chance. You might turn out to be just like the rest of us." She smiled with all her teeth showing.

Meg smiled back. "I'll never be like the rest of you." Her good hand reached over and patted the bandages. "Tell me," she murmured, "if this happened to you, what would it feel like?"

Abby shook her head in despair. "How should I know? And why does it matter? A thumb torn off? I don't know. A terrible pinch, like it's in the wrong place and a shooting, searing stab in the root of your thumb . . ." and her voice droned on like a bedtime story till Meg dozed off with a peaceful face, the corners of her mouth ever so slightly turned up.

Chapter 11

The twins were totally unprepared for the news that their father was going to remarry.

"Mrs. Pearl," Meg said with disbelief.

"Well, at least we all know each other. We're used to each other." Ralph was trying to placate them, unsure what objections might be raised.

"Is that why you're getting married?" Abby's romantic beliefs were offended. "Because you *know* her?"

Ralph changed his argument. "We understand each other, like each other. We're comfortable together. It's an important thing," he said, with sudden perception, "to be comfortable. To be at ease." He paused thoughtfully. "I haven't been at ease since your mother got sick." He nodded his head. "Yes, that's it, that's how I'd describe it. Ill at ease."

Abby was appalled. "With *us*?"

Ralph blinked and scraped his hand over his chin. "Well, no, I don't mean you. I'm not talking about you, I'm talking about me. My life."

Meg and Abby exchanged shocked glances. They had always assumed that they were the most important pieces of their father's life, that they *were* their father's life. He had them totally off-balance; they had no idea how to react.

The marriage was going to take place the next month. "You girls can stay here as long as you like," Mrs. Pearl told them, "after your father moves downstairs. Our fortunes are all together now." She blinked and beamed. The twins, astonished, blinked back.

It had an extraordinarily inappropriate tone to it. They liked Mrs. Pearl—or at least they had never even bothered to wonder if they liked her—but a landlady seemed the right role for her, not a step-mother. She was nothing like Enid; it seemed almost like they should point this out to Ralph, as if he were in danger of replacing a table with a piano bench.

And moreover, their father was about to leave them. Surely they were the ones who were supposed to be leaving home under protests and tears. Or soon, anyway. In fact, they didn't feel ready for it. They felt deserted, as if this all-around reasonableness was the most impossible demand they'd encountered.

"Well," Abby said, trying to be as straightforward as possible, "maybe for a while. Until we figure out what to do."

"You don't have to figure anything out," Ralph said, somewhat alarmed. "I'll be here. Just a floor below."

"This is your home," Mrs. Pearl said, trying to reassure them. "Stay as long as you like."

Even Ralph knew that this felt flat, though Mrs. Pearl was trying her best to be kind. She had no experience with stepchildren or live-in relatives, only tenants, so she had a businesslike approach to living arrangements. She was kind but didn't know how to be gracious. "I'm not leaving you," Ralph said quickly. "It's just a smaller apartment downstairs, not enough room for all of us on one floor. I thought you'd like it, being almost on your own. But if you don't like it this way—if it doesn't make you happy, either one of you—well," and here he looked nervously at Mrs. Pearl, "—well, I'm sure we can think of something better. More like a family."

"We could keep the doors open," Mrs. Pearl said in surprise, trying hard to figure out, and solve, the problem. "Upstairs and down. Not like separate apartments, you see, but like one big house. Why," she said, her face lighting up, "we could all sit together in my living room!" She looked around hopefully.

"I think," Meg said slowly, "it's okay the way it is."

"We can certainly think about it," Abby agreed. "We'll see how it feels. In the meantime, congratulations, I'm happy for you." She kissed each of them. Meg leaned forward and kissed them too, whispering congratulations in exactly the same tone as Abby.

The wedding was small and matter-of-fact, taking place in front of the city clerk. They went for photographs afterwards, walking across the street to the same office that did passport photos. They stood, all four of them, looking hard at the camera, each of them wearing some effort at a smile. Ralph and his new wife stood at the center, almost the same height. They were both in their early forties, and looked closer to sixty. Ralph's suit was too big for him: he had lost weight since Enid's death but didn't pay attention to it. Mrs. Pearl's hair was still dark, but she wore it in a matronly style, and her glasses were a matron's glasses, and she wore sensible shoes and clothes.

The twins stood half a head taller than their father, and they were very conscious of standing straight, since their high school yearbook had come out recently and caught them looking stooped. They had discussed it and decided to straighten up no matter how tall they grew. They wore little bolero jackets (different colors) over plain linen shifts that did not reach their knees.

Anyone who studied the picture carefully could see that Abby was actually an inch taller than Meg, who had injured her spine so often that many intervertebral discs were squashed flat, just as repeated breaks in her legs had given her an odd, sloping walk. It was a good thing she couldn't feel pain, the doctors said, because otherwise she'd be crippled.

Their faces, too, seemed large in the photograph, mainly because they were so remarkably square. Their jawline was wider than normal, their brow more pronounced, as if they were designed stylistically or emblematically. Their hair was so curly that it tended to get out of control, pushing away from their scalps like a mass of springs. Too short, and it looked naked and nappy. Too long and they looked like Einstein. Their hair was dark and their eyes had deepened into a dark gray-blue.

The twins placed their copy of the wedding photo on top of the TV console, next to the framed picture of Ralph and Enid that Ralph left behind. The bedroom he once shared with Enid remained intact; he merely removed his clothes. The twins cleaned it occasionally, putting everything back in its place as they'd known it for the past six years. They continued to share their old bedroom. At first it all seemed strange, and then it began to feel normal and finally, within two months, they resented it when their father came upstairs too often or when Mrs. Pearl invited them to dinner more than once a week. "She does it for show, she does it because she thinks she *should* do it," Abby charged.

"Well, of course," Meg said.

It was September, and they were eighteen. They were starting college with nothing definite in mind, assuming that a year or two would translate into better pay, or at least give them time to find a direction.

Abby insisted that they take all their classes separately. After the briefest pause Meg agreed. They both understood that Abby didn't trust Meg around her friends—boyfriends specifically. After Danny, Abby kept quiet about dates. She learned to call boys and she kept their names and numbers under a code in her address book. Meg broke the code immediately, but she kept it to herself. Sometimes Abby and her date went to a movie or dinner or dance and found Meg already there, barely suppressing a smile, waiting for them. Once or twice Abby invited Meg on a double date, but it was unpleasant. Meg mimicked her. She opened her mouth, she cocked her head, she laughed when Abby did—all a split second behind, as if she were deliberately using the mirror game to mock her sister. She made Abby feel plastic and superficial, and Abby snapped at her because of it.

"But I'm not making fun of you," Meg insisted. "They like you, and I want them to like me."

Abby didn't fall for it. "That's fine, Meg, but you make everyone feel funny, you know. Just be yourself, they'll like you."

"No one has so far," Meg grumbled.

"Quit watching me. Enjoy yourself. Relax."

"How can I relax? You told me to make sure they're having a good time."

"You know," Abby said seriously, "I don't believe you anymore. You act like you've been on a desert island all your life. You're the same species. We all have a lot in common."

"Then what about Danny? He thought I was you, and everything was fine until that accident. Then he collapsed."

"It was disgusting, ripping your thumb off like that. It came out of nowhere."

"Yes, but you didn't see the look in his eyes. He thought I was a monster."

"He didn't. He never told me that. It's all in your imagination."

"It's what I *am*. It's what makes me different. I can't discuss it with anyone but you. They look at me differently, something goes click in their eyes and their voices get louder, just a little. They want to nudge each other with their elbows, or just come out and say, oh, so *that's* it. Well, you know, there is a difference, and I don't despise people for their weakness, but I get the feeling they look down on me."

"There it is," Abby sighed. "You 'don't despise people for their weakness.' That says it all."

"But I *don't*."

"It's your attitude. You think you're superior. It shows, you know. You do everything a little too much—laugh too hard, give your opinion too fast, change the subject too often, as if you were in some kind of show. You don't act normal, you 'act' normal, and it's exaggerated, as if to show everyone that you can do it. But it's the externals you've got down, the preliminary stuff, you don't know where to go after that."

"Where *do* you go?"

Abby flung her hands up. "Haven't you ever *liked* anyone?"

"Just you."

"Why?"

Meg shrugged. "No one else understands."

"I do understand. I do, really. But you're not enough for me anymore. I love to be with other people, I love looking at them and having them look at me, I love their laughter and their stories and the way they think. They think like I do."

"You're separating us," Meg said in alarm.

"I feel I can relax with them. Pain isn't a machine to them. There's nothing I have to explain."

"I'll never ask you anything again, if it bothers you." For the first time, Meg looked frightened.

"You will," Abby said simply. "It's a fascination to you, a sideshow."

"No, no," Meg said hastily. "I'm the sideshow."

"It's a question of perspective. Which one of us is the *right* one— you know what I mean? Is it you? Is it me? I get confused when I'm with you, I'm divided, I can't concentrate."

"Abby," Meg pleaded.

"I liked Danny a lot, and look what happened. He got suspicious, you know, he doubted. Even when you were in the hospital he would suddenly stare at me, at my hands. He would ask me about things we'd done together on our first date. Even when he knew he was with me, he was afraid it was actually you, that you had that much power."

"Oh, Abby," Meg said plaintively, "I have no power."

"And then the way you act when you're with me. Mimicking me. Mocking me and my friends. You make everyone uncomfortable."

"Not you."

"Yes. Even me. You get annoying. I don't like your games and I don't like the way you keep chasing people away from me."

"I'm sorry. I really am."

Abby shook her head. "I've thought about it a lot. You either stop it or I'll move out."

Meg's mouth dropped open. "Move *out!*" she blurted. "Leave me?"

"Yes," Abby said firmly. "Leave you. I won't even tell you where I'm going."

"How can you leave me?"

"I can do it. I'll get a job."

Meg stared at her for a moment. "When I open a door, when I enter a room, you're the first one I look for."

Abby breathed in deeply. "It's not a good way to live."

Meg's hands seemed frozen by her side. "You must feel the same way."

Abby shook her head. "I want my own life."

"I've never interfered with your life."

Abby was annoyed. "What have I been talking about?"

"You've been talking about other people." Meg said firmly, convinced Abby would get the distinction.

"Oh, Meg, come off it. Other people *are* my life. That's what I mean, that's what you don't understand. You keep wanting to be too close."

"Too close! We're twins." Meg stood in the middle of the room, her arms held out helplessly. Her voice lacked her normal assurance. Abby was glad to hear it, was heartily glad to hear the progression of disbelief and anxiety in Meg's voice. She wanted to hurt Meg, had always, all along, all her life, wanted to find Meg's soft spot so she could get even with her for acting so superior, for making her feel second-rate.

So there was a smile, small but distinct, on Abby's lips; she finally had the upper hand. Maybe she would move out no matter *what* Meg did—move out, start over, free and clear. No one would think of her as a twin, the new people she met would assume she was unique, that there was no one just like her on this planet. She liked it, she liked the feel of it.

Meg watched the smile on Abby's face. Her heart pounded in fear. Could Abby really abandon her? Why? For what? Those other people offered Meg nothing; they were slow to understand her; slow to like her; they seemed to expect some performance from her. And she got nothing from them, there was no secret sympathy or knowledge with those others, no intimacy. Sometimes she wasn't even sure they were really people, the way she and Abby were; they seemed so shallow.

But she felt warned, certainly, by what Abby said, put on notice. She would not do anything to risk Abby's displeasure. She wouldn't know how to breathe without her, she was so necessary.

Over the next weeks she stopped some of her spying and was rarely caught by Abby at the same movie or walking along the avenue towards her. Where previously Megan had wanted to be seen— had wanted Abby to be reminded of her—she now paced herself patiently behind Abby on those occasions when she wanted to know what her sister was doing. In this way she found out who Abby was involved with, where they went, how happy she seemed. It had happened, twice, that Megan stood outside a window, in the shadows, watching Abby eating dinner with a date. A car passed, the lighting shifted, and a startled Abby saw Megan's face briefly and then her own as the car moved on. A fleeting disquiet touched her until she forced herself to be calm. It was only her own reflection, she thought.

On the other side, leaning carefully out of the light, Megan watched Abby, who seemed comfortable enough without her. She stepped deeper into the shadows and turned home.

One day, however, Abby came home early, deciding at the last minute to skip a class. Relations with Megan had improved over the past two months. Abby occasionally suspected her sister of following her, watching her, but she was afraid she might have been too harsh. She would actually prefer to stay with Megan; they still shared a private world, even if it was now mostly in the past. After all, she did want to believe that the problem would disappear. Gradually, Megan seemed to relax, to release her. She discreetly disappeared, she did not press Abby on any aspect of her personal life, she seemed content to leave Abby alone.

When she reached the upstairs apartment she didn't call out a hello or notice anything out of the ordinary. Megan was supposed to be at the Institute—for what, Abby couldn't recall.

She put her books on the kitchen table, hung her jacket on the back of a chair, and walked down the hall to her room. Halfway there she became aware that she wasn't alone and her gut slowed and the back of her neck prickled. She proceeded cautiously, but she could hear, faintly, sounds from the bedroom—recognizable sounds.

It surprised her that Meg would have brought a boy home; Meg had given no sign of involvement with anyone. There was only a second of hesitation; it seemed so strange that Abby stepped stealthily forward, to confirm the sounds.

The bedroom door was open, and the overhead light was just strong enough for her to see in to where two figures occupied her bed.

She listened only long enough to verify that the one in bed with Megan was her own boyfriend Bobby, and then she turned silently and went out the way she came, leaving her books forgotten on the kitchen table.

She told herself she wasn't angry or hurt. What she felt was dread and an immense clear-headedness. She walked for awhile, and went to a movie she'd already seen, arriving in the middle and leaving at the end, all the time thinking that the betrayal was not Bobby's but Megan's; that it was deliberate; that Megan would always be like this; that seeing them in bed was like seeing herself in bed with him in some twisted way (a thought that kept occurring to her but which she couldn't, in any way, face). There was no way to change Megan. She had to leave or accept the fact that Megan would always nibble at her life, leaving the edge of it rotten.

She regretted having to leave Meg—but the regret was endurable. She had all along wanted to be separate, even though there had always been the pleasant, astonishing symmetry of the two of them, the jointness of their existence, the unimpeachable importance she maintained just by existing for her sister, something she was now about to lose.

Once she left, she would no longer be essential for another person—and Meg's obsession with her had always been an undercurrent in her own life, it was a steady though irritating source of confirmation. There was no doubt about it, she was giving Megan up, and it was like deciding that Megan was dead—sorrow at the loss of Megan, anger at the necessity for it, and a terrible doubt that she could replace the quality of Megan. No wonder she was reluctant to go home. Did she want to see Megan looking at her, appealing to her, when she knew that however much she needed Megan, Megan needed her more?

It was midnight before she returned home, and she crept upstairs, hoping against hope that Meg was asleep.

But she was sitting at the kitchen table, next to the pile of books Abby had left there earlier. Meg looked up, her face filled with both hope and guilt, but it flattened into blankness as she watched Abby come through the door and sit across the table from her.

"You were here earlier," Megan said, nodding towards the books.

"While Bobby was with you."

"Ah." Meg nodded her head once, ending with a deep bend of the neck. She looked profoundly concentrated, her hands clasped on the table, her shoulders hunched.

"I'll just pack my things and leave tomorrow," Abby said.

"I could go. It's my fault." Meg was deferential.

Abby gave her a cold smile. "I'd always suspect you of sneaking back."

"Of course."

"So I'll go."

"He didn't know anything about it. He thought I was you."

"It doesn't make a difference."

"I just said it to be fair."

"To be fair?" Abby was contemptuous.

"I saw your books after he left, and I spent a lot of time trying to think what you would do, and how I could make it up to you. I couldn't come up with anything I thought would work. I figured you would draw your own conclusions. I didn't think there was much of a chance. You like to judge me. I'm sorry."

"I don't care."

"I don't want you to leave. I'll agree to anything, any rules. I'll move out and you can do what you want. But if you go I'm afraid you'll refuse to see me." Her voice shook and it chafed Abby's heart, but she kept her fingers tightly clenched. "Let me leave so I'll know there's a chance we can make this up, be friends again."

Abby stared at her as if she were a bug under her shoe. Megan got up and knelt by her sister, taking one hand between the two of her own. "Forgive me. On my knees, Abby. I beg you."

Abby got up and shook Meg's hands from her own.

"I never feel like I'm anywhere until you're there too," Meg cried.

But Abby walked silently down the hallway, willing herself not to feel anything at the unfamiliar sound of Meg crying.

Part Two

Chapter 12

Megan ended up working at the Institute as a research assistant in the animal labs. She had been drawn back to the Institute because it was a familiar world that had always valued her. She marked up slides from animal tissue samples, doing a lot of the paperwork that actually certified the test results. She was especially interested in brain grants, and knew quite well by now that since the money motivated the research, it was always the money that determined the research. In the five years she'd been there, she'd discovered that the trials that got the most money were the safe ones, variations on previous trials. Research pursued grants, not cures.

Megan was tall, with big bones and a broad face, and she limped badly. She was not easily overlooked in the basement corridors—the same corridors where Greif had led her as a child. She knew Greif was wrong about the Dundee monkey; the Institute never tried to match, or clinically reproduce, the illness of any individual patient. That would have been pure research, and there was no money in it. The biggest grants came from government, and government was cautious.

Meg had nothing personally against any of this. After all, the paychecks came in her direction as well, and there was always a very real chance that someone would find something useful or arresting. Her boss, Raymond Bulicki, requested samples from human autopsies for her; he knew she was particularly interested in excesses of sensation, either pleasure or pain. Meg cleaned her counter and inserted one of these slides into a microscope. It was brain tissue from

a neurasthenic corpse, as Raymond labeled it; it was the kind of joke
he made.

This particular subject, X, was a man—neuresthetes were usually men—who, like Proust, had lived in a cork-lined, soundproof,
odorless room. In fact, his neurasthenia might have been psychologically modeled on his identification with Proust. But which was
cause and which effect? Was Proust attractive to him because he was
a fellow neurasthenic, or was he neurasthenic because Proust was
too attractive to him? Was this a psychological or organic problem—
and was there a firm difference?

She moved her slide around, then replaced it with an anonymous slide.

The anonymous slides were all from people who had died in accidents, and not of a particular disease. She and her lab mate, Pandit,
had once discussed whether a study should be made of violent-acci-
dent victims: perhaps there was a common pathological element. And
if there were, should they look for it in the seat of the conscious or
unconscious mind; in the realm of distant or immediate memory; how
about motor responses; reflexes; semiotics? Perhaps these accident
victims were slower than others to be aware of danger; if so, was it
organic or circumstantial; had they always been this way or had they
just been distracted by unemployment, divorce, anger, a flood of lust?

The pure scientists among them, questioning the pertinence of
animal-tissue samples, wished to set up a bank of human tissues.
They dreamed of getting one-page biographies with twenty pages of
multiple-choice questionnaires attached, providing the subjective side
of disease. They wanted to *know* their tissues. After all, only humans
could describe their dreams, their obsessions, the odd uncalculated
recurring thoughts, even the existence of a phantom pain or an irra-
tional fear.

Well, of course fear and pain were fascinating topics, emotional
states that had physical symptoms: piloerection—the hair prickling

on the back of the neck; the racing heart and dry mouth; the sudden adrenaline bursts. The body was prepared in an instant with a spring-loaded surge for existence—and it was almost oblivious to pain at that instant.

At the most critical, desperate times, the body is wholly given over to assessment and fight; awareness of pain, at this point, would interfere with the body's job of survival. Raymond casually offered his belief that people who met violent deaths—crashes, stabbings, falls—could not feel the pain of their deaths. Violent situations divert the consciousness. No, he proposed, only the ill could really feel the pain of death, because of the self-consciousness of illness. In fact, he wasn't altogether sure that pain of death was separate from the fear of death.

"Even for people, say, in a coma?" Meg asked.

Raymond shrugged. "How can we know they aren't afraid?" He was, she thought, immensely detached; what any other organism *felt* was an academic exercise.

Raymond himself walked to her side, leaning companionably with her over her slides of the neurasthenic corpse. "You wouldn't believe this one. Wouldn't cut his nails or hair. Said it was too painful. Anything show, anything fun?"

Meg shook her head. "There must be excited cells somewhere, I think. Or do we just keep missing them?"

"Excited cells. I have a few of those." He beamed at her, his large head with its well-combed hair placed deliberately close to her own head.

She could smell a chemical funk on him and drew back casually. "I'm looking for the threshold of stimulation. For instance, which sensations are ignored because they are too small; and what does 'too small' mean for an individual? What is insignificant for one may be problematic for another. We all fall into a bell curve for sensations." She smiled.

"The curve merely describes it; it doesn't explain it."

"Sure."

"I could draw a bell curve to show that more people freeze to death in certain months. The physical reality is that we have winter."

"I know." Moments like this, when Raymond dissolved into pedantry and obviousness, didn't bother her. She looked, then, mildly interested, or at least as if she were paying attention. Raymond was her lover and she actually liked the fact that he was transparent. She could figure him out completely; she knew his bell curve and had a certain satisfaction in seeing it, much as a computer programmer enjoys seeing a well-designed program run.

Raymond was in his late 40's; he was a well-groomed man with a slightly thick but not pot-bellied silhouette in a well-fitting gray or slate-blue suit, a large ring, and a wife who was equally well-cared for. Meg preferred married men like Raymond, who had compart-mentalized lives that weren't subject to vague emotional fugues. Men such as Raymond did not doubt themselves. They did not ask many personal questions.

"There must be monkey money in hypersensitivity," he mused.

"Induced by what?"

"Excitability and irritability," he said thoughtfully. "Chemical imbalance? Overexposure to repeated stimuli? Perhaps we should start with mice and inbreed the sensitive ones."

"That would save time."

"We never want to save time in research," he said, shaking his head. "It reduces the staff."

"Mice will save time in getting to the real, physical component of the experiment."

"Well put. There it is." He looked at her as if she were a meal he could taste. "Can you write up a proposal?"

Meg swiveled her chair back so she could look at him completely. "*My* proposal?" There was no hint of greed in her voice. Raymond would have liked a hint of greed; it would have given him some sense of control over her. He had assumed her vulnerabilities would be the same as other women's—other people's, he mentally corrected himself, since feminism was in the air. But he found her exotic and baffling.

The neutrality in her voice disappointed him. "No, my dear. Your name doesn't bring money. Although it is time, perhaps, to add you to an extended author's byline."

"Alphabetical?"

"Last. You would be junior."

"I would be honored," she said in exactly the tone of voice that always persuaded him she was unique and indifferent. It frequently annoyed him at the time; but later, in recollection, he found her manner and attitude arousing. His wife and his former lovers tried to achieve that tone, that cold hardness, as if his actions and intents couldn't touch them—but for them it had been artificial, intended as an insult, and it was never altogether convincing. Meg did it perfectly.

"But write it up yourself anyway," he said. "And just make sure your name is spelled correctly on the cover sheet." He looked at her keenly. He waited for her reply, like a man expecting a tip.

She tilted her head back and laughed quickly. "Are most people thrilled when this happens to them?"

"Always."

"Oh God. And you want me to thank you . . . in a personal way?"

He grinned back at her. "It's customary."

"Is it?" she asked, curious. "And what do you do with the men?"

"Damn it, Megan." He was annoyed. "I was joking."

She turned back to her slide, covering a smile. "That's really too bad. I mean, as far as research is concerned. . . ."

He stood for a moment without speaking. He was a loud breather: he drank often and never exercised. Curious for someone who had studied the fatty buildup in so many small corpses. But he never identified with them. Just then someone else came to the cabinet near them and Raymond came to himself, saying, "It will make a good project. We'll discuss it later." He moved away from her, down the corridor and up the floors to his own office, careful not to display any affection in front of others.

As if they didn't all know about us, Meg thought coldly. *And they don't even care.*

She snapped a pencil on her slide, however, until it cracked and broke. She swept the splinters into the trash with no concern and left the lab, limping down the hall to the library. She would spend the rest of the day determining what kind of stimulation to use—electrical, chemical; or should it be a barrage of the sensual?—and approximately how many small white lives she would need at the start.

Chapter 13

Meg took the bus on those days when Raymond didn't offer to drive her home in his Buick Regal. On this particular night she found a seat halfway down—the Institute was in a residential area and she often found a seat—and continued her thoughts on the experiment. She was musing absently about light as stimulus, watching the patterns of it as the streetlamps flashed through the bus windows, and therefore paid no attention to her fellow-passengers. She didn't see Abby sit down on the other side of the bus near the front. But Abby saw her, began to say something, and then retreated. She assumed that Megan had seen her and deliberately ignored her. Abby sat back against the side of the bus, her head straight forward, her eyes held rigidly in front of her, missing Meg's eyes by three seats.

Meg saw her then and also assumed that she was being consciously snubbed. She might have hazarded a nod to Abby; might have hoped for a look, perhaps even a word or two—after all they were polite enough when they met at Ralph's—but she became aware of the furtive excitement of a man who sat on Abby's left, whose eyes kept waving back and forth from Abby to Megan. He was waiting for them to recognize each other, and he had a smile itching on his face. Meg hated it. She trained her eyes out the window—just as Abby did.

But Meg fell back into thinking again about her experiments, and she failed to notice when Abby left. When the bus pulled out, Megan blinked and looked for Abby, and wondered what stop she'd gotten off at.

I should have said something, she thought with a stab of sadness.

Abby, on her part, almost turned to get on the bus again, thinking, *I could have said something*. It seemed, all at once, so simple, so possible. But then she remembered Meg's forcefulness, her railroading certainties, that possessiveness of hers that seemed to leave no room for Abby to breathe. Abby decided—as she always decided, time and again, when she missed Megan—that freedom was best, was always best. The bus pulled away from the curb, Meg looked over to the seat her sister had been sitting in, and Abby turned deliberately on her way home, thinking, *And she pretended not to notice, anyway. It's what she wants, too. I wouldn't beg. I'd never beg. There's something twisted in the way she thinks, anyhow. Whenever I see her, we fight. It never works, it never works.*

She went home to her three dogs and her husband, Charles. She had married him a year after leaving Meg, about the time Meg took her first lover. Though she didn't regret her choice, she knew that she had chosen Charles principally as a replacement for her sister, and she knew that Charles was exactly the kind of man Megan would hate—kind, thoughtful, content. He was ideal, a real treasure, and if he lacked a certain edge that Meg would have required—well, it was not Meg's choice. Abby was happy with him.

The dogs had been let out to the back yard and Charles was studying the paper. "I'm in the mood for a movie," he said.

"Fine by me. Eat first?"

"Depends on the time." They considered the choices, brought in the dogs, and made the next show, stopping afterwards for a quick meal. It was on the way back that Abby saw a woman on the street who looked like Greif.

The woman was muttering to herself, shaking her head, and she had a smell.

Abby stopped in her tracks and stared. Charles hooked her arm gently and gave her just enough pressure to continue moving. Abby kept craning her neck, dragged along like a child.

"Abby?" Charles asked.

She knew that it wasn't Greif; the woman must be at least fifty—twice Greif's age. She couldn't put her finger on the resemblance. Maybe there was none; maybe the woman only fit some fantasy Abby had about Greif's future, some image of madness.

"It's nothing, Charles," she said finally. "I thought I knew her."

"Did you? Know her, I mean?" Charles's steps slowed down. He was a compassionate man.

"Not this time, no."

Her answer did not surprise either of them. They had each confessed their fear of finding a familiar face among the homeless—and they admitted that their fears centered on the mad-homeless, not just the poor-homeless.

Of course Abby had more faces to attach to these nightmares—faces she had seen in the waiting rooms and corridors of the Institute. She had never, as far as she knew, ever thought of Greif as one of them, perhaps because, all along, she believed Greif was lying, that madness had sounded more romantic to Greif than whatever her real problem was.

Charles rested his hand on her shoulder and they continued walking, without comment. Abby knew her husband would be going through the mental list he kept of people he knew who might end up on the streets. This was true even though Charles had lived in three different cities before they met and married four years ago, and the people he imagined all lived somewhere else.

They both knew that Charles' fears were really rooted in the terror he had of ending on the street himself. It was one of the things that kept him calm and reasonable. "If I stopped doing any one thing—going to work every day, shaving, eating breakfast—I would stop doing it all."

Abby was glad he had this fear; his perfection sometimes annoyed her. She deeply distrusted people who were too comfortable.

"Don't you think it's the real reason people are indifferent to the homeless?" he asked. "They may become part of you, they may *be* part of you. So you turn them into dirty, smelly lunatics or simple lazy hustlers; you make them too different to be you."

"There were a lot of people like them at the Institute. I keep expecting to see some of those faces. I suppose my fear is that I'll see Meg—though *that* must be projection because Meg is above everything. She has a job, she blends right in. She still has all her fingers. So it must be me I expect to see."

"In one version or another, it always is ourselves."

"Well, versions count," Abby said.

It was only a half hour later that Megan—having gone to a different movie—stopped in the light of a streetlamp and stared at the dirty figure staring back up at her from the pavement.

"Greif?"

The woman glared and told her to fuck off or give her a dollar. Meg clicked over into a clinical attitude. She knew it wasn't Greif. "I'll give you a dollar," she said, "if you'll tell me what you'll do with it."

"Stick it in my pocket," the woman sneered.

Meg gave her the dollar. Greif had always said her mother was mad, she remembered; this woman looked like an older, used Greif. "Do you have a daughter?" Meg asked.

The woman looked at her warily. She moved inside the cocoon of blankets and newspapers she'd wrapped around herself. "A beautiful girl," she said finally. "Your age. Different hair."

She's lying, Meg thought, as the woman eyed her craftily. "And a little boy, too?" Meg asked, but too sharply.

The beggar scowled. "No boy. Only a girl. Sweetest girl you ever saw. Give me a quarter for my little girl. A quarter for the phone."

"You don't have a daughter," Meg snapped. "You're lying for money."

"I'm lying for love," the beggar snickered, "just like everyone else. I had twins, two girls who looked just like you. The other one gave me five dollars."

"Then she gave you too much," Megan said, instantly annoyed at being outdone.

"I always loved her best," the woman crowed as Meg turned and hurried away, seeing the bus lights coming down the avenue.

What had become of Greif? The pretty little girl with the curtain of blond hair—how had she turned out? It seemed all too likely that she was mad and abandoned somewhere out there. The image of Greif buzzed at the twins—alone in the world (if she was to be believed), and doomed to madness (if she was to be believed). Meg and Abby felt odd after seeing each other again. It was unnatural to be apart, it was wrong. But their pride refused to admit what the problem was, and it was easy to find a substitute. They diverted their nagging, bothersome thoughts by thinking about Greif.

So first one week passed and then another as Meg and Abby wondered where Greif might be. Both twins found themselves downtown more often, searching for the homeless woman they each thought of as Greif's mother. Abby gave her money when she found her, and asked the woman's name.

"You tell me your name first," the woman squinted at her.

"Abby."

"That's my name too."

And then, of course, Meg came around, limping slowly and peering into the shadows, and she, too, asked the woman's name.

"Abby. And I look just like you."

Meg's heart stuttered. She was not oversensitive. She did not imagine things. But for an instant she saw Abby's face—her own face—inside the dirt and wrinkles laughing in front of her. Her vision cleared, she shook herself, she threw a quarter at the woman's feet.

"That's all you get tonight. I don't like liars." She thought, *So Abby's been here. We think the same thing, even now. I'll never be sure if I had the thought first or simply picked it up from her.* She squatted down next to the beggar. "Now listen to me. The next time you see her, tell her, 'Megan sends her love.' Just like that. I promise you she'll give you a lot of money. I know her that well, because it's what I would do. Not for a lie, no I won't give money for a lie, but a salute—that's what it is, a salute, and she'll recognize it, after a minute or two. Did you hear me?" She stood up again.

"Megan sends her love," the woman said, grinning.

"I can see you'll do well at it. Here," and she handed the dollar she had originally set aside for her, "take this until you see her. It doesn't matter enough to me, to keep it."

The woman took the dollar as if it were a quarter, as if all money were equally important, and she lost her interest in Megan just as easily, looking past her to the traffic on the street.

It warmed Megan, thinking that Abby would get her message through the beggar. Oh, how her sister would be stunned—frightened—annoyed—emotions ricocheting across her face. Megan recognized her own vindictive gloating, and knew Abby would be aware of it too. They thought the same thoughts; it didn't require intent, it never required intent, it was simply and naturally unavoidable. They were streams that must inevitably flow downhill to join each other; it was in their nature to join eventually and all obstructions, all diversions, were incidental and unimportant.

Chapter 14

"This proposal of yours is well presented," Raymond said, beginning to get dressed. "I ran it past one or two people—just feeling things out. There hasn't been enough research in that area, not enough by half. I think there's money in it. It'll take a week or two more—just to make some calls, you know, to some of the major universities. We wouldn't want to duplicate another project."

"Why not?" Megan laughed. "That's how most of it gets done."

"We wouldn't want to sound like something already funded," he amended.

"Or unintentionally sound original. Give me the nice middle of the road."

He knotted his tie slowly and silently. "Yes. It surprises me how much you like the middle of the road—at your age, with your . . . ah, abilities."

"Next time I'll warn you before I'm sarcastic."

He smiled. "You'll have to learn the difference, someday, between sarcasm and truth."

She shrugged, pushing his comment aside. She watched him finish dressing, dusting his suit into shape, pulling it all into neatness. It was his custom to dress and leave at an ordered pace. He had external rhythms rather than a timetable; he reached an end to things—discussion, food, fondling, sex, relaxation—irrevocably, and moved on.

Meg had, at first, been offended by this because he required so little from her. She watched him and analyzed his systematic habits, his deliberate progressions. She was reluctant and annoyed and then she decided to see if she could beat him at it. She found, after some experience, that she could anticipate his actions, sometimes only by seconds. She would stop eating, and then he would stop; she would stop speaking and begin to undress before his hand reached his tie. She found that it actually suited her, it suggested a person who was aloof from indulgence or artificial intoxication; it projected a suggestion of austerity she approved of—as long as it was hers. But there was, also, an occasional perverse streak that wanted him to be provoked by this, to notice it. If he did notice, he didn't let on, and the small smile that sometimes appeared on his face could have been about anything. She told herself she had no need for him, that he was merely a convenience and a human necessity. She did not love him the way she loved Abby, for instance; he provided no sense of herself. But the sheer rhythm of his movements provoked a dependence on him that could have developed into affection, had Megan not learned to stop that feeling long before it became dangerous.

She disliked, however, the way he got up from her bed, dressed himself carefully, and continued an earlier conversation while she remained undressed, her eyes following his movements automatically. She tried to ignore him, lying on her stomach, not looking at him; she felt childish.

"I'm bored with this, Raymond," she said finally.

"With what specifically?"

"With the way you come here and the way you leave."

He regarded her patiently. "You knew I was married, I never tried to deceive you. I go home to my wife and that's where I live. There's nothing new here. I'm surprised any of this bothers you. Are you getting fond of me?"

"I'm sure I feel as much for you as you feel for me," she said evenly, "but I never thought my life could get so completely dull for such a long time."

"Throw yourself into science," he said seriously. "You're thinking about yourself too much, that's why you're bored. You maintain a distance from things. I suppose it's from your condition. Science is a great adventure; so much is still undiscovered. Every autopsy, every microscope slide—there could be anything there. Doors. They are all little doors. Some of the doors go nowhere, some lead back to the start. But there's always a door somewhere that takes you someplace totally new."

"It's such an abstract excitement," she said dryly.

"But it is an excitement." He finished his tie. "You've never experienced the sense of freedom, the thrill you feel when absolutely anything is before you." He checked himself in the mirror. "Once you taste it, there's no end to it."

"It would be fun to figure out the chemical components of *that* belief."

"It's like a series of vanishing mirrors; you have to be careful. You can go one step too far with the analysis; you can watch yourself too closely, trying to catch the cause of a thought." He checked his watch. "I have to go. I told her ten o'clock and I'll just make it." He came to her, bent down to place a kiss on her cheek (never on the lips unless he intended to make love), and patted her shoulder. "Remember I won't be in tomorrow, I've got a budget meeting and then a lunch."

She smiled sweetly. "I probably won't miss you."

"You probably won't. I'll try to make dinner with you on Thursday."

"Just remind me of it again please." She leaned over the nightstand, found a magazine, and began to read.

He sighed indulgently. "I'd love to discuss this with you further, but I have to go." He made one last visual sweep around the room and left.

Meg found herself relieved to hear the apartment door close.

Why was she irritated? It didn't matter that he was married; she even preferred that. Had she reached the stage of a relationship where everything about the man simply annoyed her—his complacency, his neatness, his dubious imagination and his undeserved self-confidence? It was possible; they were annoying things that in the past had given her a sense of satisfaction, since she could imagine his intelligence to be equal to her own. But external achievements mattered to him too much; to her he operated in a world of toys.

It must be time to end it. Even the thought of him, now, set her teeth on edge.

Of course, discarding a lover you worked with was difficult, especially if it was your superior. She had left her last job because it had become unpleasant after the breakup—no, unpleasant didn't do it. She had been hounded, nibbled at, denied a raise, had been subjected to complaints about her work and "attitude"—none of which annoyed her enough to suit him. She wasn't interested enough to fight back, and she might have regretted her own lack of interest, if she hadn't noticed how much her indifference drove her ex-lover wild.

So she must get some emotional satisfaction from it, after all.

Meg assumed that she lacked excessive emotions because she wasn't subject to pain. She was a superbeing, an evolved and perfected state. She had yet, however, to find a vehicle for this perfection. So many achievements seemed, from her point of view, to be childish or empty. She was not interested in exotic travel or fringe adventures. "Interested" was indeed her most-used word, her litmus test. She hoped to be interested in someone or something; she was not, except for sudden exalted moments that she learned to distrust and suppress. For the most part, she was simply walking an earth filled with other species. This must be for some purpose, and it was impatience for the purpose that drove her. Some day the call would come, the recognizable explanation for her distinction, and then all of this would cease to matter.

Until then Raymond was just a substitute for Abby, who was the only one so far capable of understanding her. It was terrible, sometimes, to be away from her, it took a hard will. Their fight was, in retrospect, too thin to continue for so long. It was hard for Megan to believe it would continue—surely Abby felt as she did, incomplete— but she had convinced herself that she was the aggrieved party. Abby had to change before all would be well again. She wouldn't call it pride, but she wanted Abby to come to her, asking forgiveness in any language, subtle or blunt. After all, Abby fit into the world and should be more giving, because everything was easier for her.

Lying in bed, already having dismissed Raymond from her mind, Meg put down the magazine finally, no longer pretending to read it. She stared at the wall, remembering Abby and missing her, remembering being a child with Abby always beside her, the two of them thinking the same thoughts except they were so slightly different. The world had been stitched together then, securely navigable—she, and Abby, and that imp called Greif.

Each, in her own individual but parallel way, had found her thoughts drawn to Greif, and what might have become of Greif. Free of Raymond's presence, Meg decided to go to central files and trace her. Taking a chance, Abby called the hospital information line, which also had her records.

When Meg entered the hospital room on the fifth floor, she found Abby there already, standing somewhat indecisively beside the bed. Their eyes flickered to each other, registered each other, and turned back to the patient.

Greif sat up in bed, her hands clasped in her lap. She had a stretched-out smile on her face—it was the first detail, after Abby, that Meg took in. This smile had an alert, eager, almost hungry quality to it—as if Greif were about to lick her lips but knew if she started she wouldn't be able to stop. She leaned forward slightly as Meg came in, gave a short, deep laugh of delight and cried, "Visiting day and no one told me!"

"Hello Greif, Abby. Just like old times."

Greif snickered. "Maybe not *just* like, you know. I live here now."

Meg beamed, a little too ostentatiously, at Greif. "It's funny. I work here, now—down where you used to take me. In research."

"Oh God. With the monkeys."

"No," Meg said. "There are very few monkeys there now."

Abby frowned. "But there are animals?"

Meg looked at her blandly. "I work with microscope slides. I'm just an assistant."

"Do you remember my monkey?"

"Of course."

Greif closed her eyes for a moment. Meg worked to shift Greif into focus. The years apart had turned the beautiful girl into a young woman with pasty skin and stringy hair and just the faintest suggestion of an odor. Every once in a while Meg could see the old Greif peeking out from this other woman's face, her eyes slanted in gleeful discourtesy. But for the most part, this Greif was flat and it was hard to adjust to it. Meg saw Abby's uncertainty. *Of course*, Meg thought. *She didn't know Greif as well as I did, but even Abby can see they've emptied her out, somehow.*

Greif opened her eyes. "I never felt the same after the monkey died. I knew I didn't have any more time." She sighed and Abby shifted. Meg hadn't gone through all of Greif's records—they had been filled with pharmaceutical and psychiatric abbreviations—but she knew the general diagnosis of personality disorder.

Abby said bluntly, "It was terrible, what they did to that monkey, but it wasn't your fault."

"You know, I checked the records and the monkey had nothing

to do with you. I always wondered if you knew that." Meg sat on the edge of Greif's bed.

Greif squinted up at her. "The dates always matched. And that number. It was the same as the last four numbers on my chart."

"It was just a cage number. It's still a cage number. There's a white rat in it now."

"A white rat. I don't think a white rat can be right. But, then, they give me drugs now, pills twice a day, and maybe they know a monkey couldn't stand it."

"Stand what?" Abby interrupted.

Greif shook back her hair and lifted her chin, the old Greif, with the old flashing smile. "You know I'm here because I'm violent?" Her eyes darted back and forth between the twins. "Didn't you have to sign a sheet to get in?"

"Yes," Abby said.

"Everyone has to sign in on this floor," Meg pointed out. "Except me, of course, I came on the employee elevator. There's security here because the patients are not considered responsible for themselves."

"*Or* for others," Greif squealed, "or others. It's because we're all mad, here, officially mad, signed-stamped-and-sealed mad. I'd be in prison otherwise, you'd be talking to me through bars."

Abby found this to be too much like the old boasting Greif. "For what?" she said sarcastically.

"I killed my mother," Greif said conversationally. "When I wasn't quite right in my head. My mother was mad too, much worse than I am, and I only hope someone comes by to kill me when I get that bad—and I'm sure I will, it's hereditary, she killed her mother too, out of pity and I suppose she couldn't take it either. But it's not an easy thing to do." She flopped back against her white pillow, flailing her arms out. "Killing *or* being killed."

Meg and Abby showed no visible reaction to this story. They

both suspected Greif of engineering an effect, enlarging on some real but different event.

A nurse passing by the door told them visiting hours were over.

"I have to go," Abby said promptly.

"You'll come back?" Greif was suddenly anxious. "No one visits me now; just doctors. I'll be here forever, you know."

"We'll come back," Abby said. Meg noticed the "we" instantly.

"That's good, that's good," Greif said, relaxing. A thoughtful expression took hold of her face. "And which one did you say you were anyway?"

Without answering, Abby walked out of the room and Meg followed.

"I've never been sure of her," Abby said carefully as she signed herself out at the nurses' desk. Meg showed her identification to the nurse, who studied their faces with interest but said nothing.

"Well, she's here, so there's some truth to what she says."

"There's *some* truth to most lies or they wouldn't work," Abby objected.

"I can get information from her records. Will you come back to see her?"

"I said I would." Abby was careful to avoid Meg's eyes.

"You never seemed to like her very much."

"No. I never did."

"So I think it's odd you would visit her."

Abby turned to face her. "She's alone and she asked me to come back," she said impatiently. "It's exactly the kind of thing I *would* do."

"Sorry. Of course you would. And you'll resent her for it."

Abby walked in silence for a moment. "But I'll still do it. And she'll get what she wants."

Meg allowed Abby the last word on this. She walked her out of the building, turning as she turned so they marched in step—exactly as it should be, and she was sure Abby felt the same. The problem was in how to suggest a reconciliation. "Do you have to go somewhere now?"

"Yes."

"Maybe we could meet the next time you come. Here, let me give you my number at work."

"I'll probably come when I can fit it in, without any notice."

"Give me a call. I work in the next building. I could come right over. You never had anything to say to her and you won't now. It'll be much better if I'm there."

Abby took the number and Meg grinned. Just don't go overboard, she warned herself; just don't go crazy. "Maybe we could get together for coffee or something, next time." She stood next to Abby at the bus stop, her face much too close to her sister's, almost leaning into her.

"This is my bus," Abby said, stepping up and into it. She didn't turn back for a wave or a final glance.

I went overboard, Meg thought as she retraced her steps, limping back to the lab.

Chapter 15

"So, word is that you have a proposal here," Pandit said serenely to Megan. His desk faced hers; they had shared the same lab space for two years.

"Yes, that's true. But I don't think it will even have my name on it."

"Oh, it will have your name," Pandit said reassuringly. "Here they are good enough to put your name on it. I myself have my name on two dozen proposals. That is the easy part. But I have not been appointed to a research team." He shook his head sadly. "There are many ideas, you see; the thinking itself is cheap. But getting the professional people who can make an actual reality out of your dream, that is the hard part and requires people with reputation." A slow smile slid out from the corner of his mouth. "I am convinced of this. Or else there are just so many people of reputation that there is no room for anyone else."

"You're very funny, Pandit, but I think it bothers you. I think you want to be a person of reputation too."

"Sometimes I think the very same thing. But you see, at heart I am attracted by ideas. I sit at my microscope and look at my slides and my head buzzes like a garden. It's a very pleasant sensation. And then, you know, I think someone must pay with his soul for what they do back there." He jerked his head towards the labs.

"Really? Do you think it matters? They're only animals after all."

Pandit looked unhappy. "Animals have souls too. They make

me uneasy when I see them. I liked it very much better when I ordered tissue slides from a catalog, it was an innocent thing. But I should know what they come from. I am happy I do not have to kill them. It is my job to make sure that their deaths have some meaning. I want to help, you see. Since I was a very small boy I wanted to defeat sickness and crippling. I was very foolish, I imagined a room where learned men paced among their books and deplored suffering."

"Well, perhaps there aren't so many books as you imagined, but that *is* what everyone wants."

"Is it?"

"Don't get too spiritual, Pandit. Disease is very earthy, it's unpleasant. Sometimes I think Raymond makes the same mistake, trying to make a disease into a problem in logic."

"Well, this is what I think," Pandit said eagerly. "I wonder if they are careful with these animals, if they are thrifty. Sometimes I think that there shouldn't be such numbers of them, as if the secret were hidden in quantity. Instead of this, I think it is a question of observation and, and . . . discovery. Yes! That is the very word, to break through to new ground. But I don't see discovery here; they keep themselves so busy with reports and theories." He returned to his slide. "But these tissues are beautiful things." He adjusted the focus. "So beautiful to look at, and so perfectly they hold their secrets."

Like so many of the research staff, Pandit was seduced by possibilities. Once a question or an idle thought popped into anyone's mind, it was only natural to consider, not whether it was a good question, but how to test it. They got excited by every new twist or variation, losing sight of their goals or simply abandoning them. They were the kind of people who would make a monster just to see what kind of monster they would make.

Megan wasn't surprised to notice that this omnipresent desire to *find out* sometimes slipped past the laboratory walls. In fact, it had slipped into her own bedroom. Occasionally, Raymond stayed with her when his wife was away. A few months earlier, she had dozed off after making love, waking up to find Raymond seated next to her on the bed, with a hypodermic in his hand. What had woken her was the cold feel of alcohol being rubbed on her arm, not the needle itself. She shifted uneasily, and Raymond turned to find Meg's eyes wide open, staring at him.

"What was that?"

He continued to dispose of the needle and the vial. "Nalaxone," he said. "I was curious."

"Nalaxone," she murmured. "It's an opiate suppressant, isn't it?"

"Yes. It counteracts the natural painkillers the body provides."

"This is a test of some kind."

He smiled. "I don't believe it will matter. I don't think your condition is a result of overproduction of natural painkillers."

"Then what?" She was interested. It didn't immediately occur to her to question his experimenting on her without permission. She, too, had explored the literature. People like her were rare: there was a known spinal condition which blocked the path of the pain transmitters; there were pain experiments that proved that excision of certain parts of the medulla interfered with pain reception; a tumor might do it, a deterioration of nerve endings might. She had none of these conditions.

"But it's only half the test," she said in a low voice. "How were you going to judge the effects?"

He sat on the bed patiently. "A slight cut on the buttocks. You wouldn't notice it, if you didn't feel it."

"I've heard the soles of the feet are tender."

"You're very understanding. We'll wait a little, I think." He looked at his watch. "Another fifteen minutes, say. For the spirit of the thing."

"I love research," she answered. Her pulse, however, was racing slightly. She was curious. Every experience was defined along a continuum, but her graph line was shorter; all her experiences stopped short of the full spectrum. What was "fullness," then? What was at the opposite end of the line, what was that territory like? To be superior to something was also to be apart from it. Sometimes she fantasized about a world filled with people like her, a world of superior people, none of whom cared about death. It was odd how she equated pain with death, when she knew very well they were different. But it was hard to think herself as capable of dying; she belonged among the immortals. Unfortunately, there were no other immortals around.

She checked her breathing; she had to be calm. If the drug worked . . . if the drug worked, wouldn't she taste the apple, the delicious apple of pain, and then return to being a god again? It was hard to imagine pain, the impact of pain; pain itself was evanescent, even to those who experienced it. They were impressed with its devastation, its immediacy, its addictive self-consciousness. Pleasures evaporated, but pain pulled the body into itself, shocking the body into existence. She looked at Raymond through half-opened eyes, barely moving, keeping her body still as she listened, tasted, looked and felt for it: pain, the common touch.

"How do you feel?" he asked. His eyes barely blinked, locked on her. He sat composed at the foot of the bed, his hands folded over his knees. He was in his underwear and socks; only the large watch on his wrist betrayed his professionalism. He never removed his watch.

After ten minutes he took a scalpel from his briefcase and said, "Your choice. It will be a small cut. I'll try not to leave a scar."

"Scars don't matter."

"Then, your hand." He picked her hand up and opened it. He ran his fingers over her palm, light as a feather. "Feel that?"

"Of course."

"Relax. More than likely, this won't hurt a bit." He smiled genially at his own joke, then he cut a line along her palm. It welled up immediately, a series of spots along its center.

"Anything?"

She shook her head.

"Give it a minute. Sometimes you don't feel it right away."

She snorted—she told herself it wasn't in relief. "Do you imagine I'm in shock?"

He went back to his briefcase, taking out a small bottle of antiseptic and a bandage. He dabbed the liquid on her palm and sighed. "I didn't really think so, you know. But one hates to miss the obvious. Your body isn't working overtime on endorphins—natural painkillers."

"I know what endorphins are."

"Sorry. Of course you would. Do you mind if I note this?" She shook her head and he went to a small notebook in the flap of his case and made quick jottings.

"Do you have other notes on me?"

"Just superficial observations. I've read your charts. I know your reaction to various therapeutic drugs; I know they tried small doses of electrical stimulation when you were a child. But, no, this is the first time I've tried anything on you purely in the interests of science." He shut his notebook and replaced it.

"I wonder if that means you've tried other things not purely in the interests of science."

He didn't reply.

A small dark-red line was showing at the edge of the bandage. "Have you ever cut your hand like this?" she asked idly.

"Yes. It hurt like hell."

"That's why you picked my hand, then. And tell me, what did it feel like?"

"I told you. It hurt like hell."

"Ah," she said coldly. "That clarifies things."

For her project Meg sent detailed requests to all the teaching hospitals. She asked for histories of patients with persistent undiagnosed pains, and especially for those who were extremely physically sensitive. She begged for slides, cultures, blood samples, reports of any tests taken.

She sent out over a hundred inquiries and received three replies. "That is not how things are done," Pandit told her. "They won't tell you anything important because you might beat them to publication if it helped your project. You won't get anything from them unless you first have something they need." He shrugged. "You do not know anything; they will not tell you anything."

She turned to the research with a vengeance. She went to the catalogs, ordering all the literature on the subject of pain and excitability, articles with obscure titles and multiple, persistent authors.

Of course they were all deep in receptor theory. Scientists were increasingly convinced that all pain—indeed all response—was chemical. A touch, a smell or a taste stimulated molecules in the vicinity and passed the stimulation from one cell to the next, straight on up to the brain. The cells carried the information by sending the activated chemicals to sites or receptors designed for that particular combination or condition in the cell—plugging in, as it were, from one cell to the next by carrying the very specific chemical flag forward to the processing centers of the brain. It was a kind of secret handshake moving down the line.

It had been found that receptors for the malaria microbe existed on most red blood cells (not sickle-cells, for instance), and working backwards this had to indicate that if the receptors exist, there must be a physiological relative of the malarial microbe. After all, this was how endorphins, the body's natural painkillers, were found.

Opiates had chemical receptors in the body, waiting for the specific physiological key to activate them. Opium did this, by matching the recipe. But it also indicated an internal source, which had been found even though no non-addictive way to utilize it had been propounded. Chemistry was the target for the future; the body was composed of lock-and-key mechanisms—perhaps for everything, even thought.

They were deliberately opaque, these articles, as if the authors intended to claim their own territory by renaming all landmarks. One article claimed to discover a "mu-endorphin," the basis for all endorphins, a bullet which could trigger all opiate receptors. Meg could tell that the article was engineered for the drug companies—after all, it could never be cost-efficient to manufacture each specific endorphin triggering each individual receptor. The "mu-endorphin" would blanket the body with a universal, biologically triggered pain killer, if the authors could get the grants.

Finally, Meg wrote back to all her initial contacts. The only tradable asset she had was herself. She said she had a "subject" with her medical history, and pointed out that, unlike rats or dogs, this subject could fully relate all of the body's responses to a chemical, could evaluate and qualify sensations. No kittens having their eyes rotated, no monkeys having their skulls cracked. Her subject was interested in pain solely as a "matter of survival" and was willing to test any byproduct of their research that seemed likely to accomplish this.

All her letters went unanswered except for one which had been forwarded to a clinical assistant in a state mental institution, who was pursuing, without grant money, his own investigations into sensory abnormalities. He apologized for his lack of credentials. He was observing chemical anomalies, he said; he was charting the patients' reactions to drugs; he had been doing it for 15 years and he was allowed to assist at autopsies, where he snipped at brainstems and gray and white matter and froze sections of the liver and so forth. He pointed out that dopamine, first introduced as a remedy for schizophrenia, had achieved its successful application for Parkinsonism only when someone noticed that it relieved the tremors in certain patients. Its success with schizophrenia was minimal; its only real promise lay in relieving the spasms of Parkinson's disease. People tended to believe, he said, that straight lines ran between a condition and its opposite: too much produced one thing, too little produced the opposite. The only problem was in understanding which things were opposite. Parkinsonism was a condition in which the body's chemical signals misfired, giving excess information to the brain, which caused catastrophic disturbances. In schizophrenia, the thought processes misfired also, giving misinformation to the brain, causing catastrophic mental disturbances. He had seen odd reactions from these patients—an occasional contempt for pain, or an obsession with it. He had separated various organic chains in his researches and was trying to map them thoroughly. If she were interested in his explorations, he would send some of his reports and the chemicals as he worked on them.

His name was John Martin. She wrote him back immediately.

Chapter 16

"I've been approaching this all wrong," Raymond said one day. "I'm at a dead end, professionally and emotionally, and I know the cause." He stopped before the mirror to adjust his tie.

"I've sacrificed creativity to professionalism," he said with certainty.

"I had no idea you were interested in creativity."

"I'm not just a piece of bureaucratic machinery. I know that's what you like to think, but I actually have daydreams, Megan. I have a conscience—whatever that is—and a sense of history. Maybe all these things combined produce a sense of purpose, because I have that too. The work we do is routine and redundant, and most of the time it's simply useless. Money, time, and minds all wasted. I'm going to propose one project that's pure research, an out-and-out exploration."

She watched him with interest.

"I want the exact moment when death occurs," he said, brushing off his jacket. "The clinical picture. I believe there's a part of the brain that signals death; that death itself is an organic response, not just a sort of loss of power. I believe there's a point at which the brain—or the mind—refuses to live any longer because it recognizes that the destruction is overwhelming. If I'm right, then of course there's another step here, because if it's a decision—at whatever level—then it's capable of being a wrong decision, a bad call."

She shook her head slowly. "I can see where you're headed. You think it's a question of will power, at the root of it."

"No. I think death involves a decision, but I don't think it's exclusively dependent on it. We talk about 'the will to live' routinely. I'm just pursuing that logically. It's something that has been noted clinically but never investigated."

She rubbed her hand across her mouth, staring at him. "Is there a reason for this? Are you sick?'

"It doesn't have to be personal to interest me. I've always thought about it, always wondered. Don't you? Don't you think about dying?"

"Not much. No."

"But aren't you afraid of death?"

"I don't know. I think of death as a blankness. How can you be afraid of blankness?"

"Really? It terrifies everyone else. God, I would imagine you'd have to be on guard about it, you're so close at any moment. You wouldn't even know if you were seriously hurt. It could happen to you without warning."

"It could happen to anyone that way."

"But it wouldn't necessarily kill someone else, someone who actually feels their body warning them."

She was irritated. "I'm not paralyzed. I can feel."

He shrugged neatly. "You could die of a burst appendix—so many things the average person would at least notice."

"And how will you test your will-power theory? Cut open any number of rats before they die so you can watch their brains decide? It's kind of a hard theory to prove, isn't it?" She sounded—and was—spiteful. So he looked on her as a freak?

He shook his head thoughtfully. "All we can say about death is what it is *not*—it is not life. The heart stops, the lungs stop, the brain stops. But death is in us somewhere, in the brain most likely, a little seed waiting to blossom. What if we could control it, correct it? We say death has to occur because the body wears down, but cells reproduce themselves all through life; why do they degrade? What if there's a little chemical center that issues orders? Why—even manufactur-ers have grasped the concept of planned obsolescence. What if it *is* a plan, a blueprint of sorts?"

"It would get a little crowded around here without that plan," she pointed out.

"We reproduce ourselves so quickly because we die so quickly. But I don't care, I don't care about that at all. All I know is that it's a possibility. I think death is in a cell somewhere, and I want to track it down. It's the duty of the scientist to do that, to do it for the love of truth. Truth always sets out to defeat mystery; and this is the biggest mystery there is." He looked at her with his face flushed and his eyes excited.

"I just see problems with it, that's all." She felt that she should tone him down, that the hectic glow in his skin was unhealthy.

"You *want* to see problems with it."

"You may be right. What does your wife say?"

"You know I never discuss work with her."

"But this isn't work yet, is it? Only theory? 'Vision'?"

"My wife and I discuss household matters, vacations, and the children. Those are the only interests we have in common." He had finished dressing and paused to look at her. "I admit I'm disappointed in your reaction. I find this idea exciting, very exciting. Of course I have to get the details in order. I don't believe I'll be able to see you again this week."

"Fortunately I don't feel pain."

"Yes," he said. "Well, goodnight."

She listened for the click of the door shutting behind him. She longed, again, for Abby, for the old Abby. Raymond had made her feel terribly alone. It was all this talk of death, of course. He spoke to her of death, and then he left her in an empty room.

Abby took the bus to the family shelter where she worked as a recreational coordinator. Her actual title was "activities director," as if she were on a luxury cruise somewhere, dispensing volleyballs.

She had an awkward job, since she was a private employee, provided by a nonprofit organization, in a public environment. She oversaw the volunteers who came in for various after-hour programs—tutoring, arts, even gymnastics.

The shelter was overheated, ugly, and offensive. Its cheerlessness affected even the children, who were incapable of sharing or protecting anything, even toys. Everything they got they destroyed, as quickly as possible.

That day she heard the excited shouts of children in the alley behind the recreation room. The alley was littered with broken bottles. It did not belong to the shelter and the fence at the street end was constantly ripped open. The children were not supposed to play there. They were not even supposed to be out there without an adult.

She went to check and found a group of five children—four boys and a girl—huddled in a shrieking semicircle facing a wall. They were hurling bottles and pieces of bricks. She saw, very quickly, that they had cornered a rat—probably poisoned or it would have escaped—and were throwing anything they could find at it. The boy with the bottle leaned forward and aimed at the rat's head, hitting it. It shuddered. Abby could see one leg completely broken. The group squealed with glee.

She grabbed two of the children, yanking them back. "Stop that. Don't ever do that again," she said in a low, harsh, angry voice, a voice she had never used with them before. "That animal can feel pain. Get inside."

She turned away from them. They were still young enough to be worried. The rat quivered. There was blood around the mouth. She watched uncertainly. If only I knew how to kill it, she thought, searching for something among the rubbish.

"That you, Abby?" A man from the shelter staff, a security guard named Ken, came towards her curiously.

"Oh good," she said in relief. She turned and pointed. "Can you kill that for me?"

He took a step back. "How you want me to kill that thing?"

"I don't know. Can you—oh, twist its neck or something?"

"I ain't going to touch it!"

"Then shoot it."

"I shoot this gun off now and the whole neighborhood's going to jump," he argued. "Besides, that ain't a horse, you want me to shoot it like a horse?"

"Oh hell," she said, and she picked up a board and lifted it, but she couldn't bring it down. She stood there, telling herself the only humane thing to do would be to smash the rat's skull in. She was afraid, however, that she would do a bad job, increase its suffering by bad blows, and she put the board down and walked away.

She almost made it to the door when she heard Ken slam it down with more strength than she could have mustered and, she hoped, more skill.

"I got rid of that thing," he told her a few minutes later. She stood by the doorway.

"I thought the children weren't supposed to be on the streets by themselves."

He shrugged. "They go from here to the bus to the school and then back here. When the weather's good sometimes we don't look when they get off the bus. They're kids."

"It's not my rule," she said quickly. "I'm not complaining. But the streets around here aren't so nice."

He grinned at her. "Not like in here, right?" He laughed. "Anyway, there's kids living out there, too, you know. As long as it's daylight it's okay. Ain't lost one yet while I've been here."

"How long is that?"

"Five months. I had a kid once tell me he'd been here the longest of any place he'd lived. I said, how long? He said, four weeks. He said he knew about everything you could know about this place in two weeks. He was moved out the next day."

"Where to?" she asked automatically. She wasn't really listening to him; she was wondering if she should report the rat to someone.

Ken shrugged. "I don't ask them that. Have you ever seen where they go next?"

"No. It's supposed to be permanent housing though."

"These people with these kids," he said heavily. "I hear they just move around. Some of them, they're okay you know, if you find them a place they can *fit in*, they know how to fit in, but the others, they just go with their kids through one system and then the next. I asked around. Why some of these kids—I heard they had different mamas somewhere else."

"Well, they're surviving," Abby said without conviction.

Ken gave an odd sound, half like a snort, half like a laugh. "Like that rat was surviving," he said.

"Yes," Abby answered slowly, making her voice neutral and turning away from him to walk down the hall back to the recreation room. "Well—you know—rats . . ."

She concentrated on the activity ahead, an after-school tutorial. Tables and chairs were set up; the locked cabinet with the pens, papers, and donated books was opened, and the sign-in sheet was placed by the door. The first volunteers came in, draping their coats on the plastic bags of laundry piled against the wall.

Only three volunteers showed up, and she waited with them for the children. A mother arrived with a four-year-old; she was turned away because the child was below school age. She glared, her head held high, and sauntered off. The adults were not allowed to leave the shelter without their children, unless the children were in a shelter-endorsed activity. She must have had plans, Abby thought.

A seven-year-old raced in energetically. He got to the end of one table, where a volunteer sat, and lifted his head, grinning expectantly.

He had been there before; he liked the attention.

Children showed up sporadically for the next hour—some of them too young and turned away—for a total of seven children and three tutors. The children twitched and shrieked and jittered over their sheets of paper, with the exception of one 16-year-old who sat, towering above his tutors, with a bored and embarrassed distance on his face. The volunteers spent their time trying to match the children with the available books. The session lasted an hour, at which time everyone left with a sense of relief. The parents were told it was good for the children, the volunteers were told it was good for the children. Abby had been doing it for a year and a half. She thought it might be good for the children, if by good one meant only all those things that weren't bad.

There was a half-hour before the next onslaught, a play group for the preschool children. Two volunteers showed up, as did nine children, four of them still in diapers. Abby pitched in, dividing the group into "smashers" (too young to do anything but bang away), "blocks and colors," and "picture books." She took the last group, so she could jump in to help the others if needed. The picture books— *Eloise, Curious George, In the Night Kitchen, Madeline*—were fairy tales for the children, who stared at the illustrations as if they concerned foreign tribes or the way life used to be.

The noise reached an incredible pitch, but they had all agreed, ages ago, that the preschools had unlimited rights to make noise while there; they needed that as much as they needed to run around. The volunteers merely tried to direct them, out of some corralling instinct, no doubt.

"I can't come back after this," one volunteer said at the end of it. Abby nodded; the average length of time they stayed was three months. "My schedule changed at work and I won't be out early enough to get here." Abby had already started to walk away. She didn't expect excuses, though so many people seemed determined to offer them.

The room was opened after this. It had been turned into temporary sleeping quarters; the cots were folded up each morning and stacked in the hallway.

There were also wooden benches down the hall. Mothers with strollers sat there waiting for the room to open; their children raced back and forth. They glanced at her indifferently as she passed. They were mostly black or Spanish. The volunteers were usually white. The fact that she was white made Abby feel apologetic—a feeling she always had to fight. Perhaps that's why she had no patience for the volunteer's apology. Excuses didn't matter; it came down to actions. There were black volunteers occasionally, and it was their disappearance that disturbed her the most, just as, in a different way, the occasional appearance of a white child in the programs, or a white face in the corridor, also disturbed her.

Some people thought of her as calm, perhaps tending a little towards too much self-control. She simply tried to harden herself to what she saw: otherwise she would be like the volunteers who one day found they were filled with dread or despair and had to leave. Abby tried to outsmart dread by insisting on precision: she would look, and note, and look further on. She would try to keep her thoughts and her actions straightforward, because some emotions fed on themselves and led nowhere.

She passed a vacant lot on the way from the shelter to the bus; every day for the past week there had been a half-grown abandoned cat crying or just sitting in a corner. Today she didn't see it and was surprised to find herself filled with guilt. Maybe someone had taken it home, poor thing. She tried to convince herself of that, in a dry, soothing, internal voice, but she wished she had taken it herself, before it was too late.

Suddenly she saw it, huddled behind a piece of wood. She went over, whispering to it, and picked it up (its fur hung loose from its ribs) and hid it in her jacket. She took the bus home, occasionally shushing or rubbing her left breast (one passenger furtively watching her), trying to keep the cat secure and alive.

"Weren't there only two cats?" Charles asked thoughtfully.

Abby watched the cats along with him, as if equally surprised. "It's been here a week," she admitted finally. "Adjusting."

He ate his cereal slowly, obviously considering his next remark. "Is there a maximum number?"

She nodded. "Based on the number of rooms."

He chewed. "I was thinking maybe a spare room could go for a nursery."

"I don't see how. What with all these animals, it's probably not healthy."

He snorted into his coffee. "I love your sense of humor. It's so unguarded."

"Really? Most people don't think I have a sense of humor."

"You're too subtle."

"I never think of myself as subtle."

He frowned. "Look, it's okay about the cat; I just don't like it when you sneak things in on me—as if I wouldn't notice."

"It took you a week to notice this time."

"That's not the point. Besides, I noticed two days ago when I stepped on it. You weren't around and it slipped my mind."

She grinned at him wickedly. "You're bound to lose count soon. You have trouble remembering how old you are, after all."

"I like to keep an open mind." He took his dishes to the sink, stepping over the line of cats, whose tails leaned out on the linoleum like a rake. He rinsed the dishes and put them in the rack. "Other people have children and cats both," he pointed out.

"And some people have horses."

He came over to kiss her on the top of her head. "I love you."

"I don't know if I even *like* cats," she said irritably. "They're so needy. Always crying and looking at you and wanting to sleep in your lap."

"You're already having a bad day and you haven't gone anywhere yet."

"I can't think of having children. The children at the shelter have nothing. Shouldn't I give them what I have instead of just reinforcing things by having a child born to privilege?"

"You can't help them all."

"I could help one."

He stood at the doorway, gazing not at her but past her to the window. "What can I do to make you happy?"

"You can't." She felt herself settling stubbornly into self-pity.

"I happen to like challenges." He turned to go and then turned back. "Do me a favor, though. If you bring anything else home, let me know, will you? Just count me in. I like to feel as if I belonged here." His voice was even; it could have been described as friendly if the words were discounted. But it was the words that stuck with Abby, and she frowned. The cats were washing themselves, grooming their faces and paws. They had settled into satisfaction; they were saved.

The dogs, let in from the yard, made straight for the cat bowls, licking them clean.

She would bet anything that Megan had no pets. Why should she? Megan felt no obligation to the world, to any part of the world. When had Megan ever cared for or about anything but herself?

Abby was biting off her nails as she thought. She should call the vet and make an appointment for the new cat. Tests and shots. It got so annoying. She cleaned out the litter, checked all the water bowls, and made sure the place was clean before she left. There were towels on the sofas for the dogs, and blocks of wood with cord on them for the cats to scratch. Dutifully, she filled the bird feeders, though it had been months since she'd actually seen a bird. Another byproduct of having cats.

It wasn't that she didn't sometimes think of a child; she did. But then the image of twins would intrude; what if she had twins like Megan, two of them like Megan? On her worst days she thought, *Or two of them like me?* After all, she knew she was dissatisfied in some unappeasable way. There was nothing she could think of that would make her feel different. Everything around her called out for attention; there was no way to shut down the cries for attention and yet Charles—oh yes very nice indeed but deaf for all that to the clamor of voices—Charles wanted to add another voice to the begging, pleading chorus. She wouldn't have it.

Chapter 17

"I know he likes me, I've seen the way he looks at me," Greif said with assurance. "But he's afraid to say anything. He has some problem. Don't you think so?" She turned her appeal to Abby, who frowned and shrugged her shoulders.

"How do you know that? How do you know how he feels?" Abby asked sternly.

"A woman knows these things," Greif answered in a slightly breathless voice. She looked from Abby to Megan, her eyes wide open, her mouth slightly parted. "I can hear it in his voice, the way he hesitates, how sensitive he is. But he comes and goes so quickly, he's barely here and then he's gone, it's a sign of his hopeless confusion."

"If you think he's in love with you, then he must be," Meg said encouragingly.

"Oh crap," Abby snapped, and waved Meg aside. "Greif, I don't know whether you see these things because they're true or because you want to see them. And Megan certainly doesn't know. You're here because your judgment is not sound; you're here because you don't always work with reality. How can you be sure he has any feelings for you whatsoever?"

"You can't be much of a woman if you ask a question like that," Greif pouted. "A woman always knows. Some things *are* obvious, even if you're crazy part of the time. Are you telling me that there couldn't be a man here who's attracted to me? There's someone for everyone, usually more than one. And these doctors, they spend so much time here they have to choose from the nurses or the patients. And I can be charming too, you know, just the way everyone can be charming and sometimes more so." She crossed her arms under her breasts and stared hard at Abby.

"Of course he could be in love with you," Megan said smugly. "And of course he would hesitate. The doctor-patient ethics problem. It would worry anyone."

Greif smiled and closed her eyes. "Ethics. That must be it. A torment for him—crushed between his heart and his conscience. And not knowing how I would react."

"Well, I can't believe you wouldn't have tried giving him some sign."

"I have my ethics too."

Abby snorted and Megan smiled cheerfully before turning to Greif. "Of course you have ethics. So many people have them who don't want them, and so few want them who don't have them. A great national irony in that."

"And life is passing me by," Greif said with sudden conviction.

"Strike while the iron is hot."

"I don't think this is helping her," Abby hissed.

Greif opened her eyes. "Positive thinking always helps. And thinking positively in a romantic sense is the only way to get things going, isn't it? The problem is not that I'm insane, or that he's a doctor, but that the signals have been wrong." She sighed. "It would help so much if you could bring me a robe of exactly the same color as my eyes. And makeup. And a razor. They never let us have razors here. Even an electric one would be okay." Her hand reached up. "I can tie up my hair. And my shoes won't matter." She settled back with an ecstatic look on her face. "Don't forget: the color must be the exact color of my eyes."

"I don't think this is a good idea," Abby argued later.

"Greif knows what she's doing. She'll probably be confined all her life; I think it's better for her to have an affair if it's possible. For all the usual reasons."

"But is she making it up? That's what worries me."

"She won't rape him," Meg amiably pointed out. "She'll just try to seduce him. Sounds like a reasonable thing to do."

"I don't know," Abby said reluctantly. She looked through her things, however, and found odds and ends of makeup that might do very well for Greif. And she bought a small electric razor and some nail polish. Megan bought a robe.

Greif never asked about the cost. She stretched her arms out eagerly. "Tomorrow," she murmured. "I'll be ready then." She held the robe bunched in her fists. "Makeup, nail polish. Time to see how I look. I'll tell the nurses I'm in the lounge. There's a window there, and a kind of view. I can look out the window and wait for him." She sucked her lip. "Yes. That will be good." She smiled at them, as if looking for confirmation.

"What time will that be?" Abby asked.

"He usually stops by around two."

"I think I'll be here around then."

Megan nodded.

"I don't know," Greif said doubtfully. "Won't it be better if I'm alone?"

"It could be better if he saw you surrounded by friends," Meg said. "We could leave, discreetly, when it seems right."

"That would explain why I'm in the lounge."

"Yes," Meg agreed. "With two friends to show him you're still in touch with the outside world."

"What do I care about the outside world?" she answered stiffly.

"Why nothing, nothing at all. And no one else cares about it either," Meg said soothingly.

"Do you think this doctor even exists?" Abby asked, somewhat worried as they sat over a cup of coffee in the cafeteria.

"Yes, I'm sure of it."

"I wish I could be. I have a feeling something's wrong here."

"You know, I'm beginning to think you have that feeling about everything in your life."

"That's not true!" She thought for a moment. "Not entirely true, anyway. I was raised to watch out for danger, you know, I always had to watch you. It's natural I should be aware of the potential in things. Contingencies. I'm not like you, I'm not immune. I had to feel your pain for you so I felt twice as much."

"And I suppose by extension I had to take your strength."

Abby drummed her cup. Her head was lowered. These pauses, these moments of concentration, were like a physical tic, as if she were internally surveying her signals in order to guess the right answer.

"Yes, I wish I were braver," she said finally, "but I don't know if I can blame that on you."

Meg read some more research articles at work and then went to ask Raymond, "Have you heard of the P factor?"

"Well, of course. The question is, do I believe in it?"

"All right. Do you?"

"On the surface it seems likely. Every aspect of human life has a chemical basis. So the theory is that there's a chemical that actually carries the pain response along the path. The human body." He hummed. "The human body. An amalgam. A chorus. A balance. Right now someone is hard at work tracking down the particular formula for depression. I believe in the next century they will do away with psychiatry. Trauma has its chemical makeup; it alters the balance of the body. They will unravel schizophrenia, too. But these things are hard to test in rats. Pain and pleasure are so much easier—and of course pain is easier than pleasure. Look at the fuss over endorphins! They think they've found a free, nonaddictive painkiller! The problem is that it's ephemeral. There was a Nobel Prize in it, but where's the pill? Where's the cure based on these endorphins?" He smiled. "A lovely idea. The drug companies were excited and surprisingly supportive. A free painkiller. My." He rubbed a spot on his wrist, a spot he was fond of ever since he'd looked into acupressure. "I believe all they'll end up with is confirmation of ancient Chinese medicine. The body produces it naturally for the practitioner, but in low and specific dosages. To manufacture it . . . a few needles are much cheaper."

"They may find a way."

"More likely they'll just find more funding."

"*You* believe there's a chemical for death," she said quietly.

"The D factor." He laughed. "I've told you, I think, that it's a side door—a sister, should I say?—to the orgasm?"

"No, you didn't say exactly that."

"Oh, but I should have," he said generously. "I think death comes with delight."

"I see. But this P factor?"

"Your own personal crusade. Are we defined by what we search for?" It was unusual to see him so jubilant. Had he discovered something about death, then? Meg dismissed his confidence. After all, his topic could not be proven one way or the other. The literature on death was interesting and extensive, but wholly anecdotal.

"I think it makes sense, this chemical adjunct to pain."

He came to her and stroked her cheek once, with the back of his fingers. "You would like a little prescription? You would like to be one of us?"

She sighed. "This mood of yours is very irritating. It's a serious question."

"The problem," he said seriously, "is the discrete differences in pain. They want a pathway that carries all pain messages; they think it separates in the brain, preferably in the limbic region. That's okay, it's a sound experiment. You could even argue that masochists, for instance, have their pathways mixed up. Pleasure and pain can get confused.—But why should anything be so simple?" he asked suddenly. "What happens to the metaphysical when we end up with nothing but chemistry?"

She eyed him warily. "I wonder what you mean when you say 'metaphysical'? You know that even when we map everything we'll still be wondering why two people with the exact same chemical makeup act differently."

"Will we?" he wondered. "Won't it all break down to cause and effect, key and lock?"

"Why should it?" she snapped. "Why should we be strictly anything? There's always an animal factor, an individual factor, in play. Two people experiencing the same experimental events will probably react differently."

"They'll have individual chemical maps," he pointed out.

"Twins, then," she said stubbornly. "I think even twins will act differently." She felt a certain sardonic pride in saying it.

"Except to death," he said deliberately, ignoring her ploy. "Everyone reacts the same way to death." He paused weightily. "And I'm talking in the purest sense. I mean physically."

The next day the twins waited with Greif in the lounge. Her nails were polished, her hair was washed and brushed; she looked normal and healthy and expectant. The blue robe was cinched tightly around her waist, and she sat on the edge of the chair, playing with the skirt of her robe, straightening its folds so that they draped smoothly.

"But do I look good?" she kept asking. "Am I beautiful today?"

Abby rushed to reassure her. She sat next to her, leaning forward and clasping her hand. "Oh you are beautiful. No matter what happens, you are."

Greif unhooked her hand from Abby and returned to smoothing her robe. "What does 'no matter what happens' mean?" She had a fixed smile on her face, and though she tried to keep her gaze on the twins, her eyes kept straying to the door of the lounge.

"Abby only meant that you can't control how other people will react." Meg sat on Greif's other side. She was not as concerned as Abby was about Greif's emotional state. Emotions, like pain, had an etiquette to them. There were words that applied to every occasion; the words were formulas and easy to learn. "Does it hurt very much?" was in Meg's personal guidebook, as was, "That must have been very upsetting." She was an efficient hostess for human ills, and her efficiencies rolled forth effortlessly. She liked to flip through her mental list regularly so she wouldn't forget the appropriate responses.

"It's always a question of decision," Greif answered, keeping her chin high and her smile fixed and her eyes roving to the door. "I knew I should kill my mother, I knew it for a long time. It was being unable to decide to do it that was the hard part, every day wondering, 'Will it be today? Do I have the nerve?' She watched me all the time, she knew very well what was going on. Each day there would be the faintest sneer, just the slightest look of contempt along her mouth. You know, there's a certain kind of insight in madness, you see people's thoughts more clearly. Or their intentions. Sometimes I get confused between thoughts and intents, it's always been a problem for me. But deciding to do a thing—anything, it doesn't matter what— always gets rid of confusion, doesn't it? Take this. I believe it's been worrying me for some time now. I know I've been feeling low. But as soon as I figured it out, I felt uplifted, endlessly uplifted." Her smile stretched outward.

"Have you spoken to anyone here about it?" Abby asked. Meg could see her unease.

"I've spoken to them so much I don't have to tell them anything ever again. I know all their answers, I know all my answers too. Shouldn't they let you go the minute you get bored? Aren't all the truly sane people bored to tears and isn't that the only real test?"

Meg laughed. "Or is it *being* boring that shows it?"

Greif took the question seriously; she stopped the incessant smoothing of her robe. "No, that can't be it. Most people are boring, even the crazy ones. But when you're mad, you're always somehow . . . interested." Her eyes stopped wandering for a moment. "Nothing is ever quite that intense again." For an instant she looked unhappy; it was just at that moment a man's voice said, "Greif?" and three pairs of female eyes turned to the doorway.

"Dr. Smallwood," she said, standing up with her hand still clutching her gown. With a start, Meg realized it was the same doctor Greif had smacked her lips over years before. It was disturbing to see him still here—as if he, too, had failed to qualify for the outside world.

"Oh, you have visitors," he said with a smile and a nod. "I'll see you another time."

"Wait!" She raised her right hand out towards him. "There's something I have to say—to tell you. The time we've spent together has been very important to me. It has given me life again." She stopped then and smiled radiantly.

"Well, thank you, Greif. That's always nice to hear, but we can just discuss it at another time. I'll stop by later." He nodded again and waved his hand.

"No—wait!" she cried. "That isn't what I meant to say. I love you. I love you deeply, passionately." With this, she slipped out of the robe completely, standing before him naked.

His mouth dropped open and, almost reluctantly, his eyes swept over her, up and down. He reached a hand out behind him and drew the door shut.

"I love you," she said again. "I had to speak for both of us."

"You've made a mistake," he said in a muffled voice. "I'm terribly sorry."

Without a word Meg and Abby got up from their seats and stood in front of Greif to cover her. Her eyes looked out at him from just over their shoulders. Abby could feel Greif's breath when she spoke.

"Oh god," Greif breathed, "I'm desperate for loving you. Don't worry about anything. I'll switch doctors, I'll stop being your patient, we can be together."

"Greif—Miss Dundee—" He took a deep breath. "It's called transference. Patients fall in love with their doctors. All my patients do. It doesn't mean anything, anything personal that is."

"Greif, put your robe on," Meg said fiercely. "Don't you see? He's not the one you thought he was."

"Oh no, you're wrong. He's always been so kind, so understanding."

"That's just what he's paid to do. Isn't that right?"

He sighed. His face had turned pink. "Yes, of course I'm paid. I'm trained to help people. That doesn't make my concerns cheap. This is normal, Greif, and nothing to be ashamed about. We've talked about impulses before. You have to learn to evaluate them better. You feel healthy and you *are* healthy, but not all your feelings are appropriate in all circumstances."

"He's calling your behavior inappropriate," Meg pointed out.

He was annoyed. "If you really want what's good for her, you'll stop presenting everything in the worst light."

"Just tell her if you love her," Abby said. "Just tell her and leave." Meg looked at her sister with approval.

"Okay," the doctor agreed quickly. "I don't love you in a romantic way, Greif. And I don't believe you really love me either. You're testing me; or yourself."

"Now leave."

He nodded at Abby who, like Meg, had remained standing in

front of Greif.

"I'll talk to you later, then," he agreed, and left.

"Nicely done, Abby," Meg said.

"Are you okay, Greif? What are you thinking?"

Greif picked up her robe and put it on. The glitter had gone out of her eyes, but she seemed sober and resigned. "Well, he wasn't very impressive, was he? I must have been wrong about loving him because I don't mind all that much." She tightened the belt ruthlessly. "Transference, huh? I went through transference two years ago—obviously I can recognize it better than he can. No, it must be the hormones in my subconscious acting up again."

"Again?"

"Oh, it's happened before—once with an orderly and once with someone else's brother. It's amazing how quickly love can strike." She was calm again. "And how quickly it goes."

"Was it love each time?" Abby asked, soured by the sudden anticlimax.

"It was love each time."

"So fast? So easy?"

At that Greif laughed. "Love is sometimes fast and sometimes easy. That's the kind I like. If you have to put a lot into it, then it isn't pure love, is it? It's need and greed and acquisitiveness. You don't possess love, do you? You visit it." She looked into Abby's face, scanning it. "I recommend it. Try it."

"It wouldn't work for me. I'm one of the greedy ones."

"And you?" Greif turned to Meg.

"Me, I just deal in needs. That's even easier, but not always faster. There's just one thing, though: why do you think it's love?"

"If it were anything else," Greif said seriously, "it would be cheap."

"See, that's funny. I think love is the cheap thing. Everyone thinks they have it, had it, and know what it means. It's all the other stuff they deny: jealousy, expectations, disappointments, possessiveness. What if that's what love really is?"

"It sounds like you're agreeing with me," Greif said, frowning.

"Only if you stop saying it's love."

"Fine. It was lust. And it was lovely."

"Good."

"And is it lovely for you too?"

Abby watched Meg as she answered, "I think people make up a lot of stories about love. You all believe it's unique and special when it happens to you, but it's common and foolish when it happens to someone else. I don't see anything special about it, when it's so universal, so you might just as well take it for what it is—a physical response. You're all so proud of what you feel. Love and pain, love and pain. It's always the same story."

This speech delighted Greif. "You still talk like an outsider. Still watching instead of doing?" She turned to Abby. "Does she still ask what pain feels like? She was always asking me."

"I don't know. I suppose so. I guess there's no reason for that to change."

"No. No reason at all," Meg said smoothly.

"And tell me—from all the questions you've asked, and all the answers you've gotten—do you know what pain feels like yet?"

"No," Meg said with satisfaction. "Pain is someone else's problem, every single time."

"And yet they keep *me* here," Greif sighed. "When I understand it all."

Chapter 18

The packages from John Martin usually contained four vials and a plasticene envelope with almond-colored powder (powder the color of ground bones). Each vial was numbered and described in instructions that carefully suggested dosages and conditions. John Martin liked to start with a small dosage over three days, doubled on the fourth day, skipped on the fifth, doubled again on the sixth and then doubled again—the final dose—on the seventh.

He always requested blood and urine samples drawn each day and shipped to him immediately, along with her answers to a detailed questionnaire about her physical reactions. She pictured him with glasses and a clipboard that had a pen tied to it with string.

Occasionally she felt tired; occasionally dizzy. Usually there was no reaction at all. She would first pinch her thigh, then jab a needle into her hip; she slammed her fist against a wall, careful not to break anything. She stuck her hand over a flame, then into the ice in her freezer.

Nothing. She dutifully identified every sensation—she experienced *variety*—but no pain. She followed John Martin's instructions faithfully, like an exercise routine. Raymond—who had disapproved of the regimen because he felt that tests on Meg were *his* province— tried to adopt an impartial attitude. He read John Martin's letters; he would sometimes send an article about new research to Meg; he often asked to read her questionnaire before she sent it off. Occasionally, he helped her with the tests, sticking in the needle, pinching her unexpectedly, hitting her with a belt. This last had disturbed her—

and she had thought she could never actually be disturbed by any physical action; she had thought she was above it.

But Raymond looked at her avidly when she turned to him after being hit. It was his motion, seen out of the corner of her eye, that had caused her to turn. The belt caught her across the cheek; she could tell instinctively that it would leave a mark. She raised her hand to feel it, her eyes on Raymond. For the briefest moment, she had sensed danger.

"You felt that," he said. His breath came out in short puffs.

"I feel things," she answered slowly. "But no, it didn't hurt." She got a cold washcloth and held it to her face. "You wanted it to hurt."

"Well, of course. It's what you want. And I have a clinical interest. Naturally."

She tried to direct all her attention to the questionnaire, determined to cover the fact that her hand was shaking. *This is fear,* she thought automatically. *Fear of harm.* Because, if John Martin's little experiment had worked, she would have felt pain, and not just pain in the interests of science, but something more personal. No one had ever been capable of doing that before.

"Tell me again why you want me to feel pain?" she asked Raymond after completing the questionnaire. She kept her voice level.

"Because you want it. I believe in fulfillment."

"Most people, from what I understand, would want to make sure that loved ones didn't feel pain."

"We never mentioned love before, as far as I can remember."

She smiled dutifully. "Most people would want the people they like to be free of pain."

"Of course I want that. But being free of pain implies the possibility of pain. You are always free of pain, and it's dangerous. It's clinically morbid. You are capable of ignoring a life-threatening situation because of your immunity to pain. I want you alive; therefore I want you to feel pain. It's a complex desire, but my happiness would be more complete concerning you if you could be hurt."

She considered this. She considered how difficult it was to decipher the self-serving from the unselfish lie. She thought, too, that she couldn't untangle Raymond's impulses.

Finally, she said, "Have you gotten anywhere with your death?" She no longer said "death project"; the shortened form was acceptable to them both.

He laughed. "I'm having a slight engineering problem. Animals—even rats—are aware of death. I have to perfect a way that would present the same conditions to all the animals, but they wouldn't all die. It's not an easy task. I have to be sure they don't die of shock. I *want* it to be a fair test." He ran his hand over his face.

"I'm the only creature you know who wouldn't be afraid of death coming." That had always been true; she had always believed in her own recklessness. She decided to ignore the thin prick of—what was it, really?—surely not fear?

"Yes." He ran his hand over her cheek.

"It's to your advantage if all John Martin's tests fail."

He stared for a moment beyond her. "Well, yes, of course, you would be the ideal chemical choice if you could be tested when you died."

"And yet you want John Martin to succeed."

He sighed. "That's the problem with science. You want everything to be proved, out of greediness."

"I suppose. But don't you ever find yourself rooting for an opponent's view, just out of the desire to be surprised?"

"I have no opponents."

"Competitors."

"The surprise is always in the original thought, never in its proof. Proof is pride. And money, power, prestige. Externals."

"The externals must matter. After all, you spend years working towards them. It only takes you a moment to have the inspiration."

"I won't pretend money and power don't matter, but they're just means to an end. I'm a scientist, and a scientist pursues the truth, even things that are true for the wrong reason. I don't care what the outcome is, so long as I am satisfied. I'm sorry about using the belt, I see it's left a mark. I had it in my hand and the thought came to mind. As I said, it is always the thought that holds the most interest."

She was already searching through her makeup kit for the things she would need. She had always viewed her observable injuries as proof of her immunity: people would murmur and cluck and she would dismiss it indifferently. This time, however, she felt embarrassed.

Once she had a severe reaction to John Martin's vials. It was the double dosage on the fourth day that did her in.

She always took her dosages in the morning, orally or intravenously.

In less than an hour she was sweating and her heart was beating. She noted it calmly on the questionnaire. Then she began to vomit and the contractions spread from her stomach to her legs until she lay on the floor, twisted and convulsing. She was alert enough to grab towels from the rack and tie them around her head and spill them on the tiled floor in case of convulsions.

She was sweating even though her arms were covered in gooseflesh. She felt no pain; she merely acknowledged that she was at the mercy of a bodily event, like a hiccup. She hoped it would end soon. She considered the possibility of poison seriously. John Martin was conservative; he always advised her to have stimulants and various cures at hand. Most of his chemicals were in the family of spasmotics or agents which stimulated neurological activity of one sort or another. The medications were on the kitchen counter; her attack had come on too quickly for her to consider antidotes; she continued to writhe.

After an hour it had decreased enough so that she could reach the kitchen and take an antispasmodic.

She sat, trembling, in the living room with the clipboard in hand. She stuck a needle into her arm. She had hit her head on the floor during the attack, and had felt nothing new. She made her way back to the kitchen, holding her hand over a flame and then holding it to the side of the freezer.

She made a note to John Martin of all of her symptoms, crawled into bed, unhooked the phone, and slept for fourteen hours. She had never felt this weak before. Perhaps John Martin was on to something.

Chapter 19

"Did you ever get around to forgiving me, Abby?" Meg smiled across the table in the diner; she looked, Abby thought, like she sometimes had when they were children, determined to please, eager to admit her misbehavior. Meg's misdeeds didn't stick to her, they rolled off her as if from a sheet of glass, leaving only the minutest trail to melt off in the sun.

"Forgive you," Abby repeated reluctantly. "Oh. You mean for sleeping with Bobby."

Meg frowned. "Of course. What else could I mean?"

"There are so many things."

Meg's mouth tightened, but she forced it to relax. "Let's start with Bobby then. Do you forgive me? After all this time?"

Abby stirred her coffee indifferently. "I wondered, at one point, why you did it. You must have done it to hurt me."

Meg snapped to attention. "Of course not. How could I want to hurt you? I never expected to be found out, you know; I always felt so invulnerable, as if I were magical. But you hurt *me* when you slept with him. It meant you'd found someone more interesting. If you went your own way, experiencing things I was kept apart from— well, it didn't seem like we would be twins anymore. He could only hurt me if he was a secret you kept from me. That's how I thought of him, as your secret. I thought if I slept with him I would be part of your secret." She paused. "I never thought you would come in."

Abby shook her head. "I think you *had* to make sure I found out."

Meg was eagerness itself. "Yes, yes, I see that now. In a way, it was a kind of innocence, it was just a ploy to get your attention."

Abby frowned. "I don't see it as innocent. You wanted to control me."

"I did something wrong—very wrong, I see that now. But I did it because you were more important to me than I was to you. If you hadn't made me feel so left out, so discarded, I might not have done it."

"Oh, don't try to make this my fault, I won't buy it."

"Not even a little?" Meg wheedled. Her eyes crinkled winningly around her smile. "But you knew what I was like, you can't deny that, and if you excluded me you probably expected me to do something, didn't you? I almost always did something."

Abby sighed. "You can't make me responsible. I settled this in my own mind years ago. I don't blame you, I don't blame me. You behaved in exactly the way you always had, it was a shock but not a surprise. And you're right, of course: something in me may have orchestrated the whole thing so I could find a way to be rid of you."

Meg worked hard to keep her face under control. Anger wouldn't help. "For starters," she said, "you didn't have to parade your lovers in front of me."

A faint pink spread over Abby's face and a small smirk tricked at her lips. "Oh, don't you remember what it's like when you first get hooked on sex? I couldn't stop myself, nowhere was sacred. It seemed to fall out of the sky like rain—the possibility, the unexpectedness of it. It rushed at me everywhere." She gave a quick laugh. "Oh, it was lovely, wasn't it?"

Meg's smile didn't change. "Of course we had different experiences. Sex is not quite that wonderful for me; or maybe it's the men who aren't quite that wonderful. I get hungry and I eat; that's how I think of it. Is it still so wonderful? You have a husband now."

"Sex with my husband is great," Abby said firmly. She resisted

Meg's attempt to draw her in, to talk intimately, as if no time had passed at all. "You can't pass for me any longer," she said finally. "My husband would know."

Meg shrugged. "If it didn't work then, it wouldn't work now. It wasn't who you were sleeping with I was after, anyway. I just didn't want us to be separate. But that was inevitable; I learned that the hard way. I don't own you because we're twins. We were once as close as lovers. We no longer are."

She's trying to trick me into something, Abby thought. *How strange to think I still matter so much to her.* Her eyes wandered off to take an inventory of the other customers. Most of them were probably visiting patients at the Institute; they sipped coffee with blank determination, reaching the bottom of their cups with a helpless distraction. Some of them, she thought, will not even remember eating. She swung her eyes back to Meg.

"I'm glad you see it that way."

"Yes. It's so pleasant being rational."

"Well, that's just it," Abby said. "You behave like an idiot sometimes, there's no excuse for it from someone like you."

"Because I can't feel pain you think I'm perfectly rational. But it's just because I can't feel pain that the rational doesn't interest me."

"Very clever." Abby looked at her watch and began to get her things together.

"Can you honestly tell me you didn't miss me?" Meg asked.

Abby sat back down quickly. "I missed you," she said. "I'm sorry if it seemed I didn't. But you have no honor, and I won't stand for that."

"Honor!" Meg was dumbfounded. "What in the world does honor have to do with it?"

"It's something that matters to me." Abby got up decisively. "You have no moral life. You don't even know what I'm talking about.

That's what I love about my husband. We are as close as you and I were and we look out for each other equally and I can bet you anything he'll never do anything cruel or corrupt or damaging. I love him for that." She looked at her sister with a glint of triumph in her eyes. "And I have to run now."

"I don't believe you," Meg said, remaining seated, not even turning her head as Abby walked away. "You've been waiting for me all along."

Like hell I have, Abby thought, fuming, on the bus to work. She wished Megan would stop trying to suck her in; she was willing to be friends—but that was impossible, it was not how Megan did things. Megan didn't want to be independent and separate; she wanted to be a young girl again, the center of Abby's world. It was not something Abby would ever willingly do. She was sure of that.

As Abby walked down the hallway in the shelter, a mother seated in the corridor opened her handbag, searching for a cigarette. Abby saw the hypodermic needles and glanced away. She had been carefully instructed to refer drugs and misbehavior to the shelter staff.

The woman caught Abby's glance and stared her down. Her eyes were sharp and certain.

Abby nodded with a friendly if frozen smile on her face and went into the rec room. Two volunteers had not shown up, and—just for the fun of it—more than twice the usual number of children had been signed in.

It all angered her. She had taken the job a year ago, and the orientation then had mentioned that everyone hit a wall, everyone felt exactly the way she felt now—frustrated, ineffective, elite. Halfway through the tutoring session, a young mother came in, grabbed her child without explanation or apology, and yanked her out the door. The child began to cry quietly, with a backward glance.

Abby spoke reassuringly to the other children. The remaining volunteer, Dorothy, whispered, "Should we report her?" and raised her eyebrows quizzically. They were supposed to report any suspicion of child abuse or neglect, and under no circumstances intervene.

"She has a right to take her child out if she wants," Abby said neutrally, trying to keep from forming a judgment. That particular child, Juleen, was Abby's favorite. The children were only around for a month at most—this was a temporary shelter—but even though their faces changed, the prettiest, smartest and friendliest children were always the favorites. The volunteers looked for the easy ones, hoping to be busy with them before the difficult children arrived. There were, of course, children no one wanted to deal with—dysfunctional children with uncontrollable behavior, ugly children who smelled, children with irritating voices who couldn't make themselves understood, even after repeating themselves four times. Abby knew that the unlovable children needed to be loved—needed desperately to be loved if they were not to be lost forever in the everspreading reaches of their unlovableness—she knew it, she chose them time after time, struggling with their uncontrollable activities, their incoherent and insistent voices, but always with the same heavy failure. She didn't love them, she couldn't love them, they were unlovable children because no one could. No matter what her intentions were, she would prefer children like Juleen around her, the unlovable children made her heart clamp shut. She had good intentions, but she failed relentlessly.

Her current charge, Jason, blinked his eyes at her, his hand still gripping the pencil that refused to get his additions right. That was how Abby believed Jason worked. He would whisper the numbers he was adding up, and his pencil would hover at the blank answer line, waiting. He must have learned that if he waited long enough someone would hiss the answer at him. He was a child who was stuffed full with waiting.

On Abby's other side was Ahmed, whose legs were kicking

against the table and whose pencil was drawing jagged comic-strip lines across his reading assignment. Ahmed was nice and his project was to draw connecting lines between words and the objects they represented, a chore usually given to 7-year-olds. Ahmed couldn't read, but he drew compulsively, and Abby would soon bring out the picture books and colored pencils. He was uncommunicative and spoke only in monosyllables. He had come to tutoring twice and was bound to be moved on soon. She didn't know if she—or anyone else— could do anything for him in this setting. Maybe, she thought as her attention turned back to Jason with his poised pencil—maybe if Ahmed came again she would drop the pretense of studying and set him up with notebooks and inks (could she get inks? he liked sharp lines) and pictures of objects with edges.

She looked over at Dorothy, who had Babe on her lap. Babe was six and dressed in a starched and ironed red-and-white dress. Babe's hair was cornrowed with a ribbon at the end of each braid. The child was polite and bright and used to being petted. Her mother was just as neat and well-dressed (perhaps overdressed, given the circumstances); she spoke with a heavy island accent; it was the accent which made it hard to talk to her. Abby wondered how Babe and her mother had ended in the shelter. Abby would bet Mrs. Babe was a serious churchgoer, and church groups usually handled members-in-crisis with a sure and helpful hand. Perhaps Mrs. Babe, like a number of the shelter residents, had left a jobless home state to follow a relative who, without blame, found him- or herself out of a job and unable to cope. Abby had heard that story already, and what amazed her was how matter-of-factly the story was told. These families— some of them including fathers and boyfriends—lived on a fine line. Sometimes the line tipped up and they had enough; sometimes it tipped down. Given a chance, any chance, they would make it. But they were borderline; they had left school early, had children early; they fought against each other for the same low-paying jobs and poor housing; they knew they would lose.

The next day Abby brought rulers and some drawing pads and very sharp pencils for Ahmed. She had ripped out pages from magazines, collecting pictures that contained sharp lines, most of them advertisements. Many of them showed rooms that were almost empty, clean and white, but even in their emptiness (maybe especially in their emptiness) they seemed wealthy. In the sharp corner of one white room stood a single end table with a vase of pale long-stemmed tulips. A shadow from an unseen lamp cut through the corner at an angle. This was the picture that caught Ahmed's attention.

He held it in his hand after leafing through the other pictures, and looked at Abby expectantly.

"Do you want to try drawing that? You can draw it any way you like."

He nodded and chose a pencil, bent his head low, and concentrated.

The first drawing was squeezed into the lower right quadrant of his paper, as if he were worried about taking too much space. He finished, looked at his drawing for a moment, then looked up at Abby and smiled.

"It's very good," she said seriously. "It's so good I think you can do it again, only bigger." She took the used sheet away, placing it carefully next to her side of the table, and pointed to a new sheet.

"You can start in the middle if you want." He stuck his tongue out slightly and pulled his lip back in a tentative smile.

This time he used the ruler to draw a box in the middle of the page, and in the box he drew the picture again, only occasionally referring to the magazine ad. The first drawing had been compressed and timid. This one was formal; the uncertainty was replaced by a confident series of edges. The shadow cut through the table and the flowers with precision.

But in the lower right hand corner of the box he'd drawn he hesitated and drew in a squiggle. He put it in at the last minute, when Abby thought he was finished. She couldn't see that the squiggle suggested anything in particular, and she was uncertain whether she should try to guess what it was or just leave it unremarked.

Ahmed, for his part, looked up at her, ready and alert.

"It's a beautiful job. You have talent, Ahmed. I want you to do it again, just for practice, only this time make it as big as the whole page." She held his drawing in her hand. "You're an artist." She put the drawing down. "And you can add anything you want. Just start with the table and flowers like you did, and you can put in anything else you want to."

This time he drew a box just slightly smaller than the edges of the paper, as if his drawing needed to be locked into place, and the table and flowers and the bold stroke of the shadow leapt out larger than magazine size. But on the lower-right corner another figure began to appear, and she saw that it was part of Ahmed's face peering out over the edge of the paper.

She was surprised because Ahmed drew without a mirror, and drew with confidence, as if he'd practiced it often. She didn't expect it of him, this clear self-presentation. She had thought him capable only of small cramped boy-drawings akin to the rockets and machines he'd always doodled before.

She picked it up and Ahmed's image looked back at her from the corner of a luxurious room. His eyes, dark irises filled in with shading for pupils, smiled out at her. His head stopped at the nose, but it wasn't hard to picture the smirk below it, a small boy's joke.

"Do you want to keep this one, Ahmed? It's beautiful."

He shook his head. "It's for you." The words were breathy.

"The mothers are here," a volunteer turned to tell her. "It's time."

Ahmed's mother appeared. She was a small, uneasy woman who always seemed nervous or angry, a shifting alliance that could change abruptly from an ingratiating sentence to a hostile, abrupt snatch at her son.

"Look," Abby said. "Ahmed did this wonderful picture."

"How nice," the woman said. "He's always drawing."

"He's talented."

Ahmed hung his head.

"He can't read. Not much. He's bad at school, he don't do well."

"He does well at this."

"He can draw all the time. I thought you'd be reading with him. Or maths. His maths is bad."

"We do that, usually," Abby said, beginning to feel defensive. "But sometimes he draws, too. Can you get him some drawing lessons?"

The woman blinked and Abby flushed. "I mean, this is important too—maybe even more important, because he's so much better than children his age."

"He's got a dreamy head," his mother complained, laying her hand on Ahmed's arm and pulling him from his seat.

"We'll work on the reading. Maybe I can find a drawing book of some kind, too, it's important for him."

"He don't need it," his mother said, looking at Abby unhappily. "He needs his schoolwork, he flunks and then what?"

"I know," Abby said carefully. "I understand."

Ahmed's mother looked at her with contempt. "He spends all his time in the same grade," she said. "They don't care about his pictures."

Ahmed left his drawings behind, including the third one. Abby wanted to treat them with respect, even if Ahmed's mother found it a bad use of time. She took them home and hung them on the refrigerator. Charles raised his eyebrows at her. "We have a kid now?"

"I took your picture home and hung it up," Abby told Ahmed.

He grinned at her peacefully. He held a sheet of lined paper in his hand. "My mama said to show you this."

The teacher had marked a red F on the page, which contained four math problems, all of them circled.

"Well, let's see what we can do here," and she pushed aside the drawing pad she'd brought, spending the next hour laboring with him over subtractions. At first she thought he'd simply never been taught how to borrow from the next column, but even when he did that he failed to add it to the number he'd started with. He had no interest in learning and she had no interest in teaching him subtraction. What she wanted was to watch him draw, to see how he would interpret what he saw, to find out whether he would insert himself into another picture. She had ended up looking forward to it, even though she knew that schoolwork was important, and Ahmed's mother had a right to determine his studies. But from what she knew of the shelter children, Ahmed would continue to fail in school. He might find one or two people willing to concentrate on him for a while, but he and they were parts of different systems; he or they would move on and he would have little chance. He would move around too much, and too much of his time would be spent adjusting to different teachers and students. Because of this—because she saw this particular little boy being lost, either now or further along the way, in too much change and too much frustration—because of this she wanted to make sure that he would have at least one thing to be proud of, one talent that might rescue or console him. She thought of him and felt disconsolate, lonely beyond bearing.

But none of this was her call. For all she knew, Ahmed's mother might be able to find her way forward. She might.

Noting the time, she quickly gave Ahmed a set of problems to do. She made them easy enough for him, to get them right. Was that cheating? There were no clear guidelines, but surely a boy who saw a red F more often than not deserved an occasional A.

She debated the A. Ahmed's mother might not believe it. She turned it into a B.

Chapter 20

"The problem was a conceptual problem," Raymond said. "How do you control the cause of death so that it fits the criteria? It's so haphazard—poison, shock, disease. I realized of course the point was to expose all my animals to the same conditions *until half of them die*! That's the only way to test my theory—get it so that half make the decision to die and half to live. Thoughts are chemical—or at least thoughts tied to a physical impulse are. Maybe it's true for all thoughts, even the thought for a play, a poem, a painting, a song. All of it capable of being induced. I really think everything is, even scientific breakthroughs, energy solutions, cures for cancer. The idea is enormous!

"Would it surprise you if I said I believe I've found it?" Raymond laughed gleefully, nodding emphatically. "The mice were a disappointment; no matter how many died I couldn't find anything distinctive. But rabbits—ah, there it was a different story, just a question of getting enough of a unique substance in the brains of the ones that died to start trying to define it. Of course it takes hundreds just to get the merest trace. But it's the researcher's dilemma: I've found it with rabbits, but does it have any bearing on people? We all know that the species are too different to draw quick conclusions. No more rabbits. Up the ladder. Dogs? Cats? Primates? Oh, but we have to be careful here. Last year some fanatics burst into the head-crush labs and took pictures. Dogs unfortunately, an emotional issue. The pictures, of course, were taken out of context, that test may lead to something important." He ran his hand over his head. "But I don't want to take chances, I won't introduce an emotional issue. No dogs, no chimps. Do you remember Galen's comment on cutting animals open alive and without anesthetic? He didn't like the reproachful look in the ape's eyes when they cut it open. He preferred goats and oxen. Cows are too big, there's a space problem. But I think it must be a food animal. That makes the public less uneasy. They like these animals, you see, picturesque upon a hill or properly browned on their plates. What happens in between is nothing they want to hear about."

One afternoon Meg tracked Greif down in the lounge at the Institute. Abby was already there, sitting rigid with her face frozen and her hands in her lap. Opposite her sat Greif, and next to Greif sat a large pale woman who looked at Meg briefly and then resumed a far-off, patient stare.

"Meg, I was just telling Abby that I'm going home next week. I can't see any point in staying here much longer, can you? I mean, everything's been said on their side and mine, and all this talk can't undo the past. Let's face it," Greif smiled winningly, "I'm not a danger to society. We all do what we have to in order to survive. We're all agreed now. I killed my mother because she had an unhealthy hold over me. It was my mother who should have been here all these years, not me. In a strange way I was the victim. I was manipulated into my actions. I was not acting freely."

The look on Abby's face was resolving itself into a stricken discomfort, and because of the way Abby's eyes darted towards and around—but not on—the strange woman, it was easy for Meg to guess that it was this person's presence that disturbed her.

The pale woman looked resignedly at the floor.

"It's a terrible burden to carry, killing your own mother. Of course it's natural to do it symbolically, everyone does it symbolically in order to mature; otherwise we'd be children all our lives. You're always a child to your mother of course.

"She was sitting in the armchair in front of the TV. That's another way to remain a child, have all your attention taken up by something you can't participate in. I came into the room after washing the dishes and she was sitting there as usual—I always hated the way she sat there, filling it. I saw her and I realized she was filling my life, too. All my thoughts came from her. You must remember how I always talked about her? When I got up in the morning I had to see her, I had to tell her what I was doing. She always had to know, you see. If I told her what I did or thought, she always commented on it. No, she always *interpreted* it. And what bothered me is that she always found a significance to it that turned it into something I hadn't intended, but just the suggestion changed it into what she said. It wasn't really mine anymore.

"My mother loved scarves, she always wore long ones around her neck. And this night the ends were draped over the back of her chair like long hair. She often fell asleep with her eyes open in that chair—and that's a sure sign of an evil mind, a mind that likes to influence things, because she could never allow herself to shut me out entirely, she was always watching. You'd think she'd know better because she told me about Isadora Duncan and she read murder mysteries—of course I read them too, she left them just laying all over the place, like her books on mental disease."

"Greif—" Abby said in a stricken voice. "Greif, that woman next to you—"

The pale woman looked curiously at Abby and then at Megan, and then dropped her eyes again.

"It's all right," Greif said reassuringly, "I've told it so often that it doesn't bother me anymore. I said 'Mother?' and she didn't answer and it occurred to me that I wanted her dead because she was controlling me. And she wanted to be dead, too, because she didn't even like her own thoughts. When she didn't answer I crept behind her and I grabbed the ends of her scarf and pulled as tight as I could.

Her hands came up to her throat but she didn't make a sound and she didn't try another move. She could have knocked herself off the chair, she could have tried to do something, but she didn't. It wasn't only my choice, it was hers. So she shares in the responsibility, I think that's obvious enough. I'm very happy now, and it's ridiculous to keep me here. There was no trial, you know. Everyone understood the facts, and I admitted it all from the start. I saw her dead in that chair and I went to a neighbor and told them what had happened. Of course they called the police, and the police brought me here." She looked happily from Meg to Abby and said unexpectedly, "It's a wonderful story, isn't it?"

There was a small moment of silence. Greif leaned back against the green leatherette sofa. Her movement caused the woman next to her to move slightly too, but Greif took no notice.

"And what will you do when you leave?" Meg asked.

"I'm going back to my own house. It will be peaceful and quiet there. My mother left me some money, so I won't have to worry about money. But I would like to do something helpful, you know. I think I could help people like me to readjust. I think I have something to offer. Of course they wouldn't let me be a therapist, even though I always know exactly what the right response is to anything I might say. I mean I know the routine. But they've classified me as insane, and of course they won't let anyone like that treat other people. Just to make sure I don't, they're keeping that diagnosis on my record." She shrugged. "I'm determined to work within the system, whatever system it is."

"Medication?"

"Of course medication. And out-patient visits. I recognize I have a debt to society."

She seemed to be finished with her speech. Meg and Abby waited, but there was nothing else. Abby looked finally at her watch and got up, saying, "I have to go to work." She hesitated in front of the two women on the sofa. "I guess I'll see you at home next time, Greif?" Greif nodded.

Meg followed Abby out into the corridor and watched as her sister exhaled her breath rapidly and said in a low voice, "Who was she? She looks like a relative, doesn't she? But Greif ignored her completely."

"That was her mother, I think," Meg said. Her tone was cautious.

Abby's cheeks flushed red. "Her mother? You mean her mother is alive and you never told me?"

"I'm sorry. I honestly am. I didn't see you for a while after I found out, and then I forgot. I was used to our knowing things together. I felt you knew. I wasn't thinking."

"It amused you."

Meg's voice snapped back at her. "I didn't *intend* to do it. The only time I see you is here, and you decided that. We've managed to talk twice away from Greif. And I know you don't want me to call you."

"I never said that."

"Your number is unlisted."

Abby's hand waved in the air, as if she wanted to brush that objection away, and then she relented. She raised her chin slightly, hitched her bag over her shoulder and said, "Are you sure it wasn't deliberate?"

"The last thing I want to do is antagonize you. But it's so hard to avoid. I want to be your friend again, I want us to be sisters again. This obviously wouldn't be the way to do it." Her hand, too, rose briefly in the air as if it to wipe an objection away, and then dropped down to her side.

Abby regarded her closely for a moment and Meg was sure she was about to relent, but at that moment the woman they had just met came down the corridor towards them.

"You girls," she said quietly. "Please wait." She drew up to them, a woman who now seemed to bear a strong resemblance to Greif, whose haircut even reminded them of Greif's. Her face, however, in contrast to her daughter's expressiveness, seemed unused, as if she had forced herself long ago to betray nothing.

"You'll come to see her when she's home?" Mrs. Dundee asked. "Do you know where we live?" She handed a slip of paper with the address to them. There was only one piece of paper, and after a moment Abby took it. Then it seemed as if no one could even think of the next thing to say, until Meg finally murmured, "We were out of touch for five years. This has all come as a surprise."

"She said she had murdered her mother, and she seemed to be here permanently," Abby said, in a firm tone to cover her embarrassment. *I don't want to pretend things with her*, she thought.

"She has a delusion," Mrs. Dundee said calmly. "She has always had a delusion. It comes from her father's side of the family."

"She always said her mother was insane." Meg was beginning to enjoy the oddness of the conversation. Mrs. Dundee's seeming imperviousness intrigued her.

"That was her father. He was committed when Greif was five. I don't know what he told her before he left, but she has had a delusion ever since." Her description had no emotion in it, as if it were a piece of information only.

"More than one, I think," Abby said, slightly shocked. "She said she'd killed you."

Mrs. Dundee shrugged. "She adjusts the story a little bit every time. But I'm proud to say that all of the deaths she gave me have been easy ones." She paused to breathe in heavily. "Her sickness is that she thinks she's insane. It's organic, the doctors say. There's a part of her brain that makes her think this way."

Abby found this hard to follow, and Meg began to wish she'd read Greif's report more thoroughly. She had had to grab one chart hastily, merely skimming some of the notes. Either Mrs. Dundee understood very little of Greif's condition, or she was herself unbalanced. But if that were true, would they be releasing Greif to her? *Oh yes*, Meg thought. *Oh yes.*

"But what will happen to her?" Abby protested.

"She has her medication. It's all talk anyway, isn't it? That's all it is. No point in locking someone up for the way she talks. A story doesn't hurt anyone." She had a flat black pocketbook that she held at the top and pressed against her stomach, as if she were leaning against a fence.

"Well, as long as she isn't really dangerous in any way," Abby said uncertainly.

"Oh no, sweet as a lamb. Everyone has some quirk. It's all that's really wrong with my daughter. She can have a normal life. She's a pretty girl, isn't she? Someday she'll meet a boy I'm sure and she'll be happy."

"Yes, I'm sure," Abby murmured, grasping at this statement as a way of concluding the conversation.

"There was a doctor I was sure had his eye on her. Of course a doctor would be good."

"Excellent."

"She looks like me at her age."

"Oh?"

"I don't look like much now," Mrs. Dundee said and paused. Megan expected her to brush her hair back or smile apologetically but she did neither, and Abby wondered if the pause was offered as a chance for them to compliment her.

"You should have seen me when I was beautiful," Mrs. Dundee said in that same flat voice, her eyes wandering quietly from Abby to Megan.

Chapter 21

Abby gave Ahmed pads and pencil sharpeners and ads or pictures she thought he would like, but only at the end of the session, after they'd worked on math or reading. The two of them felt hopeless until the moment when she leaned over to her bag beside her on the floor and brought another gift out for him. His eyes watched her the whole time, waiting for her hand to move down to the floor and bring something back up again.

There had been a slowdown in the relocation process somewhere. Ahmed had been in the shelter for three months when the usual stay was four weeks. Of course she knew it was bound to end, there was no question about that.

Ahmed's eyes brightened when he saw her, his face bloomed. He was still quiet, or nonverbal, but occasionally he would whisper a whole sentence, sometimes two, to her. She found a sudden well of patience inside her; she was able to wait for him to pick his words carefully, separated by ticking seconds, without urging him to push them closer together. She looked forward to seeing him; sometimes, when there were many more children than volunteers, she had to divide her time between Ahmed and one or two other children, but he seemed to understand.

She wasn't supposed to give gifts, of course. Sometimes, when she felt guilty, she would bring in a round dozen of whatever she had chosen for Ahmed, and she would distribute them to all the children, feeling fair-minded. If she brought in pictures, however, there was

always a favorite one held back from the others that would go to
Ahmed. She might bring cookies for the others and give Ahmed a
stick of charcoal.

She refused to think about it directly—how she considered
Ahmed's mother an adversary, how she was buying Ahmed's affec-
tions away from this woman, how it was inevitably going to end
badly. Of course she'd had favorite children before, but this was the
first time a child had seemed both permanent and personal. She knew
that Ahmed would be moved on, but she didn't want to believe it
emotionally. Ahmed was growing into a piece of her, as if in some
reverse process he was the rib being placed back next to her heart.

She trusted that Ahmed was going to be an artist, that this would
save his life, and that it would be because of her. "Most women have
rescue fantasies," Charles said shrewdly one night as she talked about
Ahmed. "But they dream about being the damsel in distress, not the
Calvary."

She stared at him. Had she heard right? "Calvary?"

"Oops. Sorry. Wrong metaphor. Cavalry, of course." He nodded
at her, grinning smugly.

Abby frowned. She didn't have a Christ-complex and she thought
she was tired of rescues. Maybe she took risks; maybe she did. But
Ahmed was worth it.

Then the day came when Ahmed didn't appear. She had a book
for him, a child's guide to Cubists or something equally suspect, and
it sat nervously in her handbag, she had to keep checking on it.

She collected a small child while she waited for Ahmed. The
little girl was a talker, and she chattered happily while Abby kept her
eye on the doorway. She put a pile of connect-the-alphabet dots in
front of her, and pictures that could be matched with words, and as
the minutes passed she grew miserable. Her face felt rigid, she knew
she stared at the children around her, she stared absurdly at the little
chattering girl beside her—who had probably learned to talk her way

through terror, just as Ahmed had learned to remain still.

If her lips stretched any tighter across her teeth they'd snap like rubber bands.

The volunteers didn't seem to notice, the children didn't seem to notice, and Abby helped clear things up with a wounded, almost offended air. She tried to pretend that Ahmed had been sick, or his mother had needed him, or that it was no big deal, he was just doing something else for one day.

The afternoon whizzed by without her notice; she cleaned up the chairs, stowed away the books and playthings, and then it was time to go.

She stood uncertainly by the sign-out desk, holding the pen in her hand.

Ken nodded at her and then, as she continued to stand lost in thought, he said, "Place's a lot quieter tonight. Got to be. Shipped out a lot of families today."

Abby heard this slowly; she looked at him as the words sank in. "Oh? They found housing, did they?"

"Yes, that's right. I hear the suburbs, maybe even another state. Maybe that's where your little friend went."

Abby's lips twitched into a polite smile. "Do you mean Ahmed? Do you mean Ahmed has left too?"

"That's right, in the first group." Ken looked at the sign-out book, at the edge of his desk, at the clock on the wall. "We're all happy for him. I bet it's a good house, a nice house they got."

"Oh very nice," Abby agreed. Her mind had gone completely blank; she couldn't think of what to do next.

Ken continued. "Of course he was here a long time, hard to see them go like that." He rubbed his hand along his chin and looked at Abby through the lids of his eyes, shyly. "Your special friend."

"A child like that should have a home."

"Yes, yes, a child should have a home."

"A good home."

"With good folks."

"A back yard."

"No broken glass."

"A child like that." Abby's voice shut down suddenly, her head turned to look out the door to the street. Another minute or two fell by, and Ken said, "You're gonna miss your bus now," and Abby nodded as if she'd been waiting for this cue, and she walked out the door, down the street, and onto the bus, sitting down as her eyes darted back and forth from one face to the other in the seats opposite hers, imagining what Ahmed would have done had he been with her, drawing them.

Charles' sympathy was more than she could stand. His tone of voice was tender; he tried to do things to soothe her. He really thought she could be soothed. She wasn't sure if he was capable of taking it all seriously enough. She wondered if someday she would cease to love him; when she considered how impossible it was for her to do anything, anything at all, freely and unreservedly, his abilities unnerved her. She watched him leaning over his chili, one of his favorite dishes. He was a tolerant man—more, he was genuinely kind and trustworthy. He worked with computers, making the whiz boys' programs user-friendly. He liked programs, he liked finding the link between a utility and its useableness. It all appealed to his sense of fun. Either he was one of the lucky few who had managed to find the job that suited them, or he was the kind of man who made every job suitable. She thought it was the latter. He was an easy man. He pointed out, by contrast, how she wasn't an easy woman. "Of course," she thought, "I'm fairly casual if you contrast me with Megan. But he can't, he's never met her." Would Megan like him? Megan liked edges in people; he didn't have that. But he could be enthusiastic; he was good at enjoying himself and never lazy. Like the dogs, he looked up alertly and willingly at every opportunity and shared her sorrows with an almost palpable sympathy.

Abby finally called Megan at work and, three days later, they met at the luncheonette. Megan chatted self-consciously about movies, about Greif (whom she suggested they visit soon) and then finally, abruptly asked, "I can't get over your calling me."

"I've decided," Abby answered carefully, "I've decided to sort of see what you're doing. Tentatively."

"Of course it would be tentatively," Megan said helpfully.

"I thought I might see where you work." She kept her voice neutral.

Meg was surprised. "It's really just a room with a counter, a sink, and a refrigerator. Like the room where we found the Dundee's brain? Maybe the same room for all I know. They remodeled slightly. I look at cultures and slides and take lots of notes. There's not much to show you."

"Still, I'd like to see it," Abby said firmly.

They walked back quickly to the research building, going through a side door with a guard who nodded briefly at the pass Megan flashed at him. They took a tired, lumbering, converted freight elevator down one flight. "I've always preferred back roads," Megan explained. "This keeps us away from all the traffic."

Downstairs they walked along one corridor after the other, always bearing left. Most of the rooms, from what Abby could see through their small windows, were record rooms or equipment rooms; she didn't encounter any hint of labs until they came to the last corridor, where she started to turn left. She heard sounds as a figure walked through a door. The door shut and the sounds were muffled.

"No," Megan said, "the last turn's a right." She took Abby by the arm and pulled her away.

"It's a confusing place."

"That's part of its charm. It's like a game a child would set up, isn't it? Here we are." She peeked in and motioned Abby forward. "I share this with Pandit—that's his desk, this is mine. More space for cultures and slides than for us, but that's the hierarchy here. I don't do any of the glamorous work—I never did get a degree, you know. Did you?"

"No."

"I bet we dropped out at exactly the same time. I had enough science credits, however, to get my foot in here. If I ever really want to do anything, I'll have to go back to school, of course. I'm qualified enough to be an endless assistant, nothing more."

"What *do* you want, then?"

"I don't know. I don't look too far ahead, it's never interested me. Long plans are idiotic. If you talk to people you'll find that nine out of ten end up doing something they never even considered."

"Like you, they probably didn't have a plan."

"Oh no. The odd thing is, they *did* have plans. But then something came up, something that seemed to make more sense at the time, promised them more money or a better opportunity, and their plans got tossed. And the ones that did follow their plans seem so smug, too, don't they, about their single-mindedness? So, no long-range plans for me, they don't seem to get you anywhere. This job can be very amusing, sometimes. Mostly for what it does to people. It puts them into relief, you know, sort of overblows everyone. Pandit, who works here, has become morbidly absorbed by his own quibbles over morality. It's so intense for him that he'll never leave, there just isn't the same kind of ambiguity anywhere else. Some people get a kind of blood-lust with the animals. I'm beginning to believe what they say, you know, that the way you treat animals is a version of the way you treat people who are weaker than you. Little boys who abuse animals grow up to abuse children. There's something very stylized about the people here."

"And you? Don't you think it must say something about you as well?"

"Oh well, that doesn't worry me. I'm already a sort of totem—painless in the pain labs, totally removed. I'm the only one with an excuse for this behavior."

Abby walked slowly to Megan's desk and sat down. "I'm sure you know what you're saying. If you don't care about the animals, then you don't care about the suffering of people, either. That was your own argument."

Meg walked over to her, pulling Pandit's chair to sit beside Abby. "Oh, but I never did care, did I? Only about you. Everyone else is so alien. Oh, I like Pandit, he has the same kind of sweetness you had as a child—always looking to see what I would say. And I miss that from you, the way we were so attuned to each other. I haven't found anyone to give me that, to make me my entire self again. I miss you. I'm not going to beg—I know I can live without you, I've proved it—but I don't like it. Tell me what you want me to do." She leaned forward, her elbows on the desk.

"Take it easy, Megan," Abby said. "You make it sound like you're in love with me."

"That's the only way I know how to describe my feelings. We're more than sisters, we're pretty damn close to being the same person. I want to make amends."

"If you would just learn to back off. You always want too much from me."

"Fine."

Abby frowned and sighed. She smiled as she sometimes had with Ahmed, when they struggled through schoolwork. "What do you do here?"

"Basically, I verify slides and other data. Mostly slides, though. They get identified for the experiments. I check them and send them on, just to make sure they match the reports."

"Slides of what?"

"Animal tissue, usually rats. Some brain slices but also fatty tissues—hearts and liver."

"Do they still have monkeys here?"

"Only two now. Do you want to see them?"

Abby nodded.

Megan led her to a room down the hall, which had a wall lined with rats in cages. She looked closely and saw blind pink naked bodies about half a finger in length. "Some of these are generational studies. That's one of the major advantages of using rats. You can trace a disease or condition down through a family line. We can also keep clear family histories: we know the genetic and medical background when we start a project. I think we keep some of the cleanest studies in our field."

"Clean studies?"

"Some labs are unaware of occasional contaminations, innocent or not. We're willing to take extra time in our studies. When we get something unexpected we circle it and prod it, we don't attack it."

Abby nodded. Megan led her down to the two last cages, each about three feet square. The monkeys stared back at her. They were smaller than she remembered, and they were curiously still. It was a minute before she realized that they couldn't move their legs.

The two cages were side by side, but there was an opaque plastic wall between them, so they couldn't touch.

"What's wrong with their legs?"

"A nerve-severing experiment. To see if the brain would try to compensate by regenerating brain tissue. These are the only two left. The others were destroyed, of course; they had to analyze the brain."

"Why weren't these destroyed?"

"It was a bad experiment; it had already been done. Some animal organization got hold of it, it hit the papers and went to court.

Once it goes to court you can't do anything."

She dug into her pocket and handed a piece of dried fruit through the bars. A tiny brown hand curled out and grabbed it. In the other cage another brown hand reached out and an angry chittering exploded. Meg pushed a piece through the other cage.

"Everyone comes to feed them," she said absently. "We're not supposed to take them out of the cages, but they've been here so long . . . as far as we're concerned the experiment's over. They cling so hard when you take them out it's hard to put them back. Watch their teeth."

Abby had stuck her fingers through the other cage. The monkey grasped her, hard. Meg watched.

"It's the hands that get you, isn't it? Just like ours."

"And the eyes. The eyes look like a child's."

"Oh well," Meg shrugged. "They have lots of visitors to keep them company." She turned to go, already ready to leave. "I don't know why, but I feel bad for those monkeys."

"They're not in pain, are they?"

"No. But you can see, can't you, that there are things besides pain that can hurt you."

Abby was impatient. "Of course. You don't have to tell me."

Meg smiled. "I wouldn't try to tell you. What do you want to do next?"

"Do you remember how we would sneak down here when we were kids?"

"Sure."

"Which way was it? Can we go back that way? Sometimes I dream about it, and in my dreams I can never find the way out."

"I can show you that."

At the end of the animal corridor was the heavy door they had hid behind as children, peeking out carefully for guards before creeping to see the monkey. Abby noticed a surveillance camera aimed at the door.

"We're on television," she said, pointing.

Meg turned and waved. "I don't even know if anyone watches those."

The stairs were faintly lit and still echoed metallically with each footstep. The stairwell stretched above and below them.

"How many floors are there here?"

"Five above, two below. The one below the lab is heating, air conditioning, emergency generators, plumbing, that sort of thing. The upstairs floors are administrative and teaching floors. Not general teaching, you know: teaching for the staff. Staff reviews, legal developments, financial regs. Grim stuff."

They tapped their way downstairs and then to the corridors that linked the buildings. The lighting was dim, with leftover signs for fallout shelters near the doors. It seemed as if there had been no intervening years, no separation, as if Greif was only just a step ahead of them, her upturned chin defying anyone to challenge her. A lot of people passed by them. "It seems like rush hour," Abby said.

"Shift change. A lot of the nurses use the research parking lot when the main one fills up. After that it's pretty dead down here. It's so creepy; I guess that's why we loved it so much."

"I didn't."

"Are you sure? I know Greif and I did. It was delicious, in a way. There were always things lurking. I miss that. I miss being a child."

"It wasn't so great. Remember, mother was dying most of the time."

They walked quickly down the long corridor. "It always struck me as odd," Meg said reflectively. "How she seemed to empty out at the same time that she loomed over everything. It was always so horrible to go into that house."

"She suffered."

"*We* suffered; she died."

Abby drew her breath in sharply, thought of saying something, then decided against it. Maybe Megan did have her own variety of suffering; maybe she did.

Chapter 22

Pandit came in from the corridor, looking sick. "I can tell you this, I am looking for work elsewhere. It is terrible what he is doing now, I must write a letter, I must expose this or I will lose my soul."

"And I thought you liked working with your interesting slides."

"Oh I know what you mean. One little letter will cure nothing but cost me my job. Who will read my letter? Who will say that maybe not everything is justified in the name of science? This man, I am afraid to say, is corrupted, his morality, his duty, his sense of compassion has collapsed. I expect to see blood dripping out from his doors. There are bags of dead animals from his experiments just sitting in the corridor. Some of the bags twitch. He does not even bother to make sure if they are dead now, he loses interest."

"I haven't spoken to him in over a week."

"He is obsessed, I tell you. I admit, I was interested in his idea at first. It is a way to explain things, is it not? Three people have a heart attack, and one dies. It is apparently the same condition in all, but for one, and one only, it is too much. A very interesting problem."

"Of course nothing is ever exactly the same for two different people."

"Ah no, of course, but that is what is so interesting. If you can keep the physical stimuli the same, on physically similar models, then you are encountering a contributing element we are not aware of. It was a beautiful hypothesis."

Megan, who liked to listen to Pandit, almost never looked directly at him. She listened with her head cocked, picking up pages of reports and organizing them. Her index finger brushed against a corner of a paper and began to leak blood. She stared at it, because there was an odd—and new—and unpleasant—sensation.

"He is cutting into their brains now without anesthesia," Pandit said, his voice lowered. "I heard it from a friend who is one of the lab assistants. He believes he has found his magic area—he calls it Bulicki's Point, just at the tip of the pituitary—and he keeps the brain out until all but ten percent of his animals have died, and then he takes the last ten percent of the brains, cuts them off and grinds them down. He compares them with the brains of those who died, which he also grinds down."

Megan had frozen, staring at her finger. The neat red slit of the paper cut burned in a sharp line. Her heart pounded and all her thoughts were concentrated on her finger. Was she really feeling this or was she imagining it? Did this indicate danger? Would it stop soon or continue indefinitely? She lifted her finger to Pandit. "Look at this," she said carefully.

"A paper cut, Megan. It is nothing to worry about. Wash it off and put a BandAid on it until it stops bleeding."

"Oh yes. I remember that," Megan said, slowly turning to go to the sink.

"Why does a paper cut bother you?" Pandit asked. He seemed annoyed that his complaints were interrupted by Megan. "You leave prints of your blood all over the reports, you never even bother about such things. I am speaking about the death tests." He nodded, suddenly enlightened. "Perhaps you defend his test? You never paid much importance to it before, but perhaps you are insulted for him?"

She came back to him, her hands wet and her finger wrapped in a paper towel. "No. I don't pretend that these projects are important. Maybe one or two are, either intentionally or accidentally, but the rest are simply business. Raymond is increasingly obsessed with death, but there is no law or moral regulation that keeps him from erratic behavior towards lab animals. They are commodities."

"Commodities," Pandit said morosely, and sighed. "It is hard for me to understand this, coming as I do from a culture that gives a great deal of thought to morality throughout one's life, that believes in . . ."

"Please don't say 'soul' this time. Only foreigners say 'soul' in conversation. It's embarrassing, it's so unsophisticated." She continued to look at her finger.

Pandit's face tightened and flushed. "I apologize for my primitive standards. My nephews, I am sure, will be properly American. They already, I believe, laugh at cripples and torture cats."

"Don't get so mad at me, Pandit. When you start throwing souls around the way you do there's no way to answer you. We don't really have spiritual arguments here, it all has to be logical or practical. Souls can only be mentioned in religious surroundings; we're very strict about keeping things separate. I didn't mean to be offensive, but you stop all conversation when you do that. Find another word."

"It is so strange that qualities are not considered in this country. It is not true, you know, that people can be satisfied with purely material goods. You Americans consider power and lust only; you never mention satisfaction, purpose, joy, good will."

"No," she agreed. "They're hard to pin down. You can't prove that good will exists all by itself, without a measure of self-gratification or something."

"And these animals that are in a bag down the hall—no one has to account for them?"

"There's no category for it. Everyone understands scientific research; it is something that will reduce suffering and put off their own deaths. Against that—what is an animal they don't hear or see?" She shrugged. "I myself find it easy not to think about it. For me the issue is not whether the animals suffer—everyone suffers, don't they?—but whether the whole procedure wastes time and resources.

The money comes because they use animals in familiar ways; it doesn't matter that it's all redundant. If you propose a different approach you won't get funded because you can't show good round numbers of autopsied animals. What bothers me is that it's so unintelligent. So many discoveries were accidents, and here they are deliberately getting rid of the possibility of accident."

Pandit suddenly smiled. "I have never been sure of your position. I am happy to hear you have one. And this one suits you. You do not consider morality—very American—but only the practical aspects. And how interesting it is that both morality and materialism end up in the same corner."

"Except, of course, that neither one of them has changed the way the research is done."

Pandit waved his hands in frustration. "That's the problem with a good conversation. Among one's friends it is possible to understand the world and correct it. But you leave these friends and the world doesn't move at all." He leaned over his microscope resignedly.

Megan leaned over her thumb. It had stopped bleeding, and the startling sharpness of sensation had receded. She frowned; sometimes her sensations were deceptive. Sometimes she dreamed she felt pain, and in the dreams it was suddenly foolish to think she *wouldn't* feel pain. And it was always possible that she had simply imagined the feelings she thought were pain, relying on Abby's descriptions over the years. Was this sensation "burning"; was this one "throbbing"? The worst of it had passed, now she had to concentrate to recall the degree of response. That satisfied her momentarily—if she had to concentrate in order to remember what her finger felt like, then she was dealing with the realm of imagination, she judged, not physical reality. She assumed the idea of pain was very specific.

A letter from John Martin waited in her mailbox at home. He was very interested in her reaction to the last set of chemicals he had sent. Had she tried it? He believed that he was getting very close now, he was sure he was on the road to isolating an excitability factor at work in his examinations; it was a chemical that started a sequence, much as a seed started to grow. It was an unlocking mechanism. He found it in brain tissue from autopsied infants and fetuses. He hoped she had no objection to that? She had none.

The letter from John Martin cheered her up. She was a partner in an experiment; she could stop, she could continue. She could taste how the other world lived and reject it. She could judge what it was like to be human; and be able in future to debate its merits judiciously. She could not be viewed as bizarre—and in some sense untested—if she could say truthfully, "I felt pain." She could please Abby; she believed that Abby had always resented her condition, had been somehow annoyed by it.

She kicked her toe against the wall tentatively. But even her weak kick shocked her with incredible sensations. She hobbled over to the sofa and clutched her foot, rocking back and forth. Tears leapt to her eyes. She was overwhelmed by what her body was feeling, she was sucked into it. There was that throbbing again, and a crushing sharpness. It expanded from her big toe into the joint and halfway to the ankle. She could think of nothing else; it astonished her; it went past her expectations; she had no idea when it would end, how it would end, if it would end—or if indeed it was one of those accidents she had been warned about which could have fatal consequences. It was out of all proportion to her movement, which had begun and ended in a fraction of a minute. She tried to gather her thoughts by analyzing what she felt. When she concentrated on the pain she could almost pinpoint the exact area; but then the area seemed to expand. She moaned, as much in frustration as in pain. After five minutes or so the pain seemed to relax, until she walked on her foot, when she cried out in surprise. She inched her way over to a pen and John Martin's questionnaire. She began to record her sensations for the earlier paper cut and her recent kick.

She hesitated at her words. Pain also involved the concepts of degree of pain. Her pain, however, was the first pain; she couldn't rate it against a lifetime of similar experiences. It hurt tremendously; it concerned her, it made her wonder if she'd damaged her foot permanently, broken something. She moved it tenderly, big toe between her thumb and forefinger. It hurt, that was all she knew. She couldn't find a break. If this pain did not even involve serious damage, it amazed her. Tentatively she checked off "Medium" on John Martin's list. She could only assume it was possible to be worse.

Clutching her questionnaire, she waited, almost without moving, for another hour. She was determined to follow John Martin's regimen. Her foot still hurt, but at a level she would describe as "Mild" as she went to the kitchen and turned on a burner. Tense, staring at the flames, she moved her finger towards it. She had done it dozens of times before for the test, and she knew exactly how long she would have to hold it to get a blister. Before, however, she had needed to concentrate; now she felt it immediately and her hand trembled as she forced it to the flames.

She whipped it out again and ran it under cold water, something she had seen her sister do and something she had never needed to do before. She understood the word "burning," the heat of it, a quality or condition she had noticed merely as warmth—the heat of it was immense, concentrated, as if it attacked individual elements in her skin, a forest fire in miniature, a continually changing and inventive bursting into sensation. She went back to the cold water tap, moving her finger in and out for minutes at a time, finally soaking a towel and taking it with her.

She considered, once again, John Martin's rating system. Her finger was red, but that could be due to the wet towel as much as to the burn. She had to leave her finger exposed to the air—gritting her teeth, counting the minutes—and the burn itself then looked like a minor burn that wouldn't even blister. She checked "Moderate" on the list, then erased it and circled 'Mild.' She was unsure; she was worried that she was exaggerating the pain, that she had not developed enough fortitude to accept even the most minor damages. Was she—despite a lifetime of arrogance—a weakling, a wimp, unable to compete even with the crybabies in the world?

She put her other hand into the freezer, leaning it against the icy metal sides until it stuck.

The nicest thing about that was that the pain did not last as long as a burn's pain did. It was sharp but clean, intense but under boundaries. She held her hand under cool water and gradually warmed it— she had been told how to do these things and had done them haphazardly before. Now she followed suggestions religiously, with great concern.

The cold pain she judged "Mild," with confidence in the evaluation. Her other hand still burned, and the paper cut faintly throbbed, and her toe occasionally sent out a hammer of pain and all in all, having filled out the questionnaire as best she could, it seemed a wise and even scientific decision to remain seated on the sofa, surrounded by wet towels and bandaids, listening acutely to the rhythm of her skin.

Abby woke up, night after night, imagining she heard whimpers and cries. She got up and searched the house, room after room, patting the heads of dogs, stroking the backs of cats.

She decided not to tell Charles; she didn't want his sympathy or his self-contained understanding. This business at night annoyed her, it left her irritable and resentful. She knew she missed Ahmed, but Ahmed wasn't at the heart of it; Ahmed was simply a symptom of it.

When she sat in the living room in the darkness, listening wide awake for the whimpers to define themselves, the cats came by, one by one, to rub against her. The dogs came, panting, snuffling, slowly wagging their tails and sitting down to stare at her.

"Do I have to save them all?" she wondered unhappily. She sat hunched forward, her arms crossed over her breast, animal eyes watching her and blinking peacefully, the joint humming of the cats replacing the click of the dogs' nails on the floor. The animals shifted in turn, settling down. "Do I have to save them all?" she asked herself again, without conviction, and her hand reached out and found a warm throat and began to stroke it.

Chapter 23

Megan's limp was getting worse. Her back ached, her leg ached. She held her shoulders hunched, her spine rigid.

"Do you know how you walk now?" Pandit asked in concern. "Do you know something is wrong?"

"Trust me," Meg said bitterly. "I know."

Pandit looked at her in confusion. "You are not yourself, Megan?"

"I am not." She laughed. "I've gotten mixed up with someone else."

Pandit continued his concern. "You should take some aspirin, you know. Something simple. And see a doctor."

"He'll only tell me I've been cured."

"That would be a cruel doctor. I can send you to an Indian doctor, a man who is gentle."

"Never mind. I just have to get used to a new viewpoint." She sighed, easing herself down next to her microscope. She was moving carefully. The day before, she had knocked her elbow in the shower, and that morning bent a fingernail back while closing a drawer. She was used to pushing doors open with arrogance; but now she twisted her wrist doing that and it hurt. There were few things, in fact, that did not hurt. She could only hope that the newness, the consciousness of pain, would recede into the background, that her newly awakened body would stop being alarmed at the overwhelming barrage of sensations. When she combed her hair, tears came to her eyes.

"Have you ever bitten your tongue?" she asked, focusing her

microscope.

"Ah yes," Pandit said. "Not only does it hurt, but you feel so stupid, too, don't you?"

"I don't know about that. But it hurt. How do you avoid it?"

"Focus. It is true for most accidents. Focus. Concentrate. If you think about what you are doing you can control it."

"It seems so limiting."

"After a while it becomes more natural, and you cease to notice."

"How long?"

Pandit shrugged. "We learn it as children."

"Childhood can last a very long time," she said sadly.

Pandit nodded in sympathy. He was interested in Megan's transformation, being one of the few who knew of her condition. They had worked together for two years and his was a patient, accommodating personality. He thought her very interesting indeed, and he went about his daily business with an ear cocked to Megan's mutters and exhalations, those grunts she was adopting as a response to the mutiny of her body. He noted how the sounds had become almost automatic now, a kind of running dialogue Megan carried on with herself.

"Is it getting better or worse?" he asked finally.

Her head turned woefully to him. "I have teeth that hurt, Pandit. They wake me at night."

His voice was kind. "We go to the dentist for that."

She shuddered. "The dentist strikes me with terror. I never liked that drill, but I never even felt it before. Tell me, is it as bad as I imagine?"

"They can give you a shot so you won't feel anything."

She shook her head in wonder. "If only I could have that shot— you know, permanently."

"Perhaps there is such a thing. Have you spoken to the man who gave you the medicine?"

"I left a message for him to call. Apparently he's not even full-time there. He doesn't have an office, I had to leave a message with an assistant of some kind."

Meg moved her alarm clock as far away as possible from her bed; the noise, even on its lowest setting, distressed her. She was passing through an acute phase, she hoped, where every sensation triggered too much of a response. She had finally reached John Martin—who, as it turned out, had fewer academic credentials than she did, but who was obsessed with his research—and he didn't know, he just didn't know, what would happen next. In fact, his unexpected success elated him, enthralled him, he did not seem able to comprehend that it was a *problem*, that her body's overreactions were making her life difficult.

"Write down everything," he said jubilantly. "Keep on rating it on an imaginary scale. Keep testing yourself."

"I don't need tests anymore. Everything hurts now. My clothes. My toothbrush. The food I chew."

"Oh excellent! Such sensitivity! It's very encouraging, I can't tell you how overjoyed I am."

"John!" she cried. "Listen! I have to know how to stop it! I can't live like this, I can't bear it! You've got to give me the antidote!"

John Martin sounded astonished. "But it's a simple protein of some kind, a peptide; it's a hormone-releasing factor, that's all. Your disease was just a stalled development, nothing else, the peptide that issues instructions for pain interpretation had never triggered. I'm sure of it; I just have to put it in more elegant language. I'll need a whole set of fluid samples from you. I have the thing in theory, but it's the chemistry I have to establish."

She took a breath. "Please listen to me. How do I stop it? I need to stop it."

His voice sounded slightly subdued. "It's a trigger, Megan. It set the pain system going. Like when a baby is born and starts breathing on its own."

"I want to be the way I was."

"I could be wrong—maybe I am. But I've been looking for the hormone that would do it—all the other things I sent were hormones of some kind or other—I'm not that good at breaking down structures, I'm more of the intuitive type—variations of the known protein chains. I can get rid of the known ones, you see, and I can separate the unknown ones out. I expected to find a releasing factor for the pain system, and I did. But I never thought you'd want to un-do it. You see, that's a different theory, and a different problem. The baby's been born, it can't go back in the womb."

His voice had gotten slightly apologetic, but it did nothing to help Megan. "I don't believe everyone lives like this," Megan said between clenched teeth. "My hair hurts, I can feel it growing."

"I've never heard of that as a complaint."

"It's impossible to chew, it sends pain through my jaws."

"Look, this is all new to you. Maybe it just takes time to adjust to the experience of pain. Maybe your brain hasn't learnt how to regulate the responses it's getting; this is a new routine for it, at a comparatively late stage."

"Each day the sensitivity increases. Light hurts my eyes, sounds hurt my ears, some smells are like a fist in my head."

"Ah," he said, "you could be allergic to something."

"What can I do about it?"

"It might go away," he said brightly. "I don't mind at all if it goes away. The theory won't be harmed. Maybe there's a life to the trigger action; maybe it will need renewed hormones at some point. We could try it with half the amount then. You know, maybe it's the amount; there's no way I could know in advance exactly what the dose should be. I bet that's what the problem is—you're just overloaded with the trigger mechanism, it's seeing every response as a trauma. You're out of balance hormonally. I'm sure your body will adjust soon, what you're going through right now is a hormonal flood, it's bound to settle down. I know it's hard for you, but it's a great help to me." His voice became pleading. "Send me blood, urine, as much as you've got. Can anyone there do a spinal tap? I know it's a lot to ask, but it can do as much good for you as for me, we need to know what's happening to your chemistry. Your blood should be loaded with activity and your spinal fluid . . . well, maybe that's too much to ask but it would be the most significant of all. My career will ride on this. If I do it right, I'll even get the credit for it, unless someone with a reputation steals it from me." His voice dropped low. "Did you give any samples of the extract to anyone?"

"No." She was exhausted by the conversation, and her voice registered hopelessness. "There's nothing you can do to help?"

"Time will help," he assured her. "Your brain will figure out how to deal with your body and you'll be back to normal."

"My normal or your normal?"

"Oh well, I'd just be guessing at this point. Let's give it a week and see where it goes."

She hung up the phone very carefully and laid herself back down on the bed. The various pains throbbed into the forefront and she began to cry, though she had to do it carefully, for the salt in her tears burned invisible channels on her skin.

Megan was absent from work almost constantly. She showed up for a day or two at a time, and then disappeared again. Pandit was more concerned than Raymond, who had a distracted air to him now, who shrugged when he came to the lab and found Meg gone, as if he had only come out of compulsion rather than choice.

"There is a problem with her health," Pandit ventured to Raymond after the third visit.

"Strong as a horse," Raymond said absently. His suit was impeccable; there was only the merest stray strand of hair to suggest he was distracted.

"She has been trying an experiment on her pain center." Pandit was determined to persevere. He felt it was important to get Megan's lover involved.

"Oh yes. Experiments."

"It seems to have worked."

Raymond's mouth moved as if he were chewing vigorously. "I wanted her opinion," he said finally.

"She's not well. She comes in when she can," Pandit said without much hope. Raymond—his eyes carried away to the wall and then back to his watch—said, "I think I have news for her." His complexion was even redder than usual, a color which caused Pandit uneasiness.

"You could call her," Pandit said, but Raymond was already on his way out, his hand rubbing his jaw thoughtfully, as if he had a toothache.

Pandit carefully straightened the desk where Raymond's careening fingers had moved Megan's papers. He was concerned about her and wondered if he should call her. He had never called her before, and a shyness that surprised him kept him from dialing. He had checked her number four times when the phone rang. Megan had mentioned a sister, and when he heard a voice that so clearly sounded like Megan's but wasn't, he drew his breath in and asked if it was Abby. "It is I, Pandit," he said apologetically. "I work with your sister, who has been out ill very often now."

"Sick? What did she do to herself?"

"There were some drugs," he said hesitantly.

"She takes drugs?" Abby was shocked.

"My mistake. I mean she has taken a drug that has cured her, and now she feels pain. Unfortunately, it is more than she can bear."

He fiddled nervously with the coil of the telephone.

"Do you have her address?"

"Of course." He gave it to her immediately, feeling relieved at first that someone was going to check Megan's condition. Then he thought how strange it was that the sister wouldn't know Meg's address. He frowned and shook his head in resigned wonder. And—surely he had gotten this idea from Megan herself—weren't they in fact twins?

Abby hung up the phone. It had been purely an impulse, trying to call Megan, but an impulse that was at the tail end of a series of increasing urges to get in touch with her. When they were children they had often felt it when something was wrong, no matter how far apart they were. They just *knew*; it was nothing to discuss or fight; it was merely another aspect of their life, and Abby should have recognized it and not fought it. Too much of her time was spent rationalizing her feelings.

Abby was let into her sister's apartment by Greif, which quite unnerved her. "Come on in," Greif said, "but don't talk too loud, it's like a hangover and then some." She wrinkled her nose and winked.

Meg's apartment was relatively empty—at least, it seemed the furniture in it was all token furniture—the table seemed to be on guard as a table, the chairs seemed lined up self-consciously as chairs. The walls had nothing on them, being reduced conspicuously to walls. Greif led her through the living room (a sofa, a coffee table, an empty magazine rack, a side table) to the bedroom where Megan, dressed in a slip, lay on the bed, curled on her side. There was a plain lamp on a bureau across from the bed. The shades were drawn down, and this lamp was turned on. It hugged its frail light to itself. On a chair next to the bureau (a chair that obviously belonged with the table in the next room), sat Mrs. Dundee. Her hands were laid out quietly in her lap and she nodded and smiled at Abby as if they were old friends who didn't need words.

"Quite a change," Megan whispered, lifting her hand to indicate everyone in the room.

"I don't understand how it happened. I called you at work and Pandit said you were sick."

Megan explained, as quickly as she could, about John Martin and the little vials.

Abby felt her resistance fall away as Megan talked. It was the sound of Megan's voice that had the most effect—a voice that had never been cautious before, but now it paused and listened internally, waiting for echoes and warnings. That kind of voice was a shock, coming from Megan. Abby sat and listened, clenching her jaw to keep it from dropping open. Megan lay on the bed, only occasionally shifting to relieve her back, which ached, Megan said, from everything she'd ever done to it in her life. "Remember that tree I fell from years ago? I've landed from it a hundred times today," she said, holding in a laugh. "They said I'd be a cripple if I ever felt it. I feel it."

She turned her new face to Abby, who asked, "Is it permanent?"

"Apparently. You're looking at a medical miracle."

Abby fought hard to keep her eyes on Megan; moving them away would have indicated pity. She hated it; what would Megan be without her arrogance? What would Megan be, just like everyone else, just like her?

"She doesn't have to ask us anymore," Greif said cheerfully. She leaned over Megan. "How does it feel, Megan? What is pain like?"

Megan smirked. "Like an invasion, Greif. An army sticking it to me."

"That's how it is being crazy, too."

Mrs. Dundee shifted in her chair.

"Do you still consider yourself mad, then?" Meg asked.

"It's like an Alcoholics Anonymous program; even if you're not currently mad, you have to accept your identity as mad."

"Do you ever want to be sane, Greif?" Abby asked suddenly. She felt ashamed even as she asked, but she was unnerved; everything in this room was out of kilter and suspect.

"She chooses how much she wants," Mrs. Dundee said, somewhat savagely.

Greif smiled at them winningly. "I choose how much I want," she said, as if she hadn't just heard the same words. "You have absolute freedom once they put a label on you. Because everyone is suspicious, you know; they think that insane people just don't compromise with what they see. Oracles. They keep waiting for us to be oracles."

Abby returned to her sister. "Do you have painkillers?"

Meg waved at some pill bottles on the dresser. "I'm a newcomer to aspirin, so it *does* work, but it screws up my stomach. It comes down to a tradeoff: If I take something strong—something that lets me be a little bit like I was—then I can hardly stay awake, or my head turns into cement. If I want to think I have to be in pain. There isn't any relationship there; I think it's just a chemical coincidence, but it's a choice."

"What will you do, Megan?"

There was genuine sorrow in Abby's voice: it provoked a smile on Megan's face. "Why, I'll try to be like you now," Megan said, with a coaxing edge to her voice. "I'll learn to live with it—why, everyone does, don't they? How bad can it be?"

"Pretty bad," Greif said cheerfully. "Even when you haven't gone around breaking every bone in your body. You used to boast about that."

"Greif, that's cruel," her mother warned.

Greif appeared not to hear her. "But I imagine it's worse at the beginning and then it gets better. Things run in cycles, don't they?

That's what I've always found."

"Does your doctor say anything?"

"He wants to see me twice a week. He's very excited. He had to clutch his desk when I told him. He's been talking to John Martin, and there's obviously going to be a paper in it for him. He tried to suggest that I keep it to myself for a while—spare myself, he said, from being swamped by the Institute. He'll try me on different pain-killers if I follow his orders and keep him informed. His face lights up when he sees me, it's a little bit like love." She shifted slowly. "But not much."

"Can you stay out of work indefinitely?"

"I'm an asset to science one way or the other. You know, it's the funniest thing—but I think everyone *likes* me better now. My doctor patted my shoulder, Pandit sends me cheerful little cards—and look at this. Greif came. And you came. What should I make of that?"

"People in pain lose a little of their self-sufficiency. That's why other people step in, to help."

"Not to gloat?"

"Oh, in your case," Greif jumped in, "gloating is essential."

"She only says things like that for attention," her mother insisted. "Everyone lets her get away with it. She likes effects. Don't mistake it for the truth."

"I think they do gloat. Greif gloats. On the other hand, I think Raymond *would* gloat, and Raymond hasn't been around at all."

"Who's Raymond?"

"My lover and a well-paid sadist. I wonder how he'll feel about a medical breakthrough that didn't even get funded. And no animals died. I wonder if it will count." She was pleased with herself, having made a joke.

Mrs. Dundee very pointedly raised her arm and looked at her watch. As soon as her arm went down, Greif looked at her own watch and said, "I've got to be on my way or I'll never get organized. I've got a therapy session in an hour, and they check our fingerprints on the way in, that's how strict they are." She shook her hair. "There are men in the group."

Abby walked them out and stopped in the kitchen to get Megan something to drink. Megan's wallet was next to the refrigerator, and laying right next to it was her ID for work. Unblinking, Abby got a glass, opened the refrigerator, poured out some juice, closed the refrigerator, picked up the ID, and went back to Megan.

"So," Megan said.

"I guess you won't be going back to work soon."

"No. Not unless it all suddenly goes away."

"I want to rescue the monkeys at the lab," Abby said when she sat down again.

Megan shifted subtly. Her arm moved across her stomach, stopping absent-mindedly. "What monkeys?"

"The only monkeys I know personally are at your lab."

Meg cocked her head gently. "Why do you want the monkeys? What will you do with them?"

Abby took her time answering. "It's a miserable life, isn't it, crippled and confined? I hate it when anything is made helpless, when it doesn't have a chance."

"They're certainly used to it by now," Meg said noncommittally.

"They can't even touch. That's what drives me crazy. Monkeys are so social, and they put up a plastic wall between them."

"Sometimes we let them touch. They hug. It's very moving."

Abby glared at her.

"I like those monkeys," Meg admitted.

"I didn't think you liked animals at all."

"I like animals."

Abby raised her eyebrows.

"Well, not as pets. But they can be amusing."

"You work in a lab."

Megan raised a limp hand to dismiss her. "It's just a job. They get fed. They were bred for it."

Abby didn't answer and Megan frowned. "The monkeys don't serve any purpose now."

Abby nodded, and Meg smiled shyly. "Do you have a plan?" she asked.

"I have your ID," Abby answered. "How hard would it be?"

Meg laughed very quietly, as if she were afraid a sudden move would surprise her.

"I might be able to do it," Abby said, "if you just described a few things to me."

Megan's smile grew a little deeper. "This is more like it. We always had plans when we were kids, didn't we?"

"You'll help me?"

"It wouldn't be hard at all," Meg said. "And the best part is they'll never think it was us."

Chapter 24

The metal stairs clanged under her feet no matter how softly she tread. The banister was rough, with layers of paint chipped off then coated over, giving it a pockmarked feel. The paint was a dark, oily green halfway up the walls, and then a washed-out green. The bulbs were dim, and at the landings there were floor numbers that had overlapping edges of paint from preceding coats.

Abby hoped she wouldn't encounter anyone, yet the sheer emptiness of her route soon began to rattle her. Was there a reason no one was here? Was it dangerous? Would she end up in a dead end somewhere, locked out or locked in? She crept down, trying not to make a sound, telling herself, however, that she should walk more confidently; looking sneaky could be fatal.

The long underground corridor between the buildings was dreadful. There were leaking plastic garbage bags piled in heaps against the walls, and the dirty signs for air-raid shelters added to the atmosphere of dereliction. There were unpleasant puddles accumulating under cracked walls, the lighting was poor, and her steps sounded hollow and doomed. She slowed her pace and muffled her steps, she could imagine someone hiding behind one of those leaking mounds of garbage, ready to leap out at her.

She got to the end, looked through the door, and tried the handle. It slid open easily.

She made a point of not looking at the cameras, attempting an easy nonchalance. She was, in fact, leaving a documented trail of herself, having logged herself in at the main entrance. ("Hi, Megan, kinda late tonight?" "Got home and realized I left my bag here." "I know the feeling." "Stupid?" "Stupid.")

She walked down the corridors. Left, left—and then left again instead of right. She opened the door to the monkey room and put a wedge in to keep it slightly open. She had brought clippers with her, and with them she opened two cages. She gave the monkeys dried fruit laced with a sleeping pill. They grabbed the sweet and crawled to the back of the cage.

She left quickly, turning back to Meg's office, which she unlocked, leaving a purse on the desk. She overturned a shelf of slides, spreading them around for effect, then she took the corridor to the back parking exit, to find the guard. She was exciting herself dramatically, trying to achieve just the right degree of alarm for the guard's benefit.

She passed a lit room with an open door, and felt compelled to glance inside. Her step slowed. The room was big and clear; and a man lay spread out on the floor.

Her steps carried her one door beyond, but then she stopped, closing her eyes, raising a hand to her forehead. Oh god, what was she to do? The plan she and Meg had laid out was exact; it had a rhythm to it, it had a timetable.

She looked again. A man lay on the floor, his eyes open; she couldn't be sure whether he was breathing. Tentatively, she made a noise against the door—not quite a knock, but something that would get attention. After all, she argued with herself, she didn't want him jumping up at the wrong time. She knocked again, more firmly.

He didn't respond. She banged heavily, then pushed the door open. She went to him, saying, "Hello? Hello? Are you all right? I saw you as I passed by," but there was no answer. She dropped to her knees beside him, picking up his hand and letting it fall down again.

He was breathing, that was certain. But his eyes were open and he didn't blink. His stare was directed at the wall. She looked around and saw only a counter with cultures, bottles, vials, nothing that meant anything to her.

She stood up, wringing her hands together—actually wringing her hands together, she noticed—and went quickly down the hall. She told herself, on the one hand, this was perfect—and on the other hand, this was entirely unexpected, and should she change the schedule?

She stopped, panting, at the desk by the door. She was careful, even then, to stand clear of the camera. Amazingly, her mind seemed to be able to calculate advantages to having the man on the floor. An actual emergency would confuse things. She looked up at the camera. It would be even better to get rid of that. A wire led from the camera to the floor and disappeared into a wall. This wall, however, turned a corner, and the cord came out again. It was looser here, and led to an outlet. Checking the halls quickly again, she went back and kicked it out as she walked along.

The guard still wasn't back so she called out for him. She wasn't going to touch the door; Meg had said to avoid this exit.

Finally she heard the guard coming down the hall. Meg said she didn't talk to the guards, but Abby plastered an apologetic, acknowledging smile on her face and plunged on. "There's a man lying on the floor—he's breathing, but he isn't responding."

"Did you call an ambulance?"

"No. I didn't think. I was already on my way to you because my office looks like it's been broken into."

"Jeez," he said, and he called on his little radio to the guard in the main building, saying, "This is green door, looks like we have a problem here. Break-in and possible victim. Send an ambulance."

As they jogged along the corridors, he repeated his call over the radio; the static made it difficult to understand what was being said.

Abby led him to the man on the floor, and the guard dropped to a crouch, leaning his head down.

"He was breathing when I checked." Abby was defensive.

"Still is. His eyes are open."

"Is he blinking?"

"No. What does that mean?"

"I don't know."

The guard leaned into his radio again. "Code blue," he said helplessly. "Man down. Male, around 50, breathing, not responding." Abby nodded as the man rapped out phrases he'd heard elsewhere; she had heard them too. The radio squawked back.

Abby stood by the doorway. She checked her watch.

"The room number?" the guard asked her.

She gave it to him. The guard got up. "Shouldn't you stay with him?" she asked nervously.

He paused, looking out the door and then back at him. "Don't you know something to do for him?"

"I look at slides all day."

"You don't know who he is?"

She looked down at the man on the floor, frowning. He didn't look Indian, and the only other man Meg had mentioned was Raymond. If she had to, she would say it was Raymond. But she would avoid that if she could. "Yes I do. Does it matter?" She said it carefully, as if she were a much more reasonable person than the guard was, and knew it.

The guard, who looked very young, shook his head. "I guess it don't matter to me," he said. An animal down the hall called out. "What's that?"

"These are the animal labs. They sometimes make sounds."

The guard grunted. "Experiments," was all he said.

Abby came forward, crouching down beside the man on the floor.

"I think his eyes moved when you did that."

Abby leaned over. "Someone's coming to help," she said softly. "Just hold on now, they're on the way."

The man's eyes didn't blink again, but there was a flicker, a change, a registered response, that caused Abby and the guard to lean in over him, their heads almost touching, their ears straining for the merest hope of an answering sound.

Behind them, turning into the parking lot perhaps, was the shriek of an ambulance siren.

"They've come to help you," Abby said soothingly. "Do you hear that? They're on their way."

The ambulance came, another guard came, she saw Raymond carried off, and watched the two guards decide to do a careful search. While they were gone she took the monkeys and placed them, curled asleep, in a sling she wore across her stomach. She put on a loose coat and stooped forward, limping back to the main exit, where she wouldn't have to sign out. She held a radio, having it tuned just loud enough to cover any monkey sounds. She walked as fast as she could through the door, trying to remember to limp, and she was gone.

Chapter 25

"How is she today?" Pandit asked as Abby let him in. He was inspected by the dogs, who sniffed at his ankles, and by the cats, who eyed him from their perches.

"Hard at work," Abby said. "She's so much easier to deal with since she started her project."

"Yes, yes. The mind is at its best when distracted from itself. Such a tragedy, although I see in it a parable of sorts. It is interesting, isn't it, that when she was immune to pain she had no purpose; it is only now, when she must lock herself up in a soft room, that she can focus."

"Are you drawing any conclusion?" She led him up the stairs to the room that had been renovated for Megan's needs. It was sound-proofed and the windows had shutters that could completely filter out the light. There were no sharp corners on any of the furniture; everything was padded and cushioned. All the materials were hypoallergenic and there was an air-filtering system that screened out dust. Megan now lived in a protective envelope; the least incursion could cause her excruciating pain.

"I keep having trouble with the conclusion." He laughed gently. "Was the problem that she felt isolated or that she was made to feel so? If she had been treated as a superhero, a little god, would she have been different? Maybe she would have done things to admire. She was not handicapped by the threat of pain; she might have devoted herself to saving or helping others in a very direct way. But she felt no pity for others, did she? Because she had no understanding of pain? Or because she felt accused because she was different and so had to protect herself?"

"You're trying to find someone to blame, I think."

"No. My apologies. I am considering it only from her point of view. She was acutely sensitive to her differences, psychologically, whether she said it or not. Now she is acutely sensitive in a physical sense; another parable or paradox. My point is that she felt no sympathy. That is either part of her condition or part of her personality. How can we separate them?"

"Well, you know, I always thought she felt she didn't need restrictions, that she was above them. All she could think of doing was prodding for reactions, almost to get the *size* of them. Like feeling a bad tooth to see how bad it is. She would half-crush an ant, you know, to see what the uncrushed half would do. I'm not surprised she ended up in a research lab. Some people consider that to be science, not cruelty."

There was an alcove next to Megan's room, stocked with plastic hair caps and thin plastic jackets and robes. Paper slippers were lined up on the floor. A sink with unscented soap stood by the door. Pandit, now used to the routine, removed his shoes and began to wash up carefully.

"Someone came last week from the disability board," Abby noted. "And wore a cologne—a man's cologne. She had a seizure right in front of him."

"She has seizures now?"

"It's terrifying."

"Perhaps it pays somewhat for the ants," he said meditatively. He paused with a paper slipper in his hand. "I have decided to write a letter about the experiments. I have just seen another head-trauma proposal. It will duplicate what they already know, from previous experiments and from actual gunshot wounds. I am amazed that this seems valid to them. After all, we use the animals to help establish the conditions of a human disease. We do not need to use the animals just to duplicate what we already know to be true." He bent over to his slipper. "This is a researcher with no imagination. Perhaps that is best. No imagination. It is so much easier to attack."

Abby preferred to remain noncommittal. She believed that Pandit knew all about the monkeys; she certainly knew that Megan trusted him. But he was associated with the labs and she understood from Megan that he was a moral man. Perhaps morality, for him, meant accounting for the monkeys in some way. He had said he believed in testing, done sparingly and humanely, as essential in some cases. She wasn't sure what she believed; it was very likely that she would agree in theory to something she couldn't possibly accept in practice. She would always be forced to rescue the victims of theory, any kind of victim at all—including Megan.

All in all, she had been very lucky with the rescue. It had even been easy to convince Charles to keep the monkeys; she had simply slipped them out from under her coat and laid them on the kitchen table, where they clung together sleepily, shivering. He had looked at them, rubbed his chin, looked at her and said, "I think they take after my side of the family."

She had called Megan that night, and her description of the unconscious man she'd found fit Raymond. Meg had been nervily silent, or so Abby had thought; perhaps she really did care for the man.

She'd gone to see Megan the next day and found her curled into a ball on her bed. Abby had approached carefully, sitting on the floor next to her. "Has he gotten worse?" she asked sympathetically.

"Who?" Megan's voice had no energy; her eyes were dull.

"Why, Raymond, of course."

"I don't care about him." Meg's mouth was twisted. "Abby," she whispered, "I think I'm dying."

Abby sat down and put her hand over Meg's.

"I hurt all the time," Meg said, and shuddered. Her skin was cold and her posture had sunken in. She looked like a dog from one of the labs.

"What can I do?" Abby asked.

"I don't want to be alone," Meg said. "Please take me home."

And Abby had taken her home.

Now, Abby looked critically at Pandit as he pulled on the plastic cap. He was small, he had a thin spot in his hair, his eyes were soft and attentive. "Megan always looks forward to your visits," she said.

"Ah." He tapped his briefcase. "I bring her reports, you see, evidence from the outside world. Her condition is still new to her, she wants to hear everything that could possibly supply her with some facts."

"Are there that many facts?"

"If you look hard enough you can find a great many facts. It's a question of how you look at them, isn't it?"

Abby nodded. "Yes. I know you can prove anything, possible or impossible, with facts."

Pandit smiled happily. "How delightful it is to find someone who can understand. Megan understands, too, of course, but right now she is concentrating on something else."

"Do you think what she's doing will have any use?"

"I have no doubt of it. Anything she says will be the first time such a thing has been said by someone like her. We are all so fond of hearing what the extremes of life are like." He stood up, wrapped in paper and plastic garments to protect Megan from any wayward smell of his—shampoo, deodorant, soap, detergent—and nodded to Abby. She pressed a button that released a kind of windy sound on the other side (Megan was sensitive to bells), and the door opened slowly.

Pandit blinked quickly; the lighting was so poor inside.

He heard a voice, barely above a whisper, drift out from the darkness. "I'm so glad to see you."

Pandit walked slowly across the floor, which was covered in

sheets that were taken up and washed in hot water daily. The chairs were unpainted furniture with hypoallergenic cushions coated with brushed cotton or silk. He heard the gentle hum of the air conditioner, a hum which sometimes got on Megan's nerves, but which caused her a great anxiety when it was stopped each week to clean the filters.

"I have some articles for you," he said, placing journals on a plastic table.

She wrinkled her nose. "I can smell them."

"The air conditioner will get rid of the smell."

"Move them closer to a vent please, Pandit."

"Of course. My apologies." He spread them out as she requested, then returned to sit opposite her. "And how is your work going?"

"A lot of progress this week. I'm listing all the kinds of textural pain."

"Very interesting."

"It is, you know. Do you know there was a man who could identify the feel of colors on his skin when he was blindfolded? Red, he said, was the heaviest, and easy to feel. I think he's wrong; I think it's exactly that shade of blue that's made from the wings of beetles; it has a bit of the carapace sealed in with the color."

"Made from beetles?" Pandit asked in astonishment.

"A very common practice, and a beautiful color, if it doesn't bother your eyes." Megan's voice, while low, had more shading in it than Pandit had noticed before. She folded her hands in her lap—she was careful to keep her hands and her feet together at all times to avoid injuries—and she inclined her head just the slightest bit forward, her eyes eagerly seeking his. "This man said the feel of blue made him uneasy, although everyone else insists it's a calming color. He said blue always rushed at him, but green settled on his nerves like a cushion. This was in the '50s, you know, I'm sure he never knew that there was a 'fast' pain track for instant response, and a slow one that has receptors in the limbic or emotional system. I think blue actually hurt him because of his emotional response. That's where I've decided to put my attention. Emotions and pain—well, we can't use rats for that, can we? Maybe chimps, they can be taught language. I think some birds can too." She paused, slightly breathless, and smiled. "You've caught me after a period of intense thinking."

"That is quite all right. I admire intense thinking."

"I'm unaware of the senses while I'm thinking about them."

"It is a wonderful irony, isn't it?"

"I think my treatise on pain will be valuable. Too much of the literature is exclusively scientific. It doesn't relate to people. I want this work on pain to chronicle the experience of it, not just the clinical picture. I'm placing ads to find other people who are sensitive. I want to catalog their perceptions. Not their physiological reactions only; I want to know what they believe about pain. Projects have always centered on the general; I want to know the particular. Some pains are threatening, you know, and some are exalting. There *are* those." She looked away, suddenly weary. "Still, they are pain. I believe we will learn a lot."

"I believe it will be very valuable."

Megan relaxed against a cushion, still keeping her hands together. "Of course there's a world outside. I should ask about it." She smiled.

Pandit smiled in return. "The lab is somewhat quiet now. I have written a letter about the animals and sent copies to newspapers and animal organizations. Ever since Raymond was found—" and here his eyes flicked very carefully past her "—there have been questions from the media. The Institute has decided to be concerned about the animals. Of course, Raymond's experiments have ended now." He paused.

"How is he?"

"They don't expect any change. He breathes on his own. He

blinks, but he does not signal anything with his blinking."

"Do you think he's conscious?"

"No one can say for sure. His body can no longer respond on any level. If he is conscious it is an unendurable thought. No communication and no relief."

Megan's face wavered. "I hope he's a vegetable," she said.

"Yes."

"He can live forever in that state?"

"Yes."

She paused. Her hands, carefully folded together, twitched slightly. "You know his theory about will power and death?"

"Of course, of course, we all had heard of it."

"Do you think it was his experiment that caused this?"

"No. I do not believe he was good enough, ever, to succeed with his experiment. Do you think he found out something miraculous about death? He left no record of it. They have gone through his data and the biochemists have broken down the matter in his vials—an adrenaline compound. He saved the brains of the animals that lived the longest time in his tests. They may have been physically stronger, but he forgot that they were also the animals who were terrified the longest, and therefore so much adrenaline. Other researchers have proven that the rats know when another rat is being killed and it affects the data. They are killed in another room when the experiment is sensitive. It amazes me that he forgot this."

"Still, I can't help but think about his theory. His body has given out, now, entirely. If there's anything left at all of him it's his will. If he was right. . . ." She trailed off.

"Ah yes," Pandit sighed unhappily.

"Do you believe in irony?" She smiled at her own question, gazing quickly around the soft room.

"It would be very hard otherwise. The question I ask myself is, 'Do I believe in so much irony?' " She looked at him eagerly and he continued. "Irony for the sake of irony. God—the universe—fate—must need amusement occasionally. If it is possible for human beings to appreciate wit, then wit must exist objectively. That is evidence. It has to occur, you see, because there is a receptor for it. That is how I see it today. I have a biologist's mind now. I see that a thing can be perceived; therefore I know that it must exist." He lifted his hands outward. "We are the object of wit."

"I think you're suggesting a god."

"I suspect there may be a receptor for god; it's universally perceived. But a god so clearly unbalanced? It's hard to believe that a creature could be born only to be tortured and die."

"A receptor for cruelty, then."

"I am afraid we would excuse too much if we find there are physical reasons for it. We would be confused about it. A hand, after all, has the capacity to caress or to kill. We don't excuse the hand that kills because its design makes it capable of that. But if we find there is indeed a chemical receptor for cruelty? The closer we look the more I am depressed by what it might mean, this cellular recipe."

"I don't want to find that there's an excuse for everything. I don't want to 'understand' torturers. You can explain it psychologically or chemically, it doesn't matter. Only the cruelty matters, and I want it stopped by any means necessary." She paused and shook her head. "Sometimes I think some people have been *created* for cruelty."

Pandit nodded. "But kindness exists also. And meaning. It is very easy, it is very seductive to forget that the opposite can also be discovered. Perhaps even encouraged."

"It's funny. I can feel myself being drawn deeper and deeper, enchanted by sensation, drawn into pain, so expectant, waiting for the flood of it. I have never waited for pleasure, anticipated it, or craved its approach." She shrugged slightly. "Perhaps that's always been a problem. Perhaps I was always meant to be a devourer of pain, and the trouble was I couldn't feel pain. Until now."

"You've become a sensualist."

She smiled slightly. All her responses had been concentrated since John Martin's drugs. She was no longer heedless of her physical self: her attention to her surroundings, to every twitch or response in her skin, kept her overloaded with sensation. She could feel the air flow in her room change if she moved a cushion. The world pulsed with physical meaning, and it intoxicated her. The only pity was how long it had taken her to realize that pain was not only a sign of physical weakness (there were still moments when she remembered her former self with the longing of a lover), but pain was also an accent of physical existence, it contained subtle significances. She was truly incapacitated by her body's over-excitation; she would forever blame John Martin for that. But she also had to thank him for the attention she paid to the feel of silk. Yes, she was suddenly a sensualist.

"I think it's good for you," Pandit said.

"I am a completely different person."

Pandit grinned, with pure pleasure. His eyes crinkled. "Different," he admitted. "But not completely. Maybe more complex?"

Megan carefully nodded. They gathered Pandit's gift of articles together, and for the next hour or so discussed the latest in pain research.

They sat side by side, discussing sensations. Megan gradually relaxed, drawn in by theory. She was happy at moments like this, but she never thought it and thus never had to dispute it.

Eventually, Pandit rose and excused himself. "A dinner engagement," he said politely.

"And we were doing so well," she said with genuine regret.

"We can continue this tomorrow."

She looked relieved. "I can get through this material by then."

"I will be interested in your reaction," he said, and let himself out of the soft room, removing the paper and plastics in the outer alcove, reassembling his normal appearance. "Much improved," he said to Abby on the way out.

Abby agreed. She sat down to dinner with Charles, who smiled at her and asked, "Any new animals?"

Abby thought that it was entirely possible he was disappointed when she said no. They had four cats now, in addition to the three dogs and the two monkeys in the basement. Downstairs the monkeys clung to their swings, moving slowly back and forth, their lips peeled back, their teeth displayed. They had had difficulty leaving the make-shift cages constructed for them, but recently they were attempting more moves. At the dinner table, Abby and Charles could hear their shrieks and the clang of the swings the chimps used to move around.

Above them, in the soft room, Megan pursed her lips and turned to her manuscript.

Charles pushed a fork into his mashed potatoes and peas and said, with satisfaction, "An unusual life. But it has its points." Charles was even more content now, with illegal monkeys in the basement and a sister-in-law upstairs. He rarely visited Meg but he liked to mention her, in sentences that suggested she was either a madwoman or a genius. He said he personally didn't care which she turned out to be, so long as she did it well.

Abby got a tray together with bland foods for Megan, who—finally—had turned her attention away from her; who thought of her now more as a supplier of goods than as a supplier of experience. It was a transformation Abby appreciated. She didn't have to change on her way into the soft room. Megan had no aversion to her smell, and, as she let the food grow cold, she sat across from Abby, her face animated with her own concerns, her thin wrists moving across the sheets of paper in front of her. She was listing the steps she was taking to find more people with sensitivities like hers.

"It would be so much easier if I could just do it myself, go out and find them," she said, handing Abby a piece of paper with a list of ads she wanted placed. "If only I could see these people myself." Her hand stole up to wipe her brow, faintly beaded with sweat. She closed her eyes and her shoulders collapsed in defeat. "You're so blessed, to be free from pain. You can come and go as you choose. It's an amazing thing; I never knew what to do with myself before. I never knew, but now I lie here and think: I was a god! I was a god and I didn't know it!" She opened her eyes to regard Abby humbly.

"If you became that way again, what would you do?"

"I don't think I could do enough, I don't think you could stop me. I would dedicate myself to something that would help, I really would. I have a desire, now, to help the world." She closed her eyes. "Perhaps this work will do it, perhaps my experiences will lead to discoveries of some sort, some change."

Abby waited but Megan had dozed off, probably from some painkiller she was taking. Abby collected the dishes and the half-eaten food. Her sister looked fragile; they were no longer exactly alike and it was possible to see that they were twins only if you looked for it. Their roads had diverged so much that she felt for Meg what she felt for old lovers: a twinge of regret and a wish to move on. This project of Meg's was a relief; Abby couldn't think what life would have been like without it.

She looked back before closing the door. Maybe Meg had once, as she said, been a god, but she wasn't now. Abby remembered, for one moment, what Meg had been like as a girl—wild and defiant and with a glint of disdain in her eyes. She thought of it as something she had once loved, and for a fleeting moment she could see why she loved it. Wildness, defiance, a high wind: these things sucked life to the bone. That's what Meg had once had, not godliness but indeterminate passion. How like her to mix them up. Abby turned the lights down even lower. Whether Megan slept or woke, the room always awaited her, a cocoon she could not shed, a station for the godly and the passionate in their final forms.

Photo by: Maureen Verbeek

Karen Heuler has published extensively in both literary and commercial periodicals ranging from *Ms magazine* to *TriQuarterly Review*. In 1995 the University of Missouri published *The Other Door*, her first short story collection. *The New York Times* praised these stories, saying they were "haunting and quirky . . . the line between reason and reverie is dissolved; here even the most fantastic seems possible."

She won an O. Henry prize in 1998, and in 2002 and 2003 won awards from *Night Train* magazine and *Serpentine*, an online periodical. Her stories have been short-listed for the O. Henry awards in 2001, received special mention in the Pushcart Awards 2000, and reached the ranks of finalist in the Iowa Short Fiction Awards and semifinalist for the Nelson Algren Award. She lives and writes in New York.